LIVING QUARTERS

LIVING QUARTERS

BY VINCENT CANBY

ALFRED A. KNOPF   NEW YORK   1975

THIS IS A BORZOI BOOK
PUBLISHED BY ALFRED A. KNOPF, INC.

Library of Congress Cataloging in Publication Data

Canby, Vincent.   Living quarters.

I. Title.   PZ4.C215Li3   [PS3553.A4894]
813'.5'4   74-21287
ISBN 0-394-49513-6

Manufactured in the United States of America

FIRST EDITION

TO PENELOPE GILLIATT

LIVING QUARTERS

1

The house is built on a point of land fifty feet above the sea. The swimming pool is twenty feet below the house, set in lava rocks that look like great chunks of purplish Swiss cheese. To the left of the swimming pool, steps lead down to a mile-long crescent beach, which in 1965, the summer Charles and Daisianna du Chaudrun were living there, was still a wild beach. Few people swam there except the inhabitants of the house. Today it's a beach where strangers picnic, tourists from Atchison and New York and Moline during the week and, on weekends, local families, the mothers in rubber bathing caps that fasten under their chins and have rubber flowers glued to the tops. To the right of the pool, beyond a small beach accessible only from the sea, there is another, slightly higher point whose summit is decorated by manchineel and beach plum and sometimes by a herd of free-roaming goats. The side of the point is sheer. One sees in it the accumulation of geological eras, one atop another like the layers of a strudel. In this point the sea has carved a large grotto where Charles, late in May that year, shot a moray eel with a spear gun Daisianna refused to allow in the house. The spear gun was kept in the garage next to the generator house, which is also where the servants lived whenever there were servants who lived on the property.

The house is a principal setting. The drawing room, the library, the dining room each have three walls. The fourth is the view of the terrace and gardens and sea. When one sits on the terrace and looks toward the house, one looks not at it but into it. Even the wing that is the master bedroom is a kind of gallery defined only by arches, in the daytime when the shutters are open. There are no screens and no mosquito nets except in the guest bedroom, and the nets there were installed by a New York decorator. The house is protected on the windward side by a small mountain, and it does possess exterior walls, though one is never conscious of shape or architecture, only of masses of tropical plants, none of which is allowed to die in anyone's presence. If something starts to fail, it's immediately removed and a plant in health, preferably in bloom, replaces it.

When Charles and Daisianna saw the house on their first visit to St. Constance in 1958, it seemed a place of perfect harmony. The owner of the house, Mary Magnuson, recently widowed and spending her summer of mourning on the island, had befriended Charles and Daisianna on the wild beach. She invited them up to the house and into her life, which, that summer, was mostly devoted to learning how to fly. Charles and Daisianna were enchanted by Mary Magnuson. The house was an expression of her determined serenity. What one remembers of the house is not what it looks like but what it was like to be there at moments of no importance. One afternoon before lunch, Daisianna looks up from the couch in the drawing room, through branches of jasmine, into the white sunlight, past hummingbirds the size of bumblebees, to the far end of the beach a mile away where waves are breaking as perfectly and as silently as in an ancient *kakemono*. On another afternoon, during an all-day rain that isolates the library from the rest of the house and flattens the sea and makes it gray, Charles is reading a paperback mystery novel whose pages are turning to mush as he reads them. Reading has become an act of physical consumption. He will be the last person to read this particular book. By the time he finishes, it will have ceased to exist. It will have returned to its preliterary state, a porridge of pulp and glue and ink.

It wasn't until Charles tried to take pictures of the house that he realized it is invisible. The house's identity is that of its landscape and, like all tropical landscapes, it reveals few reminders of earlier seasons. The past is always being overtaken by present. Not defeated, simply succeeded. The house is bursting through with present, sometimes splitting its seams, as when a date palm was allowed to grow through the roof that overhangs the terrace outside the master bedroom. A carpenter was called in to cut a hole in the roof for the date palm, which abruptly died. The house is furnished with a mélange of Louis XIV, left over from Mary Magnuson's Park Avenue duplex, Finnish modern, West Indian, and inexpensive Middle West. The rooms are hung with one Pollock, one Kandinsky, a very tiny Turner, and assorted objects painted, sculpted, or pasted together by children. There is an excellent sound system, a collection of 78-rpm recordings by Bessie Smith, and a collection of tapes, once privately circulated, of well-known radio personalities making obscene mistakes on the air. There are also a complete collection of Oxford reference books and a set of *The Book of Knowledge,* some of whose pages are stuck together with marmalade dropped forty years ago. The house's red tile floors are covered with sisal mats woven in extravagantly delicate, lacelike designs and, in the drawing room, by a beautifully worn, slowly mildewing Aubusson. There are family pictures everywhere, but the subjects have become anonymous. The house records nothing of the past.

2

Three black boys who worked as busboys at the Casino
found Daisianna walking along the road through Three-Mile
Sandy Ground at 4 a.m. She was wearing blue jeans, a
lemon-yellow turtleneck sweater, dark glasses, and sandals
that slid off her feet on the soft shoulders of the road. She
did not flag down the boys. They stopped because it
seemed as if she might be ill or in trouble. She showed
neither surprise nor relief. She was extremely polite. Yes, she
said in French, she would give them thanks for a ride into
Marigot. Neither of her cars would start and she felt she
ought to get in touch with the gendarmes. There had been
an accident and she thought it best to report it immediately:
the gendarmerie was always so busy in the morning with
people trying to obtain driver's licenses and working per-
mits and complaining about noisy poultry. She didn't want
to wait in line. What had occurred? I shot my husband. I
think he's dead.

The three boys thought Daisianna was crazy or drunk
and it depressed them. They drove her to the orange plaster
gendarmerie where they woke up the duty officer, Matthew
Marcorelles, a young sad-faced Frenchman from Annecy
whose wife was expecting their first child that month. The
gendarme, with Daisianna sitting beside him in his jeep,
followed by the three Casino boys in their car, drove out to
the house in the Low Lands. As they went past the generator
house at the entrance to the driveway, the gendarme shook
his head as if to dislodge the noise the generator made.
All the lights in the house were on. The lights were also on
in the garden and by the pool. They walked up the steps
from the terrace into the drawing room, through the drawing room across the mildewing Aubusson, down the outside

stairway to the terrace by the master bedroom. Most of the time it was so windy here that it was impossible to smoke in bed. The ashes blew out of the ashtray onto the pillows and sheets. Open books had to be left face down or the places marked with combs, envelopes, matches, or lipsticks. At 4:45, just before dawn, the wind ceased and although it was mid-August the air was cold. The shuttered doors to the bedroom were open, outward. The wooden louvers in one door had been torn away about four feet from the ground. It looked as if a giant had jammed his foot through it. Charles, naked, was lying on his back on the flagstones a couple of yards from the door. Daisianna again noticed the slight heat rash on his chest and the lankness of his penis. His right arm tried to hide the hole on the left side of his chest and stomach. His left arm was under his body. The fingers poked out from under his left thigh. Everything was quite tidy. A broom leaned against a canvas deck chair. The three Casino boys watched as the gendarme gently lifted the right hand and sought a pulse. Daisianna had seen all this before but she was touched by the respect of the gendarme, who seemed to want Charles to be alive as much as she did, more than anything else in the world, at that moment anyway. Daisianna was all the more touched as she remembered that the gendarme had been the rude man who'd refused to issue Charles a French driver's license several months earlier.

3

The inquest was held in the back room of the *bureau de poste* in the orange plaster building it shared with the gendarmerie. Morning. Heat. Flies. Many people, mostly black.

They sat on folding chairs and on the floor and on the sills of open windows. It was the room where mail was sorted. There was a disturbance when a black man in a black suit and dark glasses asked to read a statement. The man was told to leave. He refused. He represented the people, he said. A gendarme took the man by the elbow. Gently. People shoved this way and that. A baby screamed and some people laughed. Daisianna sat in the front row across a table from Honoré Picard, the man in charge of the inquest. On her right was Jimmy Barnes, who was always there. She held three fingers of Jimmy Barnes's left hand and squeezed them every thirty or forty seconds. Without intending to. Honoré Picard's features didn't fill the space assigned to them. There was unoccupied flesh at the sides of M. Picard's face, under the chin, and above the forehead. The face was not fat. It had been painted onto a pale blue-white balloon that had been overinflated. M. Picard was very kind. He addressed Daisianna always as Madame, with a long, slow accent on the second syllable.

"Madame," said M. Picard. "Please tell us in your own words exactly what happened."

"Well," said Daisianna. "Well." Then: "Do you mind if I smoke?"

M. Picard said no and pushed an ashtray across the table to her.

"It began, I think, when we went swimming that afternoon. All the garbage dumps on the island were on fire. The Algerians seemed to be burning rubber. You could smell it in Marigot. The garbage dump outside Oranjestad was also on fire. It covers a whole field, you know. The one in Three-Mile Sandy Ground was burning. Everybody seemed to be burning things. I don't know why."

"Please," said M. Picard. "What happened on the night of the accident?"

"Accident," someone behind Daisianna said. "Oh, là, là . . ."

Daisianna said, "I don't remember very well," but she did remember the story she had first told the gendarme, then Mary Magnuson and Fonse Devanner and Jimmy Barnes and all the others. The night itself had vanished but the repeated story had worn a groove in her memory. It was, she assumed, as accurate as any, though it no longer had a great deal to do with her. Only the Mystery, but she couldn't possibly tell that part to anyone since she knew it wasn't true.

For how long, M. Picard asked, had Charles been sleeping in the library? Since midnight, said Daisianna. No, M. Picard wished to say, he wanted to know if they always slept in separate bedrooms. Was this their habitual arrangement? Monsieur and Madame had been married for eleven years, and he wished to say he understood such arrangements. Daisianna could not remember exactly, but she thought it began four or five weeks ago last Thursday.

"It was the night after we found the first land crab in the bedroom. Until then, we always slept with the doors to the terrace open. And all the shutters. There was the land crab and there was the mongoose."

"Mongoose?" said M. Picard.

"Not in the bedroom," said Daisianna. "It walked through the dining room one morning just as we were finishing breakfast. It was unafraid. I'd never seen one before. I thought it was a possum. We'd also found a scorpion in the bath of the guest bathroom. Charles killed it with Fly-Tox. He used an entire aerosol can. The scorpion was quite beautiful, really. Very sinewy. On the bottom of the bathtub it looked like an impression in a fossil rock."

Said M. Picard: "They give a nasty sting."

"But not fatal," said Daisianna.

"No," said M. Picard.

"After that I couldn't sleep very well, thinking of all those creatures. There are also bats, you know, and lizards. The lizards leave little things about."

"Little things?"

"Shit," said Daisianna.

"That is a nuisance," said M. Picard.

"Exactly," said Daisianna. "The night we found the land crab in the bedroom, Charles closed the doors and shutters for me. But then he said it was too warm for him to sleep, especially in the early morning after the sun comes up. He began to sleep in the library."

"And why did he not sleep in the other bedroom?"

"It's at the far end of the house. He liked to sleep on the couch in the library, even though the library is worse."

"Worse?" said M. Picard.

"I've seen rats in there. Charles says they're just field mice, but they look like rats to me."

"The bedroom was not too warm for you?"

"No."

"And," said M. Picard, "if you found sleep difficult to obtain, you would take a capsule or a suppository of some sort, would you not?"

"Yes," said Daisianna. "Not all the time, but from time to time."

"They were prescribed by your doctor?"

"Yes."

"What kind of capsules do you take?"

"Seconals," said Daisianna, "and sometimes Tuinals, which, I think, are more grand. I bought them in Paris a year ago."

"Do you take any other kind of capsules?"

"Only Mithliums," said Daisianna, "which are for my health. And aspirins. And Mirealles, which, you know, are for women, and pills to control conception."

"That's all?"

"And Valiums. They are a kind of tranquilizer."

"How is that?" M. Picard said.

"They help one rest calm," said Daisianna. She said it directly in French, which annoyed Nathalie Millard, the Préfect's black secretary who had been translating M. Picard into English and Daisianna into French. Daisianna decided to speak French. She had been thinking in French, and she had grown fatigued translating everything back into English before she spoke.

M. Picard said: "Have you any idea of the strengths of these various capsules and pills? For example, these pills that make you rest calm?"

"No," said Daisianna, "but my doctor would know. I assume they are not very strong. The night of the accident, I had to take three Seconals just to get to sleep the first time."

"Three?" said M. Picard. "Three?"

"Yes," said Daisianna. "It had been a very bad day. The garbage dumps. And that morning Charles had a fight with Fernande. He said she had lost two of his shirts, and she said he must have taken them from the laundry before she ironed them. He said she was a thief and that he was tired of supporting a den of thieves. Fernande's husband, Reuban, is the gardener, and her mother is our cook. We always seemed to be missing things. We had been missing things for some time."

"What sort of things?"

"Shirts, and I lost a bathing suit, and pillowcases. And that night my wig disappeared."

"Wig?"

"It's a blond wig I sometimes wear after swimming. When I haven't had time to wash my hair. I don't always wear it. Wigs are very warm in the tropics, you know."

"You lost it that night?"

"I think so. I wore it to the Casino for supper. When we got home, I took it off and left it in the dressing room."

"Where is the dressing room?"

"Next to the bedroom. Between the bedroom and the bathroom."

"You and your husband used the same bathroom?"

"Yes. It has an outside door, for the pool."

"He could use it without going through the bedroom?"

"Yes."

"About the wig."

"Later, I wanted to wear it again, but I couldn't find it."

"You are sure?"

"I think so."

"Did you ever lose other things? Money? Jewelry?"

"No," said Daisianna, "but Charles said Fernande was stealing his underwear for Reuban."

"Did you believe this, Madame?"

"Not truly."

"Why not?"

"I don't believe Reuban wears underwear."

The room, which had been quiet except for the noises of the waving of straw fans and newspapers and wet handkerchiefs, erupted with foreign laughter.

4

Shotguns are heavy. Had Madame ever fired one before? No. Did she know anything about guns? No. The reverse thrust when a shotgun is fired can knock a man down, someone who is not practiced in the handling of shotguns. Yes. Had Madame been knocked down? No. She had rested the gun barrels on the back of a chaise, for support. Where had she been when she fired? Sitting on the side of the bed. She had not been knocked back onto the bed? No, but she had been aware of the flash, of the smell of gunpowder. Her shoulder was still bruised. She did not remember any noise. It was very quiet and then she heard the leaves of the almond tree. They drop off the tree in the night and make little popping noises when they hit the terrace. If there is any wind, the dead almond leaves on the terrace sound like land crabs. The leaves are brittle and clatter on the flag-stones.

5

When she was eleven, Daisianna had fallen in love with Carl Crow Jolly, who was thirteen and a Fox Indian, al-though he also had royal Crow blood in him—or so said his mother, who was summer cook for Daisianna's Grand-mother Overton. It was at Harbor Point, in northern Michi-gan, where Daisianna spent her summers in a three-story yellow gingerbread house that had sixteen bedrooms and two bathrooms and whose interior walls were rough, un-painted wood planks with cracks between that a child could see through. Carl Crow Jolly was short and strong and serious. He had blue nipples and he was the most beautiful person Daisianna had ever seen. His skin was the color of Galena clay, reddish brown, and alarmingly smooth. His features were very pronounced for such a young boy. The eyes were black and widely set. His nose was of such grandeur that Grandmother Overton would say every time she saw him, not always after he had left her presence: "The boy still hasn't grown into his nose." Daisianna and Carl

Crow Jolly were inseparable that summer. He took her fishing for perch that never bit, to the movies in Harbor Springs, swimming off unprotected rocks where a boy named Alfred Butts had drowned when Daisianna's mother was a little girl. Carl Crow Jolly taught Daisianna about sex on afternoons when it rained and there was nothing else to do. He also took her hunting. He owned a BB gun he had bought through the mail from Montgomery Ward, which he called Monkey Ward, one of his rare jokes. There was nothing much to hunt during the summer, not even rabbits, which he preferred to trap anyway, so they spent most of their time trying to shoot birds. Carl Crow Jolly always missed. The gun simply did not have enough fire power. The BBs, which Carl Crow Jolly loaded by putting a handful into his mouth and then feeding them into the gun's chambers with a good deal of spit, would go sailing out of the barrels one by one, traveling in a more or less straight line for seven feet before making delicate arcs to earth. Carl Crow Jolly first hunted crows and sparrows, which no one liked, but because he never hit them he began to shoot at any birds he saw: robins, bluebirds, cardinals, wrens, catbirds—the sort of birds Daisianna had been taught to love and protect. He never hit any of these, either. The birds were barely frightened. One afternoon when Daisianna and Carl Crow Jolly were on their way home after swimming at Alfred Butts rocks, they came through the woods and found a woodpecker sitting on a stump by the path. The woodpecker was pecking lazily at something inside the stump, which was only waist-high. He would peck two or three times and pause, as if exhausted. He would peck again and repeat the pause. He seemed absent-minded, forgetful of what it was a woodpecker was supposed to do. Carl Crow Jolly took the gun, which he carried on a strap over his shoulder, and loaded it. He told Daisianna to stand back at a safe distance while he moved cautiously toward the stump. The bird was either deaf or unusually reckless. Carl Crow Jolly was not a natural tracker. He tripped over an exposed root and stumbled, but the bird took no notice. The bird continued the pattern of two or three pecks, pause, two or three pecks, pause, until the Indian boy was three feet from him. Carl Crow Jolly lifted the gun to his shoulder and aimed at the woodpecker, whose head was six inches from the muzzle of the gun. The gun wobbled. Carl Crow Jolly dropped to one knee and placed his elbow on it to arrest the motion of the gun. It was creating a draft on the bird's neck. Carl Crow Jolly again aimed the gun. He steadied himself. He waited. He pulled the first trigger and the second. The bird remained upright for a moment, then toppled over. He didn't seem to have been shot. He seemed to have gone into a faint. Carl Crow Jolly whooped with triumph and Daisianna clapped her hands at his pleasure, but when Carl Crow Jolly picked up the bird, which was bleeding slightly at the back of the head, they were both overcome with guilt. "He was old," said Carl Crow Jolly. "That was why he didn't fly away." Daisianna began to weep. The bright reds, whites, blacks, and grays of the wood-pecker's feathers looked pale in death. "I'll bury it," said the boy. He took several leaves, wrapped them around the bird, and carried it off the path into the woods. He returned immediately. "You didn't bury it," said Daisianna. "I did bury it," said the boy, "as much as it has to be. Who do you think buries birds in the forest when they just die of old age?" Daisianna remained in love with Carl Crow Jolly throughout that summer. In addition to everything else, they shared a sorrow. In the winter she fell in love with the severe, thin-lipped woman who taught her French, and the next summer Carl Crow Jolly was working in Ishpeming in a factory that made cardboard boxes.

6

Daisianna was lying at the far end of the beach behind Oranje House with Dinny Murdock. It was midmorning and quiet. At the opposite end of the beach, where Captain Magruder had begun a new garbage dump, two of the Magruder children, sweet, brown-eyed half-castes whose bluish skin was inclined to freckle, were teasing a pet pelican named Juliana. They would offer Juliana a piece of fish, and when Juliana lumbered over to them the children ran to the other side of the garbage dump. Juliana dumbly followed, always on foot. She never flew unless she had to. Daisianna said, "I'm not sure it's proper to put suntan oil on in public when one is in mourning."

7

In her neat backhand script, with little circles over the i's, and with the t-crosses so long and even they looked as if they'd been drawn along the edge of a ruler—a script developed during years of practice on lavender and rose and yellow stationery at the Girls Latin School, at L'École Boulaggier, and at Dobbs—Daisianna wrote to her mother-in-law in Paris. Her French grammar was nearly perfect, though formal, and her vocabulary more than adequate:

My dear Mother du Chaudrun:

As you have been informed, Charles is dead. I shot him last week Wednesday night with a hunting gun he had recently borrowed from Mme. Magnuson, whose house we have been renting this summer. It was for our protection, this gun, and it belonged to M. Magnuson, who last spring succumbed to cancer for the liver. Charles was buried Saturday in the small Catholic cemetery by the sea in Marigot. It has a beautiful vista across the bay, past blue mountains, to the isle of St. Barthélemy, thirty kilometers distant. There is one grave in the cemetery that carries the date 1647. It is very old. I think Charles would be happy to be buried here. It is French soil (sand, truly), and although he had become a citizen of the United States he was born French and still I have my French passport I received when we were married. (Still I am a citizen of the United States but I have two passports, which, I believe, are valid, both of them. However, I have never understood these things.)

I haven't been able to cry since the night Charles died. I loved him very much, dear Mother, and he loved me very much. It seems that all the people who have ever loved me are now dead. The authorities were very kind. M. Barnes, our lawyer, came here from New York when he learned what had happened. It was very kind of him, because I could not think of what to do. He flew immediately to the isle. Now it takes only seven hours if one makes the correct correspondence in the Virgin Islands or Puerto Rico. He is a very good man and he and M. Devanner, the Minister for Inter-Island affairs in Curaçao, put things straight. The French authorities also are good men. The hearing endured three hours one day and one hour on another day. It was conducted by M. Picard of the gendarmerie in Pointe-à-Pitre, Guadeloupe, who was sent to the isle for only this purpose. M. Picard is much younger than I anticipated, although he was wounded in Indochina. He came from France last year. I believe he wants to go into the tourist business on St. Constance in some fashion. He is a lawyer but he is studying hotel management by post, and next year he is going to visit Miami if he can obtain dollars enough.

I hope it makes you content that Charles is in a Catholic cemetery. You understand, he was not a good Catholic. When we were married I said I would like to become a Catholic and he said he would divorce me if I did. Père Gollanahan, the priest here (he is a Netherlander although his parish is on the French side of St. Constance), has given me much succor. He is a tiny man—he stands only to my shoulder—and has fine bright blue eyes and a long gray beard that makes him resemble Rumpelstiltskin. Everybody loves Père Gollanahan. He always has a good word to say and often a joke. I have gone to mass.

I hope, dear Mother, that you will continue to regard me as your daughter. As you know, my mother succumbed seven years ago after a fall at her club. I will make arrangements with M. Barnes to continue to send you each month the check that Charles sent you each month. Please, let us often correspond.

With my most sincere sentiments,

Daisianna Caffrey du Chaudrun

P.S. We could not return Charles to France for burial. M. Bouché, who is the undertaker as well as the mayor of Marigot, said that he did not have the facilities for such an adventure. D.

All this happened in an earlier decade. There were then seventy hotel rooms on the island, including the four in Marigot's Belle Rive guesthouse. Today there are more than two thousand. The road from Marigot through Three-Mile Sandy Ground has been paved, and whenever a cruise ship is in port, sightseeing buses—secondhand, square-hooded school buses purchased in Miami, repainted light blue, and air-conditioned—drive a fifteen-mile great circle route around the island, from Oranjestad, on the Dutch side, over the mountains to Marigot, on the French side, through the Low Lands past the estates of the nobs and past the new beach hotels, back to Oranjestad by way of the Dutch airport named for Queen Wilhelmina. During the winter season, there are as many as five and six cruise ships stopping at Oranjestad each week. Sometimes two at a time. The French and Dutch governments have dredged new canals to give access to the sea from the Low Lands lagoon, which had been a virtual salt pond for almost a hundred years. The lagoon is now a fine hurricane anchorage and becoming known for its tarpon. For a while, anyway. The hospital in Marigot, which was rebuilt after the disturbances, and a middle-income retirement development on the Dutch side are dumping their sewage into the lagoon. Raw. It's a fairly large lagoon, four miles long and three miles wide in some parts, but the turds are beginning to shock the water skiers.

Front Street in Oranjestad is lined with stores that sell tax-free liquor, cameras, watches, cigarettes, perfume, jewelry; with boutiques named Tout Va Bien and C'est Si Bon; with wholesale houses called the Kashmir Trading Corporation and Hong Kong Suppliers, Limited. There are pizza stands and branches of banks that have their main offices in Curaçao, Paris, The Hague, and New York. Gone are the general stores that once sold bathing suits next to canned soups, batteries, aprons, hot-water bottles, 3-in-One oil, freshly butchered beef, motorcycles, and barrels of turnips, potatoes, and carrots. There are now two supermarkets, one at each end of town. There are no fish in Oranjestad Bay. It is possible to buy fresh fish on the quay in Marigot on

Wednesday and Saturday mornings. Sometimes it's possible to buy fresh lobsters, though most of the lobsters now come frozen from South Africa. The businessmen—mostly American, Dutch, Chinese, and Indian—drive Buicks and Cadillacs and Chryslers, none of which lasts very long because the roads, though paved, remain bad. The island is filling up with automobiles that have been disowned.

There was a time on St. Constance when one knew each car and its history. Some years ago when one saw Jumbo, who runs the bar in Cul-de-Sac, driving the yellow jeep (though scarcely yellow anymore, its canvas roof long since gone, its power feeble but very noisy), one would remember the winter Mark Magnuson gave it to Mary as a Christmas present. A most marvelous yellow. A most spectacular and cheering vehicle. Old women walking along the road would raise their eyes and laugh as Mary sped by, her spine straight, her concentration intense. She looked like some great white queen on a mission of blazing mercy. The yellow jeep was a gift to the entire island at what seemed to be a happy time. When the main roads were paved, Mary turned to Porsches and sold the jeep to the Pinchots, who own the electrical supply store in Marigot. The Pinchots later sold it to Bébé, the mechanic at the garage, and Bébé eventually sold it to Jumbo, who, when the end came, put it up on blocks in the field behind his Idle Days Bar & Restaurant. The yellow jeep is dead but not buried. All the cars that anyone has ever owned remain on St. Constance. A Pontiac, covered with vines and deserted at the side of the road that connects Marigot and Oranjestad, looks like an Alpine shrine. Most are left in the fields and at sundown are indistinguishable from the cows that graze around them.

Several years after Daisianna left the island there was one Rolls-Royce on St. Constance. It was painted gold, had simulated tiger-skin upholstery and a bar, and it was air-conditioned. It belonged to the man who came down from Las Vegas to supervise the operation of the casino in the Bay Grand Hotel, on the Dutch side, the first St. Constance hotel to have music piped to its lobby, pool, beach, and elevators. The man, whose name was Bernie, liked to get into his gold Rolls-Royce on a Sunday afternoon and point out to his wife, Tess, how the island's Operation Shoestring (his phrase) was coming along. Tess hated St. Constance. She hated the humidity. She hated the wind. She hated the loneliness. She hated the television reception and, if the reception was good, she hated the programs: reruns of Westerns and quiz shows she'd seen in Las Vegas five years before, now beamed from Antigua, and screechy Spanish variety shows from San Juan. There was not much for Tess to do on St. Constance except lie by the pool and write postcards to her daughter in Rochester. Once a week she had her hair done and every two weeks she would buy jewelry. Bernie was not stingy. Nor was he up to preserving a gold Rolls-Royce in an emerging society.

One Sunday afternoon, as Bernie was driving back over the mountain to the Dutch side, he came around a blind curve and ran into the rear of the 1937 Packard that Billy White used as a taxi. Billy had stopped his car in the right lane, as was his custom, to allow the passengers to get out and take snaps of St. Maarten, Saba, St. Eustatius, St. Barthélemy, Nevis, St. Kitts, and Montserrat, spread out on a horizon that looked as real as a diorama. After smashing into the Packard's rear, the Rolls climbed up it. The Packard suffered a broken bumper and a badly dented luggage rack, but the Rolls was fatally wounded. Its wheels were knocked out of line and its crankshaft was severed, though not a glass in its bar compartment was damaged.

Neither Bernie nor Tess was hurt but the Rolls never ran again. It is still parked in front of the Bay Grand, the upholstery fading, the chrome flaking off, the glasses now gone from the bar compartment. Bernie and Tess have also vanished. They left in a hurry saying they were going to San Juan for the afternoon to shop. No one is certain whether their leaving was connected with reports of skimming at the Casino, with Bernie's police record (a conviction for carrying a concealed weapon in Topeka in 1939, a story published in the San Juan *Star*), with rumors that members of the Bay Grand syndicate were involved in the running of narcotics to the States, or with Tess's petulant disposition. The hotel has been sold three times in five years. Two years after Bernie and Tess left, Lulu Benjamin, a big young black man from the French side who had been Bernie's bodyguard and then a bouncer for several months at the Bay Grand Casino, was found floating in the sea off Case's Point, shot in the head. The odd part was that Lulu had been working in St. Thomas for almost a year. No one had known that Lulu was back in town.

Lyman Rainwater, the manager of Oranje House in the early days, drifted into ecstatic alcoholism. When he was drunk he sang hymns remembered from childhood. "Rock of Ages" was his favorite when he was feeling low. "Brighten the Corner" reflected fleeting enthusiasms, but he was most fond of "Now the Day Is Over," which he would sometimes sing on the front gallery of Oranje House before lunch. Lyman would open the Oranje House bar at seven in the morning and close it four hours later, or sooner if he felt safely drunk. It wasn't that he couldn't have got drunk in the privacy of his apartment, but he enjoyed the frozen expressions of his guests and the pinched, sad expressions of his friends when he did such arbitrary, obviously unreasonable things. Everyone liked Lyman, with the exception of the Oranje House staff, but it was too much when he began playing his stereo system in the middle of the night at full volume. Twice the Sisters of St. Constance dried him out, twice he went on the wagon, twice he fell off. He grew thinner and more remote by the month, and more eccentric. At an official reception held at Oranje House on the Queen's birthday, he called the Governor "bozo" or "a bozo." Whichever it was was said to the Governor's face. Finally a brother came down from the States and took Lyman to a family home that was somewhere in either North or South Dakota.

There were others who also fell apart and others who prospered. Fonse Devanner was removed from office after the Curaçao riots in 1969, but he's now working for UNICEF in Beirut and very happy. His wife, of whom Willie or Bo had said, "She is not so clear," died and left Fonse enough money to marry a twenty-two-year-old Italian girl who had been an air hostess for Pan American. Robert Durfee—the black orphan boy who, at the age of fourteen, became the lover of Tom Donaldson, a former scoutmaster in Nashville, who had been more or less exiled to St. Constance by his family and stayed on to become rich developing real estate, pinball machines, and domestic-employment services —now runs Donaldson Enterprises, although he is still called Pig's Foot because of the fat, turned-up nose with the nostrils that give it the look of a cloven hoof. Pig's Foot is married and has two sons and is going to stand for the city council in Oranjestad. Tom Donaldson lives in Phoenix with his asthma and a new black lover, who, at age sixteen, has murder in his heart.

Notes from the encyclopedia: Saint Constance (c. 1160–1184), b. Constance Poiret in Defresney, Gironde, the daughter of a well-to-do cobbler and an indigent mother. Little is known of her early life. In 1184, she assassinated an associate of John of Puy, the heretic bishop of Auvergne whose assistant claimed authorship of the *Liber de Duobus Principis*. Constance was a member of the Bulari sect, which was distantly related to the Cathari and, through them, to the Albigenses. She first became estranged from the Bulari over the belief, adopted from the Bogomils, that souls could be transmigrated, not just from person to person, but from man to beast. She herself sympathized with the prohibition against the eating of meat and against sexual intercourse. For a while, she was one of the Bulari "perfect," as opposed simply to "the believers," and thus had the protection of John of Puy. She had undergone an elaborate ceremony of initiations, or spiritual baptism, the *consolamentum*. The Bulari did not believe in transubstantiation. They held that marriage was an organized vice, that casual vice and sodomy were to be preferred. Constance's estrangement became an irreconcilable break when she rejected the idea that Jesus was "merely" an angel "who came to indicate the way to salvation," not himself to provide it; that his human suffering and death were "an illusion." According to legend, John of Puy executed Constance by setting his pack of Irish wolfhounds upon her in the courtyard of his palace. Irish wolfhounds were at that time extremely rare in any part of France. Constance was beatified by Pope Lucius III in the same year (a new procedure, see LUCIUS III) and canonized in 1253. The feast of Saint Constance (Constancimas) is January 6th. She is the patron saint of drovers.

Other patron saints: Apollonia (February 9th), dentists; Michael (September 29th), policemen; Florian (May 4th), firemen. Benedict of Nursia was declared the patron saint of all Europe in 1964. The patron saint of the United States is the Immaculate Conception (December 8th).

10

With the clothes that were handed down to him throughout his childhood from his brothers Travis, five years his senior, and Richard, four years his senior, Jimmy Barnes was entrusted with bits and pieces of a discipline that was not his own. The Barnes boys were good boys because, as Jimmy Barnes realized many years later, there hadn't been much point in being anything else. It was more convenient to be good, to be prudent and honest and polite and industrious. It saved wear and tear, picking up things later, making excuses. Under the circumstances. The circumstances were his father, Big Travis, whose fortunes fluctuated between semi-affluence and poverty while the boys were growing up, and his mother, Edith, a tiny, busy woman who embraced the economic want that embarrassed Jimmy and was ignored by his brothers. Travis Barnes Senior came from an established Chicago family, harness makers before the fire, grain merchants and speculators afterward, whose good luck ended with Big Travis, who lost everything, the first time, in the market crash of 1929. Thereafter Big Travis vigorously pursued financial failure by investments in electric mattresses, collapsible sailboats, non-scorch aluminum-ware, white-meat chicken farming (a patented process that involved a special kind of light bulb), and central Florida real estate. In the meantime, Edith kept the family together by running a lending library in the big old Lake Forest house on Sheridan Road, transforming the servants' quarters over the garage into two small apartments for rental, representing a line of cosmetics that could only be purchased through door-to-door representatives ("Lelani Lipstick," went one of the slogans, "on everybody's lips"), making plum puddings, selling magazine subscriptions, and clerking at Marshall Field's. Only the Lake Forest zoning laws, and Big Travis, prevented her from selling the property on which there was a long-unused swimming pool.

Edith was described as "amazing," Big Travis as "charming," and the three boys, collectively, as "good." The two older boys, whose ages formed the basis of a strong, sweet, casually assumed alliance, worked their way through Choate and then through Yale. Jimmy worked his way through Lake Forest High and then through Williams and Harvard Law School. Travis and Richard justified everyone's faith in them by being elected co-captains of the Yale football team during Travis's senior year, when Richard was still a junior. Jimmy, who played football but not well enough to make any varsity teams, was thought of as the scholar, if only because he couldn't easily be thought of as anything else. He was more quick-witted than his brothers but also more shy: by the time the clothes reached him they were noticeably threadbare.

With Edith setting the tireless example the boys worked after school, during every school vacation, and throughout the summers, which, when Jimmy was going to Williams, sometimes meant that he went to débutante parties in the evenings and drank champagne on lawns he'd mowed that morning. But being good and of good family were not the only reasons for the brothers' popularity. Quite as important were their looks: sandy-haired, even-featured, attractively sullen in expression, long-boned, and lithe, so alike that only years distinguished one from another. They were handsome boys without a single truly remarkable characteristic. Jimmy learned early to capitalize on this, for he knew he fared best when he attracted no attention whatsoever.

When Jimmy was five he first came under the influence of Daisianna Caffrey, who was six. In the yard of the Bell School, during the kindergarten play period, he had kissed her. The plot, put together with two other small friends, had been designed to humiliate Daisianna, but it backfired. Daisianna screamed herself into hysterics, not because she was afraid but because she assumed it was the thing to do. The teacher tried to seem stern but laughed, and Travis and Richard were mortified. The humiliation bounced off Daisianna and splattered everyone else. Travis and Richard referred to Jimmy as "twerp" whenever they felt the need to address him. Otherwise they ostentatiously ignored him. Big Travis began calling Jimmy "The Sport" and Edith worried about her youngest son's sex life, but she dealt with such worries easily. She worked longer hours and more obsessively. She drew up plans for a tearoom to be opened on the first floor of the Barnes house and was discouraged only when she was told she'd need between two and three thousand dollars for the renovations and equipment. It was about this time that Edith began to wear blue tennis shoes.

Daisianna Caffrey became a continuing factor in Jimmy Barnes's life, though she was never in it for long at any one time. The Caffreys were the sort of people who could not settle. They were always moving into a house for a season and abruptly leaving six weeks later. Daisianna was always being taken out of school in the middle of a term to go to a school in Chicago or to accompany her father or mother or a grandparent to Florida or Europe or South America. Once her Grandmother Caffrey came into a Bell School classroom at 11 a.m. to take her on a cruise from New York through the Panama Canal to California. It seemed an enchanted existence, not to have known at breakfast that by lunch everything would be different. This was when Daisianna was eleven and Jimmy was ten. After that Jimmy saw little of Daisianna, who, he'd heard, had been sent to school in Switzerland. In the summer of 1941, when Edith had converted the first floor of the house on Sheridan Road into a collection center for Bundles for Britain and Friends of France, Daisianna, aged seventeen, reappeared in Lake Forest to stay with her Grandmother Caffrey, who was sponsoring her coming out. Daisianna was a sensation as much for driving her own red Buick convertible as for having dyed her naturally chestnut-colored hair platinum blond, which she wore long, only faintly curled, and over one eye in the style of Veronica Lake. Jimmy Barnes occasionally danced with her at parties and once he held her head while she was sick to her stomach sitting on the running board of a car in the Onwentsia Club's parking lot. She smelled of the chlorine of swimming pools, of fading perfume, of bourbon vomit. She let Jimmy take care of her because she didn't want any of her serious beaux to see her inability to hold her liquor. Later in the summer, Travis, who'd just been commissioned an ensign, returned to Lake Forest on leave and became her favorite escort. Edith was not pleased. She thought Daisianna acted too old for her age and wondered why Leola let her do such things as dye her hair that terrible color. Richard was away that summer and Jimmy pined while he watered flower beds, pruned bushes, and acted as the lifeguard at the Lake Forest beach.

One night before Labor Day he'd sat for an hour on the bluff of a North Shore park, overlooking a moonlit Lake Michigan, while Travis made love to Daisianna in her red convertible. They were on their way home from a party in Glencoe when Travis had driven into the small park, stopped the car, put the top up, and told Jimmy to get out and wait for them. Jimmy sat on a park bench twenty feet from the car and wept in fury. He'd heard stories about Daisianna but he'd never believed them. When Travis called him back to the car, he was still dressing himself. Daisianna looked as if she'd been crying. Though Jimmy barely glanced at either of them he was sure he could detect odors in the car he'd never before associated with either Travis or Daisianna. He breathed through his mouth to avoid contamination by evil thoughts but he nevertheless wondered if Travis had used a rubber and, if so, what one did with it afterward when one was in a car. One just couldn't leave a rubber on a road in a public park. He thought it might be somewhere in Daisianna's car. Probably the glove compartment. Jimmy was then a virgin.

Jimmy, who was to become seventeen in December, entered Williams that fall on a scholarship. Next to an English Jewish war refugee who was fifteen and had gone to Harrow, Jimmy was the youngest member of his class, which was a source of pride for Edith and Big Travis and a lot of difficulty for Jimmy. He really hadn't been ready for college but he had an ability to cram vast quantities of knowledge in a short period of time, which enabled him to score misleadingly high marks on examinations. He could have waited another year but he wanted to get on with things. Travis was already serving on a battleship in the Atlantic and Richard was going into midshipmen's school in October. In addition to working in the freshman dining hall and in the library, Jimmy had had to study twice as hard as everyone else he knew even to obtain fair grades. No one except Jimmy noticed he had the most meager of social lives though he was well liked, and if he wasn't sought after, neither was he left out. A Smith girl from Scarsdale told him seriously that he wore the right kind of shoes and the right kind of socks. In early November he bought a tweed sport jacket at Chipp in New York. It was the first new, seriously expensive piece of clothing he'd ever had, but the jacket turned out to be so much like the ones he'd received from Travis and Richard that not even Edith, when he went home at Christmas, realized that he had indulged himself so recklessly. She didn't notice the lack of chamois patches on the elbows. Two nights before the start of the Christmas vacation he successfully lost his virginity at a whorehouse in Schenectady.

Back in Lake Forest he was still the youngest of the Barnes boys. At parties at least one parent an evening would come up to him to ask, "Now, which one are you?" Meaning, usually, was he Travis or Richard. Sometimes the questions comforted him. They established connections and supports that allowed him a certain luxury in laziness. He permitted himself to drink to the point of getting drunk several times. He gave up trying to smoke a pipe and took naturally to cigarettes. He worked the entire vacation in the Lake Forest post office and went out every night, wearing either Travis's tails, which had once belonged to Big Travis, or Richard's dinner jacket. Neither of his brothers was home and it would have been a bleak vacation had he not been so busy. On top of all her other activities, Edith had organized a group of Lake Forest women to knit for the boys on Travis's ship, which was on the Murmansk run. Dark blue woolen mufflers and mittens and face masks were neatly folded and piled into cardboard boxes that filled the dining room, the butler's pantry, and the crystal closet. The crystal had gone years before. Their Christmas dinner of roast chicken was eaten on trays in Big Travis's bedroom. Edith talked of renting rooms to wives of servicemen stationed at Great Lakes and Fort Sheridan. His father, who had not been well for some time, talked of becoming an air-raid warden. Jimmy listened, very sad, missing his brothers more than he could have imagined. Without them, family conversation was halt.

He had seen Daisianna at a number of parties, including her own at the Cotillion Club, and he'd dance with her at least once an evening, but they didn't have much to talk about, not even Travis. She was more beautiful, more sophisticated, more unknown, more bored than ever. Also older. The way she moved her knee when she danced at first was a secret topic of admiration and wonder in the stag lines. Then of disapproval. She was indiscriminate, which insulted everyone. Two days after New Year's she achieved a small headline near the bottom on page 1 of Hearst's *Herald-American:* "DEB FLEES TO OMAHA/HEIR IS ARRESTED." There was a picture on the inside showing Daisianna being taken into an Omaha courtroom by a woman jail attendant who was wearing what looked to be a turn-of-the-century shirt-waist dress. Daisianna was wearing dark glasses and a fur coat. It might have been Veronica Lake making a personal appearance on behalf of war bonds. It was reported that Daisianna, instead of returning to school in Dobbs Ferry as her father had thought, got off the *20th Century Limited* at Inglewood, the only suburban stop on the South Side of Chicago, and joined Jay Bixby and Dinny Murdock in Jay's car, intending to drive to Hollywood. Jay's father had had Jay arrested for car theft and all three were kept in jail overnight. Daisianna told the reporter: "Some of those women in my cell were extremely rude." Further on in the story she was quoted as saying that "it was all a terrible mistake." Two years afterward, when Jimmy was in mid-shipmen's school in New York, he received a newspaper clipping from Edith about Daisianna's marriage in Chicago to a Marine Corps pilot from Seattle.

11

In January Big Travis went into St. Luke's Hospital where the doctors removed all his teeth and a portion of his lower jawbone. Edith telephoned Jimmy in Williamstown and in three minutes said his father was fine, that the doctors were convinced they'd got all of it and that radium treatments would make sure. In April Travis Senior was back in the hospital for the removal of more of the jawbone and half of his tongue. Edith called Jimmy to tell him not to worry, that Big Travis would have some difficulty speaking, but that things could have been worse. When Jimmy came home to Lake Forest in early June nothing that Edith had said had prepared him for what he found. Big Travis had shrunk from 175 pounds to 130. The lower portion of his face had collapsed into folds of skin that dragged down the corners of his mouth so that it maintained an expression of continual reproach. He couldn't speak. He grunted or manipulated his fallen mouth in ways that Edith said she understood but it couldn't have been described as speech. When Jimmy walked into his father's bedroom, he found Big Travis dressed in khaki pants, cinched around the waist with a tie, and an old shirt of Jimmy's that had been handed down when Jimmy was fourteen. Big Travis sat in a chair by the window and tried to grin. As Jimmy walked to him, his father stood up, imitating decision. Jimmy put his arms around him gingerly, afraid he might crush what was left. Jimmy's eyes were full of tears and his father made a fist and lightly hit Jimmy's arm. It was the kind of undergraduate gesture his father had never abandoned. They spent most of the afternoon sitting in his father's bedroom listening to the baseball game on the radio. Occasionally his father wrote notes that Jimmy answered as if he were talking to a lip reader, which annoyed his father. His father asked Jimmy how his golf game was and told Jimmy that he had played eighteen holes the week before with Gil Rogers. "I didn't break ninety," his father wrote. "First time club in my hands in year." Jimmy said great, great, and smiled and looked at the floor. His father was barefoot and his feet were the feet of a young man, the skin smooth and firm and the toes long and seemingly vigorous. They could have been the feet of Travis, Richard, or himself, which made Jimmy uneasy. The feet had no connection with the relic above. Gil Rogers had been killed in an automobile accident in 1938.

Said his mother later: "It's the injections. He becomes confused. He did go to the club once but he didn't play golf. I've told Dr. Wall about it and he says not to worry." She summed up: "Your father's all right. He's not even in much pain. He's *afraid* of pain. He anticipates it. Which is why he gives himself injections when he doesn't need them."

"What kind of injections?"

"I don't know," said Edith, who was knitting furiously on a dark blue muffler. "They have morphine in them, but Dr. Wall says if he gives himself too much, he'll just get sick to his stomach."

It was early evening and Jimmy and his mother were sitting by the abandoned swimming pool in old-fashioned iron lawn chairs. The main house, a hundred feet away, was hidden by a grove of lilac bushes that had grown into a forest of tangled trees. Big Travis had recently been trying to rehabilitate the area. He spent his afternoons cutting weeds and tearing away the vines that grew from the cracks in the pool sides. The Italianate, marble-faced pool house remained boarded up, but sloppily, as if to register someone's disapproval.

Edith said at one point, "I don't know what your father thinks he's doing. When he came home from the hospital in March, the first thing he wanted to do was put the pool back in condition. It's impossible, of course. The drains don't work. There is no pump. No filters. Nothing. It would take thousands, which, I don't have to tell you, we don't have." She held the muffler up to measure it. "With the doctor bills and the hospital bills, there isn't going to be anything for anybody anyway." She nodded angrily toward the pool, which looked like a small benign cavity compared with the emptiness of more elaborate, larger pools. "Look at it. It wasn't any good when it was new. It has always leaked, from the year your grandfather built it. You've never even swum in it."

"I remember swimming in it," said Jimmy. "When I was little. I remember it was filled with tadpoles and the sides were slimy."

"That was the year your grandfather died," said Edith. "The year we moved in. You certainly haven't swum in it since then. Travis and Richard tried to take care of it, but even they couldn't do it."

As was her custom Edith made sure that Jimmy would have no wasted moments during the summer. He worked from 7 a.m. until 1 p.m. with two local boys who ran a lawn and garden service. From 2 p.m. until 6, six days a week, he was the lifeguard at the Lake Forest beach. It seemed a peaceful summer with few immediate worries. Travis's ship was based in Guantánamo Bay, though his mother and her friends continued to knit cold-weather gear. This was a time when people felt nothing should interfere with the war effort. Richard was stationed in California. His father gained weight, or so Edith said, though Jimmy knew, or suspected he knew, differently. Jimmy was not sure his father ate anything at all. Big Travis took his food to his room so that no one could watch him and the efforts his eating required. As his father dwindled, Jimmy turned very tan and felt healthier than he ever had before in his life. He was aware of strength in parts of his body he had seldom thought of, in his fingers, in the small of his back. One night a week he went out with a girl from Waukegan who allowed him to go all the way, and three or four other nights a week he went out with Lake Forest girls who didn't. It was a perfect arrangement for the sort of man Jimmy Barnes was becoming. He learned not to be shocked by his father's appearance. He even forgot about it to the extent that he had something resembling a fight with his father about the amount of black-market gasoline he was using. By written note and speech. "Well, I pay for it!" Jimmy yelled and stalked out of the house. When he returned home that night, there was a note from his father stuck under Jimmy's bedroom door. It said: "You're right, son," and was initialed "T.B."

On the first Tuesday in August Jimmy came home at one, as he did every day, to fix lunch for himself and his father and to change for the beach. Edith, who lunched at a drugstore downtown near Marshall Field's, would usually leave written instructions that his father, if he felt well enough, would have begun when Jimmy returned. Baby food, applesauce, cottage cheese for his father, sandwiches for him. On this day there were no written instructions and no Big Travis. Jimmy supposed that one of his father's friends had come by and taken him for a drive or to the club. He made a sandwich and sat eating in the kitchen, wondering why he felt uneasy. Jimmy liked routine, as he knew his father did. He stared out the kitchen window toward the garage, thinking about the major's wife. She lived in the garage apartment that faced his bedroom and never pulled down her blinds when she undressed at night. For that matter, neither did the major when he was home on weekends. Jimmy was staring at the garage and realized that the side door of the garage, which was always closed, was open, and that the big double doors, which were always open, were now closed. It was, of course, the perfect time to do it. It was the way his father planned.

Big Travis had thrown the rope over one of Grandfather Barnes's mock-Tudor beams from which, in earlier years, the boys had hung their pony saddles. He had then stood on a stepladder. He was barefoot. Jimmy pulled the ladder upright and stood on it, trying to lift his father to take the weight from the rope. For no purpose at all. Jimmy held his father and cried for all his pain, for the anticipated pain and the injections, for the loss of a tongue, for having no money. There was no way to cut his father down without having him fall two feet to the concrete floor. That was the saddest thing.

Edith seemed too busy to cry. There were the efforts to be made to obtain leaves for Travis and Richard. There were the funeral arrangements. Brothers, sisters, cousins to be notified by Western Union. Not telephone. In those days, the announcement of a death in the family was always made by wire. It was more dignified, less inviting of emotional displays. There were Barnes relatives all over the country. There were old friends. The house needed opening up. There was food to buy. Late that night, after Dr. Wall had given Jimmy some sleeping pills for his mother ("She may not show it but she's wound up"), Jimmy and Edith walked out to the pool. "Travis and Richard," said Edith, "I hope they don't go to pieces." Jimmy had his arm around his mother's waist in a move toward an intimacy she suddenly acknowledged. "He was so handsome when he was young," Edith said. "I couldn't believe that he loved me. I was no great beauty even then. I was no great catch. But after we were married, even before any of you boys were born, I realized I didn't love him. He was a nice man, and he was thoughtful. He was as thoughtful as a nice man can be, a man who doesn't feel many things, whose interests are limited." Edith took a deep breath and relaxed for the first time in years. "I shouldn't say this to you, but I want to: your father was a very boring man."

12

Both Travis and Richard were able to return for the funeral. It was the kind of funeral at which people said it was better this way, that at least the pain that Edith never admitted was over. What gloom there was Richard helped to lift by his announcement that he was engaged to an admiral's daughter in Coronado Beach. She was the first of two admirals' daughters Richard was to become engaged to, marry, and be divorced from before V-J Day. Jimmy had wanted to tell Travis and Richard the marvelous thing about their father on that last day, how Big Travis so trusted him and the high value Jimmy placed on routine that he planned his suicide in just the manner he had. It was a source of increasing wonder and joy to Jimmy that his father had taken him into his confidence in a way that he had never done in all the years that had gone before. Jimmy soon realized that it was as impossible to confide in either Travis or Richard as it was in his mother. He thought about the difference between privacy of feelings and isolation.

With Travis Senior finally gone, and the house held in trust by her for the three boys, Edith became more and more of a village eccentric. She wore the blue sneakers year round and in the winter she kept warm with a sailor's dark blue pea jacket and knitted watch cap. She gave up her job at Marshall Field's to devote herself full-time to her paying guests: servicemen (preferably officers) and their wives to whom she let all the rooms but a small bedroom and bath on the third floor where she lived. The guests paid well and Edith outdid herself in providing them with services. She purchased a restaurant-sized refrigerator so that the guests —those who also paid for kitchen privileges—had adequate room for their stores of food. She bought a second stove and installed it in the butler's pantry. She had the house re-painted for the first time in twenty years and spent much of her time cleaning, disposing of garbage, washing linens and dishes, and repairing the electric wiring. When Jimmy's ship was stationed in Japan with the Occupation forces, Travis wrote him of his first postwar visit home: "Mother seems to be in her element. Full of vinegar and never better." Richard also wrote Jimmy: "Mother's turned (the house) into a boarding house and everyone treats her like a maid. I stayed one night and moved into the Deerpath Inn. Someday I'll tell you what happened when I brought Susie home on our wedding trip." Susie was Richard's second wife, to whom he was married for nine weeks when she fell in love with a submarine captain stationed in New London. The three boys had long since gone their separate ways.

13

Jimmy Barnes graduated from Harvard Law School in January, 1948, and in February joined the Chicago law firm of Banks, Travis, Dietweiller & Swift, of which a long-dead great-uncle of his father's, a never-known James Travis, had been a founding partner. He took a one-room apartment in a pleasantly run-down brownstone on Bellevue Place, half a block from the lake on the near North Side, and continued to study and work as hard as he had at Cambridge. He genuinely liked the law, though he knew he could never be a trial lawyer. He wasn't a public performer. He liked the heavy routine of the law firm and he liked the kind of discipline of the law that allowed the mind to be brought to bear in ways that Jimmy called creative. He heard himself saying this one night in a Rush Street bar, and he remembered what Edith had said about his father. He wondered if he too would someday be so boring.

Jimmy spent occasional weekends in Lake Forest. Richard was living in Santa Barbara, married to his third wife, the daughter of a General Motors vice-president who'd been helpful in obtaining an Oldsmobile dealership for him. Edith was torn between embarrassment at having a son who'd become an automobile salesman, which she seemed to see as a kind of parking-lot attendant, and satisfaction in the knowledge that he was making a great deal of money. Travis was temporarily living at home, awaiting his marriage to a Chicago girl whose parents were giving him his own seat on the stock exchange as a wedding present. The paying guests had left and Edith had immediately turned the first floor of the house into a day school for children, age two to four. She had twelve students. The walls of the entrance hall, the drawing room, the library, and the dining room had once been dark with huge, solemn, ornately framed, orangey-brown portraits of American Indians and American Indian life collected by Grandfather Barnes, who'd given in to his passion for thirty years without ever collecting a Frazer, a Nolan, or a Remington. The Indians were sent to the attic, their places taken by finger-painted murals of choo-choos going through fields of moo-moos, by still lifes of jack-o'-lanterns, by elaborate portraits of mummies and daddies holding toothpick hands by swimming pools in front of trees that looked like all-green geraniums, under blue skies that would never touch earth. Jimmy feared there might be laws forbidding Edith's latest career but found there weren't. She was all right as long as she didn't give her scholars degrees, and as long as the house had enough exits.

Mostly Jimmy stayed in Chicago where his friends were but, being unmarried, he had little in common with them,

little interest in the problems of first pregnancies. He found
the secretaries at the law firm available but serious, and he
envied his friends who worked at advertising agencies where
everyone seemed to spend at least three hours a day fucking
in mail rooms. He'd never felt lonelier. He'd felt less alone
in the ruined alleys of Manila and Tokyo, in the law school
library. In late April he ran into Cleo Graffmueller who'd
been in his class at the Bell School until she went away to
Dobbs.

"All the girls of summer are pretty." It was something his
father had said years before at a Fourth of July fireworks
party at Onwentsia. Jimmy met Cleo Graffmueller again on
a clear, unseasonably warm spring night at a Lake Forest
cocktail party. "All the girls of summer are pretty," his
father had said, "even if they aren't." Cleo was a girl of
summer. The fat, bossy little girl he remembered from Bell
had worked herself into the kind of trim one associates with
Russian women athletes. She had a good body, which is the
way Jimmy's friends described ugly girls who were not
total losses, who were retrieved by fine legs and firm breasts,
which Cleo had. At twenty-four, Cleo wore her straight,
mouse-colored hair in a spinster's bun. Her complexion was
artifice not completely disguising old acne. Jimmy found
her immediately appealing and reassuring. She had the color
of summer on her arms ("Hobe Sound in March, and I've
been playing tennis the last three weekends") and she
smelled of Balenciaga. They dined that night at the club on
Travis's membership, the first one the family had had since
1935. Cleo worked as a secretary at the Chicago *Daily News*,
where her father was an advertising executive, but she did
not intend to have a career. "I think I'll raise English sheepdogs," she said, "when I can get at the principal of my trust.
But I have to wait until I'm thirty, an age my grandfather
made up." She'd spent the 1946–47 winter in Paris at the

Sorbonne. "It was very Scott Fitzgerald," she said, and she had caught pneumonia while staying with cousins in Rome at Easter. She said, "Palazzos *are* hard to heat," paused as she heard how curious it sounded, and they both laughed. During the week she lived in the apartment of an aunt on Astor Street and she spent her weekends in Lake Forest. "I like my life," she said to Jimmy. "Do you like yours?" "Yes," said Jimmy, "I think I do. It's not terribly exciting but I don't think I want an exciting life." "Neither do I," said Cleo. "I enjoy having money and parties and well-made clothes. I suppose I should feel guilty but I enjoy them too much." In the first impulsive gesture he'd made in years, Jimmy took Cleo's hand and held it gently on the red-and-white checkered tablecloth. "The difference with you, I think," he said, "is that if you lost it you'd still be the same." Cleo Graffmueller was moved to tears, which moved Jimmy Barnes to tears. "I'm not sure," Cleo said, "that's why I want to make certain that I don't lose it." Six weeks later, after an afternoon of tennis when Cleo was wearing a particularly becoming short, pleated tennis skirt, Jimmy asked her to marry him. "Of course," said Cleo. "I've already more or less told Daddy. We can be married in December, after I get back from England." Jimmy looked surprised. "More cousins," she said in a new, frighteningly flirtatious way. "I've promised."

14

One evening in July Jimmy Barnes was walking north on Rush Street to dine with Cleo and her aunt. His thoughts were a peacefully unpressed jumble of associations: Cleo, food, well-being, the evening air that had suddenly become translucently cool when the wind shifted from south to east, off the lake. It was one of the satisfactions of Chicago summers. "Barnes," someone said. "Barnes. I know it's a Barnes." Standing in front of him, occupying the middle of the sidewalk as if to block his way, was a fat old lady with platinum hair and swollen ankles, dressed in the sort of flowered print housecoat that women usually wear in privacy when using the vacuum cleaner. She leaned heavily on a yellow cane and smiled out of Jimmy's childhood. "Travis or Richard?" she asked. "James," said Jimmy. "Of course," the old lady said. She laughed with a weighty wheeze and gave him her cheek to kiss. It was puffy and veined. "Leola Caffrey," said the woman. "My God, it's been years." She grasped his hand in a way that made Jimmy think she would topple over if she let go. "How is your mother, dear? I can't tell you how sorry I was to hear about your father. Going that way. I mean the cancer not the hanging. I understand your mother is now running a university." She laughed a cheerless barroom laugh. "My God, you've grown." She kept him standing in the middle of the sidewalk for ten minutes talking about the old days in Lake Forest, about people he never knew or no longer remembered. Jimmy finally asked about Daisianna. "Daisianna," Leola said, "the no-TOR-ious Daisianna was living in Los Angeles the last time I heard." "I thought she was living in Seattle," said Jimmy. "She was living in Seattle," Leola said, "until the divorce." "I didn't even know she was divorced," said Jimmy. "Two or three years ago," said Leola. "I can't keep track of time anymore." "I'm sorry," said Jimmy, "about the divorce." Leola laughed. "If you're sorry, then you're probably the only person who is. I told her it wouldn't last. There was something very strange about that boy. But he *was* handsome. I'll say that." The pauses between bits of information that Leola cared to give up grew longer and longer and Jimmy wanted to get away. He asked where she was living. "Under straitened circumstances," said Leola. "That's where I live." She laughed loudly without managing to sound robust. "Due to the avariciousness of my former husband and the Typhoid Mary he married." Jimmy laughed too. "No," she said, "I'm living in a darling little apartment on Division Street, over a darling little pansy bar, Snow White's. Do you know it?" Jimmy said he didn't. "I should hope not," said Leola. "But I shouldn't say that. They're very nice about extending what is curiously called credit. Which, curiously, I'm often in need of." "Well," said Jimmy, "I'd better be going. It was great seeing you." "I'd rather you'd seen *me* great," said Leola. "Give Daisianna my best when you write," said Jimmy. Leola shrugged. "I'm off to the movies," she said, "the early-bird hour, before the prices change." She prepared her cane and her feet to continue the hobble down Rush Street. "At five-thirty in the evening. My God. Fate dictates."

15

Daisianna returned to Chicago in early October. The evening before Cleo was to leave for New York and London, Jimmy arrived at the Astor Street apartment to be met by an angry Cleo. She stepped into the hallway and closed the door so they could not be heard inside. "Daisianna Caffrey is here," Cleo said, frowning. Jimmy smiled with surprise. "I didn't know you knew her." "I can't get rid of her," said Cleo. "She telephoned to ask if she could come over for one drink. When I told her about us, she insisted on staying until you arrived." "I didn't realize you knew Daisianna," said Jimmy. "For heaven's sake," said Cleo, "she used to be one of my closest friends. Just don't offer her another drink or she'll be here all night."

Jimmy followed Cleo into the living room where Daisianna

was sitting on the couch, her legs drawn up and her sandals on the cushions in a way that Jimmy knew infuriated Cleo, who was always precise about the cost of things, as well as of services such as dry cleaning. If he hadn't been prepared, Jimmy might not have recognized Daisianna. She was wearing dark glasses and her hair had been dyed a Hedy Lamarr black. She was wearing it in the same sort of bun at the back of the neck affected by Cleo, but Daisianna looked beautiful, very feminine, very small, very graceful. Her black dress was sleeveless and Jimmy was aware first of deeply tanned skin and then of something about Daisianna he'd always liked but never placed in the forefront of his consciousness: her upper arms and elbows. Daisianna had the thinnest upper arms and elbows he'd ever seen. Not only fragile, but thin. She'd be a terrible tennis player.

"Hello," said Jimmy. He smiled like a retarded delivery boy and made no attempt to disguise his pleasure. "Darling Jimmy," said Daisianna. She reached up to put an arm around his neck as he bent to kiss her. "My God," he said, dropping onto the couch beside her. "My God. I can't believe it." "What?" said Cleo. "Daisianna here," said Jimmy. "I sort of thought she'd fled from us forever." "Not quite," said Cleo. Jimmy got up to make himself a drink and asked Daisianna if she'd like another. "I shouldn't," said Daisianna, "but I will. How are Travis and Richard?" She turned to Cleo: "Do you remember how much in love with Travis I was?" Jimmy, his back to them at the ice bucket, came as close to giggling as he ever did. He'd forgotten Daisianna's manner of assuming that everyone had a share in her experiences, the way a child believes a dream has been shared with the person dreamed of. "But Travis hardly looked at me." "Oh, come on," said Jimmy. He thought of the night in the red convertible, and went into a deep, sweaty blush. "Travis took me out once or twice, but that's all," said Daisianna. "Dear Jimmy, you look exactly like him." "That's what everybody says," said Cleo, "but they don't look alike at all. Not that much, anyway. Travis looks more like an athlete. He moves like one." Cleo, who sat opposite them on a small, chintz-covered chair, at that moment looked like a lady wrestler. "I'm a boring lawyer," Jimmy said to Daisianna. "Mother told me she'd seen Richard," said Daisianna, "on Rush Street several months ago." "That was me," said Jimmy. "Richard lives in Santa Barbara. *I* ran into your mother on Rush Street several months ago."

Daisianna was in no hurry to leave. They had several more drinks and Cleo became increasingly distracted, which was Cleo's way of being impolite. She eventually invited Daisianna to join them at supper, served in the dining room by an elderly Irishwoman who wore a white uniform and bedroom slippers. Cleo talked about the wedding plans. When Daisianna showed interest, Cleo changed the subject to her trip to England. She emphasized more than once that it was her last night with Jimmy. Daisianna made several weak gestures toward departure, which prompted Jimmy to offer to take her home, in turn prompting Cleo to soften a bit and ask Daisianna to stay for at least a brandy. When Cleo said she still had to pack, Jimmy said immediately that she had packed last night. "That was my steamer trunk," said Cleo. "I'm also taking two suitcases."

Jimmy and Daisianna left at midnight, with Jimmy promising to fetch Cleo at noon the next day to take her to the LaSalle Street Station.

When they were on the street, Daisianna said she shouldn't have stayed.

"Why not?" said Jimmy. "It was a beautiful evening."

Daisianna was living with her mother, two blocks away on Division Street, but they never made it. Daisianna walked with care. "I think I'm a little tight," she said, "but also I can't see. These are the only glasses I have and if I take them off, I'm blind." They stopped at the Airliner Lounge, an overstaffed, underpatronized bar at the corner of Rush and Division. One night, sitting in the bar alone, hoping vaguely for some kind of transformation, Jimmy had been shocked to realize that the peculiarly shaped airplanes painted as a frieze just below the ceiling were really antic penises in various stages of erection, to which had been attached little white angel wings. "It should be a queer hangout," said Jimmy, "but it isn't. It isn't anything." Jimmy and Daisianna sat at the bar, the only customers. They held hands and pressed knees together. "I'm so glad you're marrying Cleo," said Daisianna, fondling his fingers. "Yes," said Jimmy, moving his right leg between hers. "Of course," said Daisianna, "she doesn't approve of me." "Why?" said Jimmy. "She never has," said Daisianna. "When we were at Dobbs I was always getting her into trouble, and Cleo doesn't like getting into trouble. Once we were caught smoking and confined to the school for the rest of the term. Cleo was furious. It meant she couldn't go riding." "What about you?" Daisianna smiled. "I was able to go to New York once a week anyway. I was having my teeth straightened. Cleo, unfortunately, had perfectly straight teeth." Jimmy rubbed his hands along Daisianna's hips. "I didn't realize you two knew each other. I mean, I'd forgotten." "It's strange," said Daisianna. "She was probably my best friend in those days, but when I think about it now, I didn't even like her very much. She was always a bit of a plush horse. She always seemed overstuffed. She's changed a lot." "Yes," said Jimmy. He paused a moment, and went on: "I remember her at the Bell School. She was fat in those days." "And she always knew everything," said Daisianna. "Yes," said Jimmy. They sank into silent depressions. Daisianna, at last: "It's marvelous how some people improve as they get older. Cleo is like that. She's going to become more and more beautiful as time goes on." Jimmy nodded. He felt terrible. Cleo would still be playing tennis when she was eighty. Daisianna squeezed his hand. He said, "Can we go to my place?" Daisianna: "Of course."

They began living together immediately but acknowledged the arrangement by installments, in the accumulation of Daisianna's clothes, shoes, make-up, and records at Bellevue Place. This substituted for plans and commitments, and suited them both. Jimmy's apartment was small but Daisianna liked it and said it had atmosphere, meaning the wood-burning fireplace. They were able to fit into it by hanging clothes on the backs of doors and from hangers attached to old sconces. It was an octagonal-shaped room, on the first floor, with mullioned windows that overlooked an immaculately tended city garden, and was furnished with a pair of day beds and other remnants of earlier tenants. Their telephone was the pay telephone in the entrance hall and, like the bath and the kitchen, was shared with the occupant of the only other apartment on the floor, a shy, slim young man who worked in a bank and plucked his eyebrows. Leola never intruded on them and, according to Daisianna, never asked where she was staying. There were occasional attempts by Daisianna to find a job, but she wasn't sure she wanted to stay in Chicago. Her most pressing problem was that she was broke. Her mother had no money to give her, and to obtain money from Dodie meant having to have dinner with him and Ida, her stepmother, an ordeal Daisianna preferred putting off as long as possible. The first two weeks were dazzling, happy ones for Jimmy. They made love two and three times a night, something that Jimmy equated with life in Sodom. They would awaken at 2 a.m., make love and drink and play Piaf records, and Daisianna would tell him fragmented stories about adventures in Seattle and Los Angeles, where, most recently, she'd worked in a dress shop, signed up for acting lessons she didn't take, and lived with a girl she'd gone to school with in Switzerland, whose father, a producer, had just been fired from MGM. Her stories were filled with characters identified only by first names, and with situations that never had resolutions. She was even more vague about life in Seattle, where she'd gone with her husband at the end of the war. "Actually," she said, "I went there before the war was over, to wait for Pete. After I was kicked out of the Marines." "The Marines?" said Jimmy. "When were you in the Marines?" "I was in the Marines for almost six months," said Daisianna. "They discharged me when I refused to cut my hair."

Daisianna's mind raced across the surface of memories like a tumbleweed:

"Pete collected birds' nests. Have you ever known anyone who collected birds' nests? They are very strange. He worked in his father's brokerage house, and every night we'd go to bed at nine so that he could get up at five to read. About birds and birds' nests. On weekends we'd go into the mountains with sleeping bags and knapsacks, and collect birds' nests. Once he almost broke his neck trying to get some sort of eagle's nest. The basement smelled like a chicken coop. . . ."

"I didn't ask for any alimony but I did get the furniture, and all my wedding presents and the family silver and things I was given by Granny Caffrey and Granny Overton. That's why I don't have any money. Everything's in storage in Seattle, and storage is very expensive. . . ."

"Pete believed in being fit. I used to be able to do twenty-five push-ups. I thought it would make me very bosomy, but it didn't. He liked big tits, which is probably why we were divorced, tits and birds' nests. . . ."

"I wonder if it's too late for me to become a ballet dancer. I love ballet and I think I'd be quite good. I'd be willing to study hard if I knew I'd be any good at the end of it. . . ."

"Jimmy, don't ever water the gin. Pete used to do that. He didn't think I'd know. . . ."

"Let's go out to dinner tonight. Please, darling, someplace not too inexpensive."

Little by little the lack of routine he found so engaging in Daisianna turned into deliberate chaos. Their room looked like a closet stuffed with clothes, records, half-read magazines, liquor bottles. Daisianna's superb tan faded and she began to drink without him during the day. The bank clerk wrote them a gentle note about the condition of the bathroom and left it in an envelope on the washbasin. Daisianna was fascinated by the envelope. It was large and square, the sort one might use for a Christmas card or, as Daisianna pointed out, a valentine. The note said: "I've bought some sponges and some Dutch Cleanser to clean the tub after bathing. They're in the cupboard under the basin." The night Jimmy bought orchestra seats for the ballet Daisianna said she loved, she slept through the second half of the program. Another night he worked late and returned to the apartment at midnight, wanting her badly, to find her drunk, improvising ballet steps to Frank Sinatra records. He'd heard the music when he came into the house from the street and knew that the bank clerk and the tenants upstairs must be frantic. "For Christ's sake," he said. He turned off the record player so roughly he almost broke it. Daisianna burst into tears and he was immediately sorry. She hiccuped and sobbed and he comforted her for having frightened her. He said, "This is the first time I've seen you cry since that time in kindergarten, when I kissed you in the yard. Remember?" She drew back from him, stared into his eyes through her tears. "Was that you?" she said. "I always thought it was Richard."

When they were making love that night Jimmy became aware that Daisianna was feeling absolutely nothing. Sex wasn't an end in itself for her. It was only a way of keeping him a little longer, a means of hanging on to the day. The knowledge that this had always been true saddened him and made him uneasy, though it didn't make her less appealing.

"I suppose you realize," Travis said at lunch several days later, "that she's the town pump."

When Travis had telephoned, he'd said he wanted to talk business with Jimmy, but when they sat down in the restaurant, the first thing he mentioned was Daisianna. "What the hell do you think you're doing?" Travis said. "You certainly don't think it's a secret, do you?" Jimmy said no. "What about Cleo? You're engaged to be married to a darn nice girl and you let yourself get mixed up with someone who's probably been fucked by every man between here and Honolulu." Jimmy could find nothing to say. He was five and Travis was ten and telling him he was a twerp for having kissed a girl. Jimmy said that Daisianna needed help. "Well, let someone else help her," said Travis. "Cleo's bound to hear about it and then you really will be in trouble. I don't understand. You're supposed to be the smartest one in the family and yet you do something as stupid as this. Daisianna is a joke."

Travis was so upset that he drank two martinis to Jimmy's one. Cleo was right about Travis. He did look like an athlete, even when he drank a martini. There was a certain clumsy grace in the manner in which he held the stem of the small glass and gulped *at* it. It was as if he were going to roll the martini around in his mouth and then spit it out on the carpeted floor of St. Hubert's Grill. A ladle of water at half time. "I don't care what you do," said Travis, "as long as you don't make the rest of us look ridiculous. You don't have to live with everybody you screw." "Or screw everybody you live with," said Jimmy. "What do you mean by that?" Travis asked the question mildly. "I haven't any idea," said Jimmy.

The reason Travis had invited Jimmy to have lunch was to make a business proposal. Travis and his fiancée, Emmy Lou Gooding, wanted to buy the Barnes house and to restore it and the outbuildings and the property itself to some measure of the estate's worth. They wanted to live there when they were married. Travis wanted his children to be born there. Edith, he said, would have the interest on the sum he and Emmy Lou would pay the estate, and then, on their mother's death, the money would be divided between Richard and Jimmy. Travis had already talked to Edith, who had come around to the idea—she would live in a new, enlarged apartment over the garage—and Richard was willing to go along with the plan if Jimmy was. "Eighty thousand dollars," said Travis, "with the proviso that if, at the time of Mother's death, the property has increased in value, that sum will be added to the original price. The value of the property, that is, not of the house. Well?"

"I don't know," said Jimmy.

"What don't you know?"

"I don't care about the house anymore," said Jimmy. "You can do anything you want with it."

16

When Jimmy returned from the office on the evening that he and Daisianna were to dine with her father, stepmother, and grandmother, Daisianna had already taken two hot baths and was running a third. He could smell the steamy scent even in the entrance hall. Daisianna acted as if she were about to appear in court. "Ida can be very critical," said Daisianna. She refused the drink Jimmy offered her, saying that they had to be prompt. In the walk to Lake Shore Drive Daisianna wore her dark glasses but took them off in the elevator going up to her Grandmother Caffrey's apartment. She looked wan, sober, and fearful. The butler, a gray-haired Negro named Felix, was waiting by the elevator door when it opened. He nodded toward Dodie and Ida, who stood waiting for them in the hallway behind Felix, as if in a receiving line. Dodie, a small, slim, dapper man with silver hair and ruddy complexion, hugged Daisianna and called her Daisy. Daisianna and Ida brushed cheeks. Ida, who had been a trained nurse when Dodie was a patient at the Crocker Clinic in Madison twenty years before, wore an austere black evening dress, the sort that lady harpsichordists wear, and a ring containing the biggest emerald Jimmy had ever seen. Her manner was still that of a trained nurse —not a sympathetic, solicitous private nurse but a ward nurse dedicated to the maintenance of discipline. They were led into the drawing room, a spectacular, two-story room that looked like a baronial hall mysteriously levitated to rest atop a fourteen-story Chicago apartment house. The wormholes in the paneling were real, as were the heads of mountain lions, ibex, rhinoceros, and black panther. Zebra skins lay on the back of a leather sofa and there was a Siberian tiger on the floor in front of the fireplace, facing outward toward the room. Through the expanse of plate-glass window one could see the rush-hour traffic curling along the Outer Drive north toward Evanston. Everything in the room was heavy but it seemed to be afloat. Ida told Daisianna to go upstairs and say good night to her grandmother. "She's not feeling very well. I thought it best she stay in bed." When Dodie indicated he would go with Daisianna, Ida stopped him: "Let her go by herself. Felix is bringing the drinks."

The drinks were ginger ale for Dodie and sherry for the rest. Felix also served potato chips as if he were presenting caviar.

"I remember you went to Yale," Dodie said to Jimmy, "and that you were quite a football star." "I went to Williams," said Jimmy. "You're thinking of one of my brothers." "One of his brothers is marrying the Gooding girl," said Ida. Dodie: "I went to Princeton. We've bought a house there." Ida: "We haven't bought a house there. We've been pricing some. That's all." Daisianna returned to the drawing room and sat beside her father on the sofa with the zebra skins. She'd been weeping. When Dodie asked her what was wrong, Daisianna showed him a five-dollar bill. "Granny told me to take five dollars from her purse." She looked at Jimmy. "She always used to give me five dollars when I came home from school on vacations." Said Ida: "I didn't know she had any money in her purse. She shouldn't have. It just gets stolen by the maids."

"She should have some money," said Dodie.

"If it doesn't get stolen, she gives it away," said Ida. She made a gesture of futility toward Jimmy. She turned her head to him but didn't look at him. "She's eighty-six and forgetful. She's also secretive. I found a dividend check under her mattress the other day."

"She seemed fine to me," said Daisianna.

"She's dying," said Ida. "She'll be dead in six months."

Daisianna's eyes filled with tears and Dodie patted her hand. Ida: "I hope all of us can live that long. It's nothing to be sad about."

The conversation at the dinner table was full of spaces. Dodie talked about Princeton again, about running into San White, the legendary Princeton football star, not long before. "He's bought a farm in Virginia." Said Ida: "It's in Maryland." There was no wine but the sherry decanter was placed near Ida, who helped herself from time to time without offering any to the others. Coffee was served in the library, which was almost as big as the drawing room and had ladders on wheels so one could reach the books on the higher shelves. Jimmy sat on a couch under a portrait of Daisianna's great-grandfather, whose fortune had its origins in garbage transformed into real estate—Lake Michigan landfill—on some of which stood the apartment building they were now in.

"Well," said Ida, "isn't it about time we discussed why you came over?"

Daisianna looked weepy again. She found the dark glasses in her purse and put them on.

"You want money, I assume," said Ida.

"Dear," said Dodie.

"I'm sure Mr. Barnes will not be embarrassed," said Ida. "He's heard money discussed before, haven't you, Mr. Barnes?"

Ida did not look at Jimmy. She wanted no answer. "Your father and I have been waiting for this occasion for some time. I trust you do want some money, don't you?"

"Yes," said Daisianna. "I have to pay the storage on my furniture in Seattle."

"Have you thought of working?" said Ida. "Or is that something you'd prefer we didn't talk about?"

"I thought I might look for a job at Saks's or Bendel's or someplace like that," said Daisianna. "I've also thought about going back to school. I've thought about studying ballet, maybe painting."

"Ballet and painting," said Ida. "One or the other, or both?"

"One or the other," said Daisianna.

Dodie was not connected to the scene in progress. He addressed himself to Jimmy. "Daisianna was very talented as a little girl. Painting."

"I don't think she's had much interest in painting recently," said Ida. "Not from what I've heard. Isn't that true, Daisianna?"

"Yes," said Daisianna. "I suppose so."

"How much money do you want?" said Ida.

"Five hundred dollars."

"Why don't you ask your mother?"

"She doesn't have it."

"She doesn't have it," said Ida. "Your father gives her money every month, though heaven knows why. She doesn't give you any money because she drinks it. She's also stingy." Ida laughed. "There's nothing worse than a stingy alcoholic. Or perhaps by necessity all alcoholics are stingy. Your mother owns property. Why doesn't she sell that?"

Daisianna said quietly, "She doesn't own property."

"She does," said Ida. "She owns an old farm down somewhere near Springfield. Your father knows about it—don't you, Joseph?"

"Yes," said Dodie. "I've seen the deed. But the income is negligible. Several hundred a year."

"I'm surprised," said Ida, "that you have the nerve to come here this way. You come to dine with your father and me, you bring a friend, and you expect us to behave as if nothing at all had happened. Your father has already spent five— eight—thousand dollars on you in the last year. You didn't even write to thank us."

"Dear," said Dodie to Ida.

"Dear," said Ida. "There's your dear. Look at her. Your dear is a whore."

Daisianna put her face in her hands and sobbed, but she made no effort to leave. Dodie looked wounded and away.

"She's not a whore," Dodie said, but he said it as if he were a ventriloquist. He threw the statement to the other side of the room so that it could not be traced back to him. He would not be responsible for it.

"She *is* a whore," said Ida. "The Bible calls them whores. Women who sell their bodies."

"I didn't," Daisianna sobbed.

"You were picked up for soliciting a Los Angeles detective," said Ida. "What do you call that? I call that prostitution."

"I didn't, Daddy," said Daisianna. "Never."

"We have all your records," Ida said. "Your complete police file. Your fingerprints. Your photographs—what I believe they call mug shots. We have those, too, dear."

"We destroyed them," said Dodie.

"We did not destroy them," said Ida. "They cost us five thousand dollars. I'd rather destroy my jewelry. They're in my safe-deposit box. Destroy them? Never."

"Please, Ida," said Dodie. He put his arms around Daisianna, but he did it in such a way that it seemed as if he were using Daisianna as a shield.

"And what about the doctor bills and the hospital bills?" Ida said. "The suicide that failed. Naturally. Do you know how much that cost your father? Do you? Not that he didn't already have enough to pay for and worry about, with the lawyers and everything else. Your vacation in that little rest home in the desert came to over three thousand dollars. Well, I hope you had your rest, because from now on you'll have to pay for any more rests yourself." Ida paused as if to calm herself, but it was obvious she did not want to be calm. "Furthermore," said Ida, "now that we're bringing everything out into the open, I suppose you know that we know all about that Mexican divorce and why you didn't ask for alimony. No alimony? From one of the richest men in Seattle? It wasn't because you were too proud, dear. It wasn't because you don't believe in alimony. Wasn't that what you told that foolish woman who writes for the *Tribune*? If you'd take fifty dollars from a Los Angeles detective, I think you'd be able to persuade yourself to accept several hundred thousand dollars from a former husband. I mean if you really tried. I know it would be difficult for a woman of your high moral principles. I know you'd have to rack your brains and search your soul, but if you thought about it long enough, I imagine you could reconcile principle and need. You didn't ask for alimony because your husband brought up the odd fact that you had given him a slight dose of gonorrhea."

Daisianna buried her face in her father's shoulder. Her body shook but she made no sound.

"In my day," said Ida, "when I was an innocent young girl in nursing school, we called it clap."

"Christ," said Jimmy. "Stop it."

He got up and went to Daisianna. He put his hands on her upper arms. "Come on, Daisianna," he said, "we're leaving." She didn't budge from her father. "Please, Daisianna," he said. He shook her gently and she sat up. Her eyes looked like the eyes of a blind person. She could hear him from a great distance, but she wasn't sure who he was or what he was saying. He pulled her to her feet. "We're going," he said. "Where?" "We're going home," he said.

Ida watched them with serenity. She said to Daisianna: "And don't come back. I don't want to see you in my house again."

Daisianna began to weep once more, but when she spoke it was less an attempt to argue with Ida than an attempt to reassure herself. "This is my house too," she said. "I was born in this apartment. I was born in Granny's bed."

"Slut," said Ida.

Daisianna made a sudden movement toward Ida, but Jimmy stopped her. "I'm not, I'm not," said Daisianna. Then she screamed, "You are so unkind!" The outburst collapsed. A feather had been hurled and missed. Jimmy led Daisianna from the library, across the marble floor of the foyer to the elevator, where Felix met them with their coats. As they waited for the elevator they heard a kind of croaking sound from the library. It was Dodie, crying.

17

The next day Daisianna received a letter from her father, delivered by messenger to her mother's Division Street apartment. Attached was a check for two thousand dollars. His script was graceful, manly:

My Darling Daisianna,

In view of what occurred last night, I deem it best that we do not see each other again. Please do not try to contact me or the result will surely be more unhappiness all the way around. Your stepmother is not a bad woman. Indeed, I credit her with saving my life. Without her love and understanding I would surely be in my grave. I console myself in the knowledge that you have your mother to help you through any crises that might arise in the future. The events of the last year (Los Angeles) are difficult to comprehend. I cannot believe them but I cannot disbelieve the records. Try as I might. Ida and I are going abroad for a few months. Where is uncertain, someplace warm. We'll roam, probably. I do not like to leave your grandmother at this juncture in her illness, but she is in good, competent hands. The best that money can buy. I pray that God will keep you safe, and that you will trust in Him as I do. I would advise you to cash the enclosure soonest. To avoid possible embarrassment should I. notice it.

Your loving,

Dodie

Her father's letter, and especially the check, filled Daisianna with optimism and resolve. As the depression vanished she cleaned the apartment and sent clothes to the laundry.

She bought a bottle of Cleanli-Mist, a new kind of liquid soap that, when sprayed on the tub before filling, was guaranteed to make post-bath tub cleaning unnecessary. She placed the bottle in the bathroom accompanied by a friendly note to the bank clerk urging him to use it whenever he wished. She made no direct reference to what Ida had said, though she did remind Jimmy that she'd warned him that Ida could be difficult. Ida believed people should be punctual. She mentioned it as if it were the worst thing one could say about Ida, and she was filled with admiration for the way Dodie controlled his alcoholism with Ida's help. "You have to give that to her," she said to Jimmy. She lent a hundred dollars to her mother, sent two hundred to the storage house in Seattle, and spent one afternoon at the Art Institute inquiring about courses. There were five she wanted to take: figure drawing, oil painting, ceramics, dress designing, and the history of cave painting. She spent almost fifty dollars treating Jimmy to a wild-pheasant dinner at L'Aiglon, and talked about the possibility of buying a car. Jimmy no longer wished to make love, nor did Daisianna apparently. On the Sunday before Thanksgiving she announced that she had decided to move to New York. She'd find a job and go to school there. She loved New York. New York was where most of her friends were, anyway. She left on Thanksgiving morning, easily, without ado, without sharing Jimmy's sadness or his relief. Jimmy rented a car to drive her to the airport and then drove to Lake Forest to dine with Edith, Travis, Emmy Lou, and Emmy Lou's parents. When Jimmy returned to the apartment late that night, he was so lonely for Daisianna that he wept. The loneliness was intense but it lasted only a couple of hours. He drank several straight bourbons, lay on her bed smelling her perfume, and fell into a deep, peaceful sleep.

18

Life with Cleo was as unexciting as Jimmy had hoped. Cleo returned December 1st. They were married on the afternoon of New Year's Eve and spent a ten-day honeymoon in Nassau where they played tennis whenever it wasn't raining. Cleo referred to Daisianna once: she said she'd been told that Jimmy and Daisianna had seen a lot of each other and she wondered if she should ask Daisianna to be in the wedding party. Since they were having a small wedding—Cleo was to have only one attendant, her older sister as matron of honor—Jimmy later assumed that this was Cleo's way of being vicious. He liked her control. At that point there would have been nothing to gain with a fight. They moved into the apartment owned by Cleo's aunt on Astor Street, Aunt Fredericka having turned it over to them when she moved into her new cottage at Hobe Sound. Fredericka left them her furniture, her silver, her linens, everything, which might have given an air of unreality to the marriage, a sense of hotel living, of impermanence, even of sin, had the marriage been to anyone except Cleo. It was, instead, as if they'd always been married and had always lived in this big, gloomy, comfortably uninteresting apartment, always observed by the taciturn Birdie, the old Irishwoman who— miraculously, it seemed to Jimmy—found things about him to disapprove of: a sudden wish to have fried eggs for breakfast instead of boiled ("They'll give you the heartburn," said Birdie), or his staying up all night to finish a brief ("The missus will make a lovely widow"). She wasn't friendly but she was supporting. She was another definition of the life he wanted.

One morning in March he received a telephone call at his office from Leola Caffrey. She asked if she could see him right away and he said yes, that she could come in before lunch if she liked. "*I* can't come in," she said crossly. "You'll have to come see me." When he hesitated she said that it was about Daisianna, that something had happened. He took a taxi to the Division Street address and felt furtive to be seen descending from a taxi in front of Snow White's even at 11 a.m. Leola's apartment was on the second floor of a building that also housed two dentists' offices, a beauty shop, and a tailor. Her apartment, in the back of the building, was a high-ceilinged, shoebox-shaped room, with small windows near the ceiling that opened and closed, like skylights, by means of chains of the sort used on old-fashioned toilets. The room was neat and desolate, furnished with a studio couch and an old sofa, a folding bridge table on which sat Leola's hotplate, several straight-back chairs, and a cardboard wardrobe closet. A small refrigerator was in the bathroom. Leola greeted him at the door wearing a housecoat and no shoes or stockings. Her swollen feet looked like white gourds and her face like a fat, bleached tomato. Her hair, he realized with a good deal of surprise, must be naturally platinum. It was casually tied up and coming loose, but no one in her condition, he thought, living under her straitened circumstances, would bother to dye it. There was a stack of paperback books on top of the radio beside her bed. Leola walked across the room with difficulty, leaning on her cane. "You see the state I've fallen to," she said. "You're one of the few white people to be so honored." She offered Nescafé or a can of beer, both of which he refused, and then sat down with evident, sighing relief on a wooden chair by the table. "A friend of Daisianna's telephoned me yesterday from New York. Daisianna was arrested yesterday morning for throwing a brick through a window at Brooks Brothers. My God, Brooks Brothers. I don't need to tell you that's where her father buys all his clothes. Anyway, the police arrested her and she seems to have had a breakdown. Nothing serious but she's in Bellevue in the crazy ward. My sister and her husband live in New York, and though they hardly speak to me, they've promised to go see her and to get her a lawyer if she needs one. I talked to her doctor, who, I imagine, is fourteen years old. His name is Dr. Phil— he sounds like a hairdresser—and he gave me a lot of crap about tests and treatment, and about money. The thing is, I need money. Her father and his wife are somewhere in Europe—nobody will tell me where—and I can't reach him. If I could, he probably wouldn't do anything anyway. To be blunt about it, I was wondering if you could lend me two or three hundred dollars." Jimmy said of course, and he pulled out his checkbook and wrote a check for three hundred dollars. He asked, "Do you think you should go see her?" "I can't go see anybody," said Leola. "It's all I can do to make it to the potty to peepee." She shrugged. "No," she said, "there's no reason for anyone to go to New York. But I wanted to be able to send her some money for whatever she might need." She laughed. "For candy and cigarettes." As Jimmy was preparing to leave, there was a knock on the door and a tall, solemn, rail-thin young black woman let herself in with her own key. She was wearing the blue uniform of a Visiting Nurse. "How nice," said the girl. "You're having company." Said Leola: "I'm having my lawyer, if you want to put it that way." The girl efficiently ignored Leola's tone and opened her carrying case. "How do you feel today?" she asked. "Right as rain," said Leola. "Are you breathing any more easily?" "I'm breathing," said Leola, "which you may want to call a good sign." When Jimmy left the apartment Leola was saying to the girl, "Would you have time today to amputate my feet? I think I'd be able to walk better."

19

Jimmy Barnes had once called down a curse upon boredom. It was shortly after he had joined his ship, an LST, in the autumn of 1944, when it was taking on a cargo of tanks and trucks in the New Guinea port of Hollandia as part of a support convoy in the Philippine operation. They spent three days loading the cargo, and had been directed to anchor in the bay to await sailing orders. They lay at anchor for weeks. At first the men had rallied to shore leaves of swimming, baseball games, and visits to the Army Post Exchange. After a while they lost interest. Eventually a sweet debilitating lethargy overtook the officers and crew. Fewer and fewer men cared to go ashore to swim or play baseball. They lay in their bunks and read small, oblong-shaped paperback books called Armed Forces Editions, reprints of almost everything that had ever been published in the English language: classics, mystery stories, contemporary novels, histories, Westerns.

When Jimmy had joined the ship he had brought with him a half-dozen worthy hardback books purchased in San Francisco the afternoon before he left: *Das Kapital, The Prince, Thus Spake Zarathustra* (as well as *Some Aspects of the Life and Work of Nietzsche*), *Life on the Mississippi,* and a Bible. The lethargy and the boredom that overtook the ship in Hollandia in those weeks made most reading impossible. He gave up on Marx and turned to S. S. Van Dine. It made no difference if his mind wandered. He needn't feel guilty. On a Sunday afternoon, when they'd been at anchor three weeks, Jimmy sat alone on a winch in the shadow of the 40-millimeter fantail gun. He stared at the shore less than a mile away where some soldiers were swimming in turquoise water next to a gold sand beach edged by palm trees, guarded by high green foothills patched here and there by compounds of Quonset huts. The distance made the soldiers inanimate. Nothing stirred. There were no birds, no clouds, no jeeps on the road that led out of Hollandia into the interior of New Guinea. Though there was a war on, there was no hint of urgency. The processes of living had been suspended.

Several weeks later Jimmy Barnes remembered that afternoon with ferocious longing. The ship had sailed first to Leyte and there had been assigned to a convoy resupplying the recently invaded island of Mindoro, south of Luzon. It took the convoy two days and three nights to make the trip from Leyte through the inland sea to Mindoro, during which time they were under enemy air attack for approximately forty hours. They sailed at midnight. The attacks began without warning at ten the next morning. When the general-quarters claxon had sounded, Jimmy ran out on deck to see a single-engine airplane dive as slowly as a paper toy into the superstructure of the Liberty ship in the column next to them. There were what looked to be the sparks of a fizzling firecracker. Then the Liberty ship simply ceased to exist. Where there had been a ship, there was suddenly substituted a column of yellow smoke. It rolled straight up as if from some gigantic undersea smokestack. Someone shouted to prepare for the concussion, but the concussion was barely a thump. Simultaneously the air was full of metal. It came at them not from across the water but from the sky. The LST and the sea around it were drenched in a rain of pieces of the Liberty ship, small bits of junk that could have been screws, bolts, hatch fittings, shreds of bulkheads. Nothing to be recognized. If there had been life aboard the ship, it had evaporated. Something that seemed to be a charred sparkplug went through the battle helmet of a man named Cousins in Jimmy's repair crew. It stuck in the top of

Cousins's helmet, looking like a handle of some sort. Cousins's eyes opened wide as he sank to a kneeling position on the deck. He was dead but he did not fall forward. He knelt, frozen with surprise. The raids were continuous after that. Never more than four or five planes at a time. The raids were thin but constant. The pilots made no attempts to bomb, torpedo, or strafe the ships. They wanted only to smash into them. If there had been the leisure the men might have been terrorized. As it was they were too busy, too edgy to give in to fright. Instead they became resentful at the fate that had somehow managed to confuse the fight. Two different kinds of war had been allowed to overlap. The stakes were unequal. Everyone slept and ate at his station. They lived on rumors and anger that effectively masked the fear. There was very little air support because the Leyte fields were locked in fog. The Japanese took their time. Sometimes they circled the convoy looking at the ships, speculating about targets, out of the range of the destroyer-escort guns. Sometimes they'd climb very high, beyond the reach of radar, and dive at the ships from the sun. The concussion from the explosion of the ammunition ship had parted the bow plates of Jimmy's ship. They took on some water but the watertight compartments held fast. Other ships had been more badly damaged. The first afternoon, three ships out of thirty had been sunk and two others left in such disrepair they had to be scuttled. Jimmy had never before considered the possibility that he might be killed and the thought came to preoccupy him. The second day they lost two more ships, including a destroyer. There were reports that support planes were coming from Mindoro, but they never appeared. The third night was worse. The convoy had slowed from seven to four knots. A burning tanker was sent off alone so as not to illuminate the others. About three o'clock in the morning they could see lights on the horizon of the base at Mindoro. It, too, was on fire. At dawn, twenty-one surviving ships sailed into the Mindoro road-stead. There were three cargo ships at anchor, two were burning and low in the water. As Jimmy's ship dropped anchor, one of the two suddenly went under, bow-first, but the roadstead was so shallow the ship could not sink properly. Its bow sank twenty feet and abruptly stopped. The stern remained high and dry and burning. Jimmy remembered his boredom at Hollandia. He wanted it back again. Boredom was the absence of feeling. It was peace and safety.

20

Cleo assured Jimmy's happiness in ways she never understood. She knew she was not beautiful so she went to great lengths to make herself attractive. She dieted. She exercised. She spent a great deal of money on clothes, her hair, her fingernails, on dental prophylaxis, all of which made her—in the words of a manual she employed—lovelier to know. She would have been extremely upset had she been told that what attracted Jimmy to her and made him the lover he was to her was nothing more or less than her orderliness, and orderliness was more natural to Cleo than any erotic impulse. She looked forward to sex. She prepared herself for it carefully, and it was always as if she were doing things because she'd memorized the rules. And she'd be damned if anyone would ever be able to call her a prude. There was nothing spontaneous about Cleo, and Jimmy appreciated this more than anything else.

In early summer, more than a year after they'd been married, Jimmy received a letter from Daisianna that had been forwarded from his old apartment by the bank clerk.

Darling Jimmy,

As you know I landed in something of a jam a year or so ago. First Bellevue, which was too ghastly to talk about, then Kings County where everyone is a terminal case of something, then here, which seems like Onwentsia in comparison. Thank heavens I was able to stay in the Marines as long as I did. If it had been one month less I wouldn't have been eligible for a veterans' hospital. This place is brand new and run like a country club. The doctors are divine and even the nurses not too impossible. We're 50 miles from New York, overlooking the Hudson, and live in bungalows named for war heroes. I live in Colin Kelly House (Sec. 2, Rm. 4-C). It's a little bit like being back in boarding school except there are a lot more men around. We see movies once a week and once a month we have dances. The soldiers here are mostly breakdown cases or people who are being reha-bilitated emotionally. The ones who've been burned or badly wounded are sent somewhere else. Just as well. Though I'm all right now I wouldn't have been up to making small talk with basket cases six months ago. The jokes people tell here are grisly. I've heard from Mother several times. She sends me clippings from Cholly Dearborn about you and Cleo, Travis and that Roosevelt girl he married, and everybody else. I haven't heard from Dodie. I guess he and Ida are still in Europe, though I think they must have come home when Granny died. Mother has hired a private detective to find out where they are. Someone told her they were living in Princeton, but if they are they aren't listed. I asked one of the doctors who lives in New Jersey to check the Princeton telephone book. They aren't in it. I'm doing a lot of sketch-ing and painting. We have a marvelous man who teaches at West Point and comes over one day a week for classes. He's very flattering, and when I get out of here (???) I'm plan-ning to go to a design school in New York. They won't let me dye my hair so I've turned that dumb brown color I always loathed when I was little. I'm also getting fat. I look like Sophie Tucker without her wigs. All double chins and things. They still won't allow me to have matches so I can't smoke, which I guess explains it. Would it be too terrible to ask you several favors? Could you send me some Piaf records? I don't know what happened to mine. The girls I was living with when I had my accident were all kleptomaniacs. Everything has disappeared and nobody answers my letters. Also some candy and any kind of make-up. I'm very, very drab. If you ever get to New York, please come to see me. PLEASE! *I can have visitors any day as long as I know in advance when they're coming. I'm through with the shock treatments, which really are ghastly.* Bride of Frankenstein *stuff, but I suppose they work. With much much love,*

Daisianna XXXXXXXXXXXXXXX

Less than a week later Jimmy received a postcard that said: "I can smoke now! Please send cigarettes too! Love, D."

Though Jimmy was making periodic business trips to New York at this time, he never found the opportunity to see Daisianna. Cleo worried about the reference to the Roosevelt girl Travis had married. "She doesn't sound cured to me," she said. Jimmy sent the records Daisianna asked for and Cleo went to a great deal of trouble to assemble a collection of candy, cigarettes, and various kinds and shades of lipsticks and mascara, as well as bath salts, cologne, and, with malice, several packets of black Clairol hair dye. They never heard whether Daisianna received the box. Said Cleo: "I knew we wouldn't. She never thanked anybody for anything in her life."

Their first child, a son who was named James Junior, was born the following February, and in the following June

Jimmy was transferred to the New York office of Banks, Travis, Dietweiller & Swift, as a junior partner in charge of Middle Western estate clients. It was an orderly move. They packed up Little James, Birdie, and some of their summer clothes and went to Nassau for five weeks. From Nassau they flew to New York, where everything had been put into the house they'd bought near Westport. It wasn't a handsome house but it was large and outside the city limits, with land enough for the day when Cleo could begin raising English sheepdogs in earnest. The furniture in their house always remained where the movers had put it.

21

"Jimmy?" Daisianna's voice came through the telephone with the same gravity she had when attempting to read a menu without her glasses. It was a nearsighted voice.

"Daisianna?"

"I hope you don't mind my calling you at the office. When I heard from Mother that you and Cleo had moved to New York, I assumed you'd still be with Banks, Travis. You don't move around much, do you?"

"No," said Jimmy. "How are you?"

"Fine. I don't have any money, but I'm fine. I've been out of the hospital for over a year. It was ghastly, at first. I mean, when I got out. I was rooming with a girl I'd met at the hospital, an ex-Wave. She was working for B.O.A.C., but she was still sick. One night she jumped off the roof of our building and I had to identify the body."

"Christ . . . Daisianna . . ."

"It was quite awful, but everything's all right now. I'm working in the Village at a shop called Corduroy Incorporated. We sell nothing but clothes made of corduroy, even bathing suits. And I'm going to school at night, the Madigan School of Design. Have you ever heard of it?"

"No," said Jimmy, "but I probably wouldn't have anyway."

"It's terribly good, though I'm the only straight person there."

She talked about Dodie and Ida ("The earth has swallowed them up. When last heard of, they were living in Tangier"), about her mother ("She's fine. She's trying to sue Dodie for nonsupport and it's given her an interest"), and about Chicago ("I don't miss it at all"). She asked about James Junior, about Cleo, who was pregnant again, and about his brothers. Then: "Jimmy, would you do a favor for me?" There was only a second's pause and she said, "It's not money. I'm living with someone I'd like you to meet."

"Oh," said Jimmy.

"Yes," said Daisianna. "He's French. I think you'll like him. He makes films—at least, that's what he did in Paris. He's working in a travel agency here. I don't think he believes that I know anybody except boys who want to design women's clothes, or people who work in hamburger stands, or bartenders. I'd like to show you off. His father's a count. His wife works for Bolon, Bates & Macauley in San Francisco. She's English but they're separated."

Cleo groaned when Jimmy told her about the telephone call that evening. "Either he's a fraud," she said, "or he's as crazy as she is. A travel agent and married. That's par for the course. It sounds to me as if she wants to borrow more money. Daisianna is a leech. If I were you, I'd just send her the money and forget it."

"I don't want to forget it," said Jimmy. "I'd like to see her."

22

"Jesus was ahead of his time," said a middle-aged man lunching at Sardi's on the afternoon of Washington's Birthday. The dining room, abandoned in a few minutes of rush by the matinéegoers, was as unnaturally hollow as an empty fish tank. The people still lunching seemed stranded. The man talking about Jesus had a broad, flat face, cheerful little slits for eyes, and thick lips. With his hands resting on the table in front of him, he looked like a frog contemplating a spring. His luncheon companion, a man in a Glenplaid suit, had his back to them and spoke so low it seemed as if the first man were delivering a monologue with occasional meaningful pauses. "I say that to everybody," said the first man. "Jesus was ahead of his time, but don't tell my rabbi." He laughed loudly at his closet ecumenism. Side by side, on a banquette near Jimmy, Daisianna, and Charles, sat two expressionless men who might have been in their late twenties or early fifties. They had found ways to accommodate the years. One was dark. One blond. Both were heavily tanned and as carefully cut and combed as show dogs. They picked at what the menu called The Actor's Salad (spinach, ground bacon, oil, and vinegar), and did not speak. Possibly words too have calories.

23

It was not the poverty of Daisianna and Charles that embarrassed Jimmy and Cleo Barnes. It was the success with which Daisianna and Charles seemed to ignore it. Their buoyancy was embarrassing. They seldom even talked about money. The two couples saw as little as possible of each other after having exchanged self-conscious visits initiated by Daisianna. She invited Jimmy and Cleo to the Bank Street apartment for supper one Sunday evening. She spent all afternoon preparing duck à l'orange from a cookbook she'd bought in a drugstore, and then, with the arrival of Jimmy and Cleo, she forgot the duck until smoke came from the oven. By the time she could get the duck out, it had melted into a sticky cinder. Said Charles: "Fuck the duck. We'll have another drink." He and Daisianna thought it was so funny they didn't notice the strain in the smiles of the guests. The rest of the food was awful, and Cleo resented Daisianna's refusal to pay proper attention to the fact. The next afternoon, she telephoned Daisianna and told her she shouldn't treat people that way. "It's rude," she said, which hurt Daisianna for the rest of the day. Charles and Daisianna went to Westport to dine with the Barneses on a Wednesday night, and Daisianna, after playing with Cleo's two sheepdog puppies for half an hour, and after drinking part of a martini, fell asleep at the dinner table. Charles didn't apologize. He got up, walked around the table, and massaged the back of her neck. "Little dear," he said to Daisianna, and then to the others: "She works very hard, you know."

In those first years Jimmy Barnes came to respect Charles du Chaudrun and then to like him. They lunched together once every five or six weeks, always at Charles's invitation and always at a restaurant near Jimmy's Wall Street office. Jimmy accepted the invitations with reluctance initially. Like Cleo, he was suspicious of Charles. He couldn't understand his motives. There was something suspect about a man who earned a fraction of the money Jimmy earned, who was a representative of a country receiving Marshall Plan aid, paying for Jimmy's luncheons. "Think of it as a kind of tax refund," Cleo told Jimmy. Later Jimmy realized that he was Charles's only male friend in New York, and that Charles had a capacity for a kind of friendship unlike any he'd encountered in an American. Charles was not interested in gossip. He did not pry into secrets. Jimmy was surprised at the amount of reading Charles managed, but then Jimmy imagined that if one worked in a travel agency, one probably had a lot of time to kill. Charles was interested in the kind of life that Jimmy and Cleo lived in Westport and had lived in Chicago. He did not pry into secrets but he was fascinated by details. He spent one entire lunch learning about mortgage systems from Jimmy. Charles apparently knew all about Daisianna's troubles in Los Angeles and more about her illness than Jimmy could bring himself to ask. Compared to Jimmy's American male friends Charles had courtly manners and, surprisingly, they civilized behavior that Jimmy would have found scandalous in himself. Completely without secrecy because confidences were understood, Charles once told Jimmy about an affair he'd been having with a German woman, now married to a French marquis, who came over from Paris twice a year to go to the theater and misbehave. "She's a lesbian," said Charles, "but she's one of the most fantastic women I've ever slept with. In her own way, she's quite brilliant. I like her." He laughed. "She'd be hell to be married to." Said Jimmy: "You couldn't trust her." "No," said Charles, "you could. She'd tell you everything." It was at the same lunch that Charles told Jimmy that he and Daisianna were being married at the end of the week at City Hall. Said Charles: "It's about time."

Two years after the marriage, the lives of Daisianna and Charles began to change radically. It was something they seemed to take for granted as much as they had their poverty, without visible traumas. Through a French film director Charles had worked with in Paris, Charles was sought out and hired to act as an assistant to the producer of a television special the director was making in New York. It started as a temporary job and grew first into a job as an associate producer-director of public service programs for a local station, and then into a staff producership for the network. When Charles's name appeared on their television screen at the end of programs about the Electoral College, forest fires, garbage, and male prostitution, programs that Cleo would not have watched ordinarily, she began to find Charles attractive, a word that was from her Lake Forest vocabulary. To Cleo, even tiny babies could be called attractive.

It was about this time too that Dodie came back into Daisianna's life. Through Jimmy Barnes, Dodie learned where Daisianna was working and telephoned her at Corduroy Incorporated to inform her that Ida was dead. He called from the bar at the Princeton Club, very drunk and very soon in tears. He'd just returned from Madison, Wisconsin, where Ida had been buried. "In her family's plot. Next to a garage." The whole thing had taken less than two months. Ida had gone into the hospital for the removal of a growth in her colon and was dead six weeks later. "She never left the hospital," Dodie said. "She was in a coma for the last ten days. She was cheerful to the end." The drastic effect Ida's death was to have on the lives of Daisianna and Charles was delayed, disguised, by the demands and rewards of Charles's new career. Though they still lived on Bank Street, and though Daisianna continued to work at Corduroy Incorporated and to go to school two nights a week, they were already looking for a place in the country when Dodie reappeared. Their transformed circumstances eventually became apparent to Daisianna, who didn't like to think of transformations, good or bad, when Dodie came to the apartment for supper one night, the pockets of his suit and overcoat stuffed with jewelry that had once been Ida's or Daisianna's grandmother's. There was so much of it that it looked fake, a tangle of pearls, pendants, clips, rings, earrings, and necklaces. Dodie took Jimmy to Chicago to make an estimate of the estate and to draw up a new will in favor of Daisianna, replacing one that left everything to Ida and, through Ida, to Ida's several nieces and a nephew in Madison. Jimmy told Cleo on his return to Westport, "After taxes, Daisianna should inherit between eight and nine million dollars. There were bonds and jewelry in safe-deposit boxes the old man didn't even know about. Daisianna, the leech, is about to become a very rich woman."

24

Within a year she was. Leola died in March, leaving Daisianna several thousand dollars in debts, the old Barrett farm in Sangamon County, two albums of family photographs, and some papers assembled by Daisianna's Great-Grandmother Ridgely when she joined the Mayflower Society. Leola fell off a barstool at Snow White's, fractured a shoulder and a leg, and died of pneumonia. Six months later, Dodie had a heart attack and died in his sleep at the Princeton Club. Daisianna grieved for weeks. The slightest reference to a mother or a father caused her to weep, even television commercials in which young women wearing unconvincing white wigs demonstrated the superiority of a certain brand of denture paste. Charles took her to St. Constance where she spent hours lying in the sun by Mary Magnuson's pool. She seldom read. She had patience for the sun. The darker her skin turned, the lighter became her depression. It vanished when her skin had begun to look leathery. One of the first things she did when they returned to New York was to buy a sewing machine, the most expensive sewing machine manufactured by Singer for home use. It was, she told Jimmy Barnes, to replace one that Charles had wrecked years before. The machine went into the closet and was never touched, but she liked knowing it was there. In quick succession they bought a co-op apartment on Fifth Avenue in the Eighties and a thoroughly renovated Colonial farmhouse near Greenwich. It had only three bedrooms but it had a heated swimming pool and a small stable and paddock. Daisianna had decided that she wanted to ride again. She also retrieved her furniture from Seattle and put most of it into storage in Manhattan.

25

In the years that followed Jimmy Barnes came to devote more and more of his time to the management of the Caffrey estate, which until Dodie's death, had been parceled out to four different firms. Banks, Travis was pleased but Cleo wasn't, even though it represented a sizable portion of their income. Cleo saw it as bondage to Daisianna, which it was. Charles and Jimmy still lunched together whenever Charles could, but at a restaurant near Charles's offices in Rockefeller Center, not on Wall Street. Charles traveled to Europe several times on special projects, usually accompanied by Daisianna. "If I leave her here," Charles once told Jimmy, "she stays in the country and doesn't see anybody except tradespeople. She knows the name of every clerk in every supermarket in Connecticut, and they know hers. They call her Daisianna." One winter afternoon Charles telephoned

Jimmy to ask him to drive with him to Sean's Pub, an expensive restaurant outside New Canaan where Charles and Daisianna sometimes entertained, since Daisianna found it difficult to keep any kind of staff in the country. They arrived before the dinner hour and went directly to the bar. Charles asked to speak to Gino. The bartender, a young Sicilian with a pretty face, said that he was Gino. He was immediately uneasy and glanced around to see if there weren't some other customers he had to wait on. Said Charles: "I'm Mr. du Chaudrun and this is Mr. Barnes, my lawyer." Gino, with a large smile: "Oh, yes, Mr. du Chaudrun." He put his hand out to Charles. "How are you, sir?" Gino turned and took Jimmy's hand: "How are you, sir? I remember you very well. Yes." Charles: "You probably know my wife better." Gino looked puzzled. "*Mrs.* du Chaudrun," Charles said. Gino smiled but shook his head. "Daisianna," said Charles. Gino beamed. "Oh, Daisianna? She was here yesterday. A very nice lady, Daisianna." Charles: "I believe she gave you something." "Oh," said Gino, "yes. She gave me a ring." Charles: "And you accepted it?" Gino: "Yes. What could I do? She insisted." Charles: "She was drunk." Gino: "Oh, no, Mr. du Chaudrun. Daisianna was no drunk. . . ." He laughed modestly. "I know when a lady is drunk. She was feeling very good. Very friendly. But she was no drunk." Gino reminisced casually. "I had no other customers. She was alone. She ask me many questions about my life, you know, in Sicily, in Connecticut. When I told her I was getting married and did not have the money to buy the beautiful ring, she gave me hers. That was all. A friendly gesture." "A very friendly gesture," said Charles. "Where is the ring now?" Pause. Gino, unhappily: "In my pocket." He put his hand in his pocket and brought out the emerald Jimmy had first seen on Ida's finger. Charles took it. He examined it. He said, "Maybe we should all have a drink." Gino poured

Scotches for Charles and Jimmy and a vodka for himself. "I did not steal the ring," he said. "She gave it to me. I swear to God." Charles: "I know she did." When they left, Charles gave Gino, who was very blue, a check for a hundred dollars. Five weeks later Daisianna gave her grandmother's antique diamond earrings to an elderly but fierce saleswoman at Bergdorf's who refused to give them back. Charles did not press the point. That afternoon he talked to their doctor in Manhattan, and when he came home that night Daisianna was sitting on the floor of their bedroom clipping last Sunday's *New York Times*. She was finding messages from Jesus buried within the headlines of the news sections. A word from one headline, a phrase from another, circled with red ink and connected by arrows that pointed in both directions at once, formed the code only she understood. Aphorisms, riddles, promises, warnings. "We must change our ways," said Daisianna. "The Redeemer tells us how." Charles pulled her to her feet and put his arms around her. She suffered him. Her body remained rigid with fear. She had been frightened before, but he'd been able to hold her until her fear subsided. This time it took four sleeping pills administered over a period of four hours. The next day Daisianna signed herself into Hickory Hollow, a highly recommended clinic near Danbury.

Daisianna came and went from Hickory Hollow in those years. Whenever Jimmy saw her alone at lunch in town, she seemed more beautiful, more serene than ever. There were no sudden gestures. No exclamation points. This languor was not new, but for the first time Daisianna herself observed it, and with amusement. Jimmy never detected the furies within, demons that Daisianna sometimes mentioned as if they were horses that lived in a far pasture. "In those days I was consumed with jealousy of poor Ida. She was difficult but I think I understand her now. She was a first-class bitch." She drank an occasional vermouth and did not fidget while Jimmy drank two martinis before ordering the meal. "It's all a matter of pills," she said once. "But whenever I feel something's not quite right, when the pills don't work, I call Mandelbaum. It's a little like having epilepsy." The year that Charles was assigned to the Continent, they lived in Lausanne so that Daisianna could be an outpatient at the Valois Clinic. She afterward described that year as one of the happiest in her life. Several years later, when Charles was in Egypt covering the Khrushchev visit and Daisianna had her scrape at the Yankee Clipper, Jimmy dealt directly with Dr. Mandelbaum. She did not ask to see Jimmy and he made no effort to visit her. Somewhere in his soul he was afraid that her disorder might be a contagion. And, in a way, it was.

26

The boys were at camp. Cleo was in England visiting cousins and looking for a sheepdog bitch of particular ancestry. Jimmy, having planned to spend the night at the Harvard Club, had dined in Brooklyn Heights with a former law school classmate and his wife who were remodeling an old brownstone themselves. The place was a mess of torn-up floors, missing walls, bricks neatly piled up and stored according to patina. The place looked irretrievably bombed out. They drank Chianti from paper cups and ate lukewarm Chinese food from paper plates in the living room. They used sleeping bags for cushions and the cardboard containers of fried rice and egg rolls sat on the tops of new plumbing fixtures that had been delivered months too early. When Jimmy left the house he lost his way until he

found himself on Atlantic Avenue, outside a Green Rose Bar
& Grill that sounded at that moment as if it were the jolliest
place on earth to be. The jukebox had been turned up to
compete with the television set, which was showing an old
movie. The bar was full but not crowded, mostly middle-
aged working-class men with a few wives and assorted, semi-
attached women. Jimmy sat on a barstool next to a frail,
ancient lady dressed in worn widow's weeds. Her hands
were on the bar, her right holding a jigger of whiskey, her
left a glass of beer. Her face was tucked down into her
shoulder, like a sleeping bird. Jimmy ordered a Scotch and
water self-consciously from the fat, paternal Irish bartender, but he drank it in sublime anonymity. Nobody paid
any attention to him. The laughter, the arguments, the
camaraderie made him invisible. "All right, you tell me what
round Baer knocked out Braddock." "Baer didn't knock out
Braddock. Braddock knocked out Baer." "All right, you tell
me." "I'll tell you." "You tell me." Jimmy was very happy.
He ordered another drink and asked the bartender directions to the nearest Manhattan subway. The bartender gave
him his change and ignored the question. He was in the
middle of an argument with someone at the far end of the
bar. "You're full of shit," the bartender shouted. The manner was jovial. "You tell 'em, Paddy." Jimmy ordered a
third drink. A pretty, black-haired girl with an intense frown
on her face entered the bar and sat next to Jimmy. On the
other side of him the old lady had not stirred. The girl wore
shiny black high heels, a bright yellow dress of thin material,
and large gold loops through pierced ears. She banged a
bunch of keys on the bar. "Paddy," she screamed, "I'm
going to be an old lady before I get my drink." The girl
turned to Jimmy and smiled as if noticing him for the first
time. "Honestly," she said, "Paddy is so slow." She fanned
her face with her open hand. She smiled again at Jimmy.

"Aren't you hot," she said, "wearing that?" She touched
the buttons of his vest. She said, "Why you wear that, anyway?" and began to giggle. "Honestly, it makes you look
so funny. You are a very funny man." Jimmy laughed too.
When the bartender finally brought the girl her gin and
orange juice, Jimmy paid for it. Said Paddy to the girl:
"Pachico has been looking for you." Said the girl, looking
at Jimmy: "Pachico is in Norwalk." Paddy: "He wasn't in
Norwalk three hours ago." The girl, still smiling at Jimmy:
"To hell with Pachico."

Jimmy: "You're a very pretty girl."

The girl: "You married?"

Jimmy: "Yes."

The girl: "What's your name?"

Jimmy: "Travis."

The girl: "Trabis? That's a very pretty name."

"What's yours?"

"Amor."

Jimmy laughed. "You're kidding."

The girl, angrily: "Paddy! Paddy! Tell this gentleman what
my name is."

Paddy, standing fifteen feet down the bar, shrugged his
shoulders.

"You see," said the girl. "My name *is* Amor."

"That's a very pretty name," said Jimmy. "Who's Pachico?"

Amor sighed, as if someone had asked her to synopsize
the plot of *War and Peace.*

"That's very long story, Trabis."

"Is he your boyfriend?"

"Yes, Trabis," said Amor solemnly. "He is my boyfriend,
and something more besides."

"Besides what?" Jimmy was delighted.

"Besides being my intended husband, Trabis."

"He's your pimp," said Jimmy.

"I help him," said Amor. "He is first time in New York. He comes from a small town in Puerto Rico, Trabis, a very tiny town, and he does not know big cities. Not even San Juan. I help him until he can speak English and get a job."

"Do you live together?"

"No," said Amor. She was shocked. "Not until we get married. He lives with his brothers. Some in Brooklyn. Some in Norwalk. Do you want to fuck me, Trabis?"

Jimmy looked her up and down. He did not want to be hurried into a decision. Amor smiled and slightly turned her torso on the barstool in an attempt to give extra dimension to her small breasts. She had the whitest teeth Jimmy had ever seen.

"Where?" said Jimmy.

"My place, Trabis. One block away. Very clean. Very quiet. No one bother you."

"How much?"

"Whatever you like, Trabis. Twenty-five dollars."

"Yes," said Jimmy.

Amor's room was five blocks away, five blocks farther into Brooklyn on Atlantic Avenue, over a Middle Eastern grocery store. The room had the kind of worn linoleum on the floor associated with places where poor girls had abortions and died. The sort of floor fetuses might be left on in a hurry. The room would have been depressing except for Amor's eager optimism. She was full of belief. She burned incense on one end of the dresser and kept an open bottle of Airwick on the other. One wall was devoted exclusively to religious pictures, mostly of postcard size, Jesus at all ages and stages of development. She also liked bleeding hearts. In a place of honor was a genuine original oil painting that vividly depicted the stoning of a Saint Stephen who looked like John Derek. A crucifix and cherry-red rosary beads were hung from Saint Stephen's frame, over the head of the bed. There was a large mirror opposite the bed on the dresser, and another wall was taken up with lay postcards and family pictures. Group photographs and individual portraits. Slim, small beautiful children with large black eyes. Squat, fat older people. In Amor's family the children did not grow up. They expanded and cracked into wrinkles. First communions, weddings, funerals, arrivals and departures at Pan Am gates. The room was full of objects: three empty Kotex boxes under the washbasin, a large plaster piggy bank on the dresser, a furry nylon jacket and a number of dresses hung from a ceiling rack. The double bed was made with fresh sheets. Said Amor when Jimmy sat on the bed: "There are no cockroaches in my room. Only when the exterminators kick them out of the room next door. Then they come here. You see, I am very clean."

Amor had a fine, smooth brown body. She enjoyed making love with a sincerity that totally escaped her smiles in the bar. At first they turned off the lights. Then they turned them on. They shifted the mirror around. They used a chair. Said Amor: "We work together very well, no?" Said Jimmy: "We fuck together very well." Amor: "That's what I mean, Trabis. But I don't say fuck unless I have to." About two o'clock they stopped. Jimmy said he'd like to have a drink, but Amor had nothing except some cans of warm beer. "What you like, Trabis?" "Scotch," said Jimmy. "You get Scotch, Trabis." She went to the window, pulled up the shade partway, and screeched at someone on the sidewalk below. She went to her purse, paused, looked at Jimmy. "Oh, Trabis, dear, have you got ten dollars?" Jimmy gave it to her and she leaned out the window and threw the bill with much laughter to the person in the street. She returned to the bed beside him. "If you want Scotch, Trabis, you get Scotch." Within half an hour there was a knock at the door. Amor called out in Spanish and was answered by a man in Spanish. She frowned a moment, then smiled. "Trabis, I would like to introduce you to my future husband. Okay?" "Wait a minute," said Jimmy. "Oh, my God." He jumped off the bed and was pulling his pants on when Amor opened the door to a short, muscular young man carrying a bottle of Scotch. The man, who might have been good-looking if his eyes hadn't been somewhat crossed, stood in the doorway more or less staring at the floor. Amor was very gay. "Come in, darling, come in." She yanked Pachico into the room and took the bottle from him. "Honestly," she said to Jimmy, "he is so shy. He is a small-town boy, Trabis." She shouted directions at Pachico in Spanish. He took off a gray fedora and offered his hand to Jimmy, but he never looked above Jimmy's ankles. Amor hugged Pachico. She stroked his cheek. She kissed his hand. "He is a good man, Trabis. Best there is. And when he learns to speak English, watch out U.S.A.!" They each had a large shot of Scotch diluted with tap water. Amor told Jimmy about her job in a cafeteria on Seventh Avenue near Times Square. "Very nice people," said Amor. "I have many many friends." "How long have you been working there?" said Jimmy. Said Amor: "One week." Through Amor Jimmy asked Pachico what sort of work he was looking for, how long he'd been in New York. Pachico thawed, and when Amor gave him a chance he answered questions at great length. He smiled once, showing several gold teeth. When Jimmy left, Amor asked him to give the twenty-five dollars to Pachico, who put it in his pocket with no embarrassment. At the door Amor said, "We do this again, yes? You see? No funny business here, Trabis. No goddamn hustlers here, Trabis. I see you next week, maybe? In the Green Rose, Tuesdays or Thursdays, okay?" Jimmy said yes and as soon as he was in the street he was mortified. He probably had syphilis.

He didn't, and ten days later he met Amor again. "Oh,

Trabis," she said, very hostessy, when he walked into the bar, "I'm so glad to see you. Pachico sends his regards too." Pachico came to the room when Jimmy was exhausted, as if by signal. The three had a parting drink together. A routine developed during the summer. Always a Tuesday or a Thursday. When Jimmy took his family to Nantucket for the first three weeks of September, he found he missed Amor. At least he missed the sex and found it difficult to make love to Cleo. She was understanding and didn't press him. Jimmy's life was in perfect order.

The routine was resumed in October. Tuesdays or Thursdays, when Jimmy worked late at the office and spent the night at the Harvard Club. For Christmas he gave Amor a small portable television set. The fact that it wasn't a color set troubled her for a few minutes; then she was grateful. She changed jobs frequently, working usually as a waitress, but people were always getting fresh with her. "Honestly, Trabis, you don't know what I put up with. I had to leave." It ultimately was apparent that her bosses became impatient at her inability to work for any five-day stretch without calling in sick at least once. "I have my period," she told Jimmy. "I have cramps. I have headaches. I vomit. They don't believe me." After a while Jimmy came to realize that he was Amor's only client. There had certainly been others before him, but she didn't have the drive for serious hustling. Once Pachico got over his initial shyness, it was obvious that he spoke English well enough to hold down any number of different jobs, but he had set his heart on becoming the computer analyst he saw advertised on television. This required a high school diploma as well as a thorough knowledge of English. First, he explained, he had to learn English. Then he had to return to high school. Pachico wasn't lazy. He was just too busy to work in a job that didn't interest him while he perfected his English. Then too he had his family obligations. He occupied himself calling on brothers, sisters, cousins. He would describe to Jimmy the smallest details of getting from the apartment of one relative in the Bronx to the house of another in Jersey City. The subways and buses taken, the transfers negotiated. He very much wanted an automobile. It would save time, he said, even though he seemed to spend most of any day just hanging around, waiting for relatives who, having got their signals crossed, moved on to the next encampment. Pachico was cheerful. He regarded Amor as a kind of goddess and he treated Jimmy as a respected equal. Never once did either Amor or Pachico ask Jimmy what sort of work he did or where he lived. It didn't occur to them. In March Pachico bought a car, a 1955 Buick station wagon that, when Jimmy saw it for the first time, was held together with Mystik tape. In teaching himself how to drive, Pachico had had several accidents. He was, of course, too busy to get a driver's license. How, Jimmy asked Amor, could Pachico afford to buy and keep a car if he wasn't working? Had Amor paid for it? No, said Amor, but she had helped. Then, asked Jimmy, where did the money come from? Amor laughed. She looked bashful. "He picks it up, here and there." "He doesn't sell drugs or anything, does he?" "No," said Amor, "he does like I do, sometimes." She shrugged. "You know, with men." She quickly added, "But don't get the wrong idea, Trabis. Pachico is very *macho*. He's no goddamn queer." That revelation prompted new fantasies for Jimmy, or, he realized, they were old ones now recognized. While they were making love one night, and after Amor had had several drinks, Jimmy made his proposal. He wanted to watch her making love with Pachico. Amor giggled. "Oh, Trabis!" "Would he agree?" Amor had such a laughing fit they fell apart. "I don't know," said Amor. Then: "How much you pay? Fifty dollars?" Jimmy: "Yes." Amor: "I'll ask him." She did not ask him in front of Jimmy when Pachico later came to the room, but when Jimmy met Amor at the Green Rose the next week, Pachico was with her, wearing a dark blue suit, a white shirt, a tie, his hair slicked down. Pachico had been drinking but he was not drunk. "You understand, Trabis," he said, putting his hand on Jimmy's arm, "we do this because we like you." He smiled. "We like the money too, but we like you, don't we?" He turned to Amor. Amor nodded her head vigorously. Jimmy had been drinking since late afternoon. He had the slightest suspicion that his life was about to collapse. They had a drink at the bar and went to Amor's room.

The first visit Jimmy did little more than watch. He sat in a chair by the bed and remained aloof, a dispassionate stage manager. He inspected, directed, and timed them, but he was not a part of it. There were surprises: Pachico, who was not at all self-conscious in action, was not as big as Jimmy. Nor was he particularly inventive. Under Jimmy's guidance, Pachico tried things that even Jimmy had never done, though Jimmy did not admit this. There was no need to. No one demanded explanations. It was as if someone who didn't know how to fly were teaching someone else from a book of theory. The theory, once put into practice, taught the teacher. Amor was as enthusiastic as only the single-minded can be. When she invited Jimmy to join them, it would have been a crime against nature not to. Initially he and Pachico alternated places. When Pachico was finished, he would read a comic book rather than watch. But after a while Pachico too became interested in seeing. He measured, timed, expressed wonder, and felt, them and himself. It wasn't long before Jimmy had a choice between Amor and Pachico. Practices that had once been unthinkable became commonplace in that room. Pachico, like Amor, had a special reverence for physical cleanliness. He told Jimmy

seriously: "Trabis, you are the cleanest person I know."
Jimmy said, "Thank you." Pachico smiled the gold-toothed
smile and put an arm around Amor's waist. They loved
Jimmy. Jimmy loved them, as well as the room's assortment
of smells: incense, Airwick, disinfectant, perfume, soap,
linoleum, Amor, Pachico. The nights became longer. Sometimes he didn't return to the Harvard Club at all. The
Trinity. Three. It was not a random number.

27

Cleo said it would sound silly to call it the Barnes Kennels.
"It could just as well be the Kennels Barnes." The operation was named the Graffmueller Kennels, and with the help
of a veterinarian from Darien, a man named Phil Krazitski,
Cleo made it into a very successful business as well as an
avocation. Phil was almost old enough to be Cleo's father.
He was a tall, thin, spidery man who appeared to have
more interest in animals than in people. He had been
married, fathered five children, and divorced some years
before Cleo brought him into her family's circle. He dined
with them one or two nights a week, worked at the kennels
on weekends, and supervised the staff. He advised Cleo
on Connecticut politics, washing machines, shopping centers,
pesticides, movies, highway routes, and biography, as well
as bloodlines. When the three of them had dinner one night,
Jimmy suddenly realized that Cleo and Phil were lovers and
that they had been lovers for several years. As Cleo and
Jimmy were going to bed that night, he asked her if Phil
had accompanied her to England two years before.
    "Yes," said Cleo. "Why?"
    "You never told me."

"I told you," said Cleo. "You don't remember."

"You did *not* tell me."

"Why should I hide it?"

"Because you're lovers, that's why."

Cleo was in the bathroom with the door open, rubbing cold cream into her face. She didn't answer. Jimmy was in the bedroom. He looked at himself in the full-length mirror. He seemed to be rippling.

"Well?" he said.

"Well?" said Cleo.

"Are you?"

Cleo came back into the room wearing the sort of satin and lace peignoir that looked ridiculous in the bedroom of a country house, especially on the increasingly stocky figure of Cleo. She sighed. She sat on their turned-down bed and looked at him. "Don't make a scene," she said. "I can't stand scenes."

"What do you mean you can't stand scenes?" said Jimmy. "We goddamn well never have had any."

"That's why," said Cleo.

"Well," said Jimmy, "are you fucking him or not?"

"Oh, James."

" 'Oh, James.' I want a straight fucking answer."

"You can't even say 'fucking' right. You sound like a choirboy." Cleo smiled, but it wasn't an entirely unfriendly smile.

"What do you mean by that?"

"I mean, I guess, that I love you, and that, yes, I have had an affair with Phil. I'm sorry."

" 'Sorry' is a poor fucking word for it."

Cleo became angry. "Stop saying 'fucking.' " She searched for a cigarette on the night table. "I said '*had.*' It's over and has been over for months."

"Why'd you stop?"

Cleo laughed. "It was too complicated. It would have been nice if we could have had some peace. I'm not interested in motel rooms, or running in and out of bedrooms in the afternoon, wondering if the boys are going to come home from school early, wondering what Birdie thinks, or if you're going to turn up."

"Do you want a divorce?"

She shook her head and seemed suddenly on the verge of tears. "No. Do you?"

"Why should I want a divorce?" said Jimmy. This obviously sounded peculiar, under the circumstances. "Are you sure you don't want a divorce?" He was trying to be civilized instead of defensive.

"No." She shook her head and wept. Cleo didn't often cry and the sight of her tears frightened Jimmy. "You have every right to, you know. And I've thought you were—well, tired of me, of us. The boys. The dogs."

Jimmy sat on the bed beside her and was more noble than he had thought possible. He put his arms around her and hugged her. "I'm not tired of you, darling. It's just that I work so hard."

"I know you do," said Cleo. "I appreciate that. And I love you." She sniffed into some Kleenex. When she spoke again, it was the controlled Cleo, with edge, although she tried to laugh. "Now we're even," she said.

"What do you mean 'even'?"

"You had Daisianna."

Jimmy continued to hold her tightly. "That was a long time ago. We weren't married then. After all."

"We were engaged."

"It's still not the same thing."

Cleo broke into tears again. "I know it isn't. . . . I'm so sorry."

Jimmy was very happy. As he held her he wanted to make

love immediately. "From now on I promise I won't work so hard. We'll spend more time together."

They didn't. The weekly visits with Amor and Pachico continued and became more demanding physically, financially, and in other not easily measurable, not easily predictable ways. Jimmy was not only keeping them. He was, in effect, keeping them together. Amor told him one night when Pachico had gone to a bar to get some ice that she and Pachico no longer made love if Jimmy was not there. She was not sad about it. She announced it as a kind of breakthrough. The three of them had become one.

28

His secretary buzzed Jimmy and told him there was a call coming through from the Virgin Islands. At first he didn't recognize the name, Mary Magnuson. Mary explained they'd been introduced by Charles and Daisianna at a dinner party in New York the previous winter.

"Have you heard?" Mary said. Her voice turned very small. "There's been an accident. You know that Daisianna and Charles are renting my house for the summer. Well, last night . . ." The voice trailed off and came back ". . . shot him with a shotgun."

"Who?"

"Daisianna," said Mary. "Can you possibly get down here?"

"What happened?"

Mary Magnuson's voice became steady. "Last night, at about three in the morning, Daisianna shot Charles with a shotgun."

"Oh my God."

"It was an accident."

"How is he?"

"He's dead. It was my husband's elephant gun. There had been prowlers around the house recently, and she shot him through the door."

"Oh God."

"His arm and part of his chest were blown away. I can't tell you. . . . You've got to come down here right away. I don't know what to do."

Jimmy said he would leave as soon as possible and Mary said if he would catch the one-o'clock flight to St. Thomas she would meet him and fly him over to St. Constance in her plane. When Jimmy telephoned Cleo to tell her what had happened, Cleo cried for several minutes and then calmed herself with fury. "I'm not surprised," she said. "It's typical. One time when we were at Dobbs, she poured a bottle of ink all over my clothes. She said it was an accident but I always knew she did it on purpose."

29

St. Constance local color: wild canaries, warblers, catbirds, gnatcatchers (black), gnatcatchers (blue-gray), pelicans that sit on offshore rocks and look sage, often when they're sleeping. Very thin cows with xylophone ribs; they walk down the middle of the highway connecting the Dutch and the French sides. They follow the white line. Tree frogs no bigger than beetles that sing after the rain, gardenias, hibiscus (red, yellow), bougainvillaea (magenta, peach, yellow, white), oleander, almond trees, lime trees, orange trees, a tree about which it's always asked, "What kind of tree is that?" (a kapok tree), azaleas, cactus, petria, manchineel (which looks and smells like crab apple, and whose fruit

and sap inflame the mucous membranes, sometimes fatally),
poison ivy, papaya, breadfruit, jack-spaniels (wasps), zinnias
(imported in pretty little packets from the United States
and do well if properly watered). The words painted on the
wall of Marigot's Catholic cemetery during one of M.
Bouché's campaigns for reelection: "VIVE LE PEUPLE!" The
late afternoon sea bath in Oranjestad when mothers bring
their children to the beach for their daily wash-ups. "The
kamms" (the calms), which occur in September and October when the trade winds stop, when the sea becomes the
color of smoked glass and as smooth, when mosquitoes appear. Also the kamm bugs, which don't bite but fly in such
swarms they get into the mouth, the nose, the eyes, and the
ears. They make reading at night impossible, even in rooms
protected by screens. They penetrate screens. They fly
around a light in rope patterns and look to be some kind of
kinetic sculpture. The Christmas winds, strong, almost gale-
force winds that blow away the kamms and can arrive at
any time between November 1st and February 28th. Between March 1st and October 31st, they're called high
winds. Lots of places on the island have French and Dutch
names, but the most practical names are English: the three-
mile-long sandbar that connects Marigot to the Low Lands
is called Three-Mile Sandy Ground. A bluff is called The
Bluff. High Point is the top of St. Constance's tallest (1,200
feet) mountain, named Naked Boy Hill. Seen from the east,
its rocky profile suggests a boy with the beginnings of an
erection. Front Street in Oranjestad is the town's main
street and runs parallel to Oranjestad Bay. Behind it is Back
Street. From a local guidebook: "The spectacular ruins of
the St. Constance Synagogue, one of the first in the West
Indies, have not yet been discovered."

30

Fonse Devanner, the Minister for Inter-Island Affairs for the government in Curaçao, spent a great deal of time on St. Constance that summer. He was a tall man, six feet five, and built like a professional football player. His dark brown hands, with fingernails fastidiously manicured, seemed as long as swim flippers. Fonse was a mixture of Negro, East Indian, and Spanish. He had been born and raised in Curaçao and had spent two years at a *gymnasium* in The Hague before attending the University of Leyden. He was very much in love with Mary Magnuson, the first woman he'd met who was almost as tall as he was. Mary had great affection for Fonse, but she was practical and she could not be sure she wanted to live in the islands twelve months a year. The Hague, while charming, was out of the question as something to look forward to. There was also Fonse's wife, a Dutchwoman several years older than Fonse, who never gave him any hint that she might one day divorce him. She liked being the wife of the Minister for Inter-Island Affairs, who everyone said would eventually succeed the Prime Minister. Fonse and Mary had a gentle, low-keyed affair that satisfied them both much more than either would have thought possible when it began. Late one night on the back gallery of Oranje House, overlooking Oranjestad Bay, Fonse told this story to Mary, Charles, and Daisianna:

"The last time I was in New York I saw an amusing—no, not amusing—interesting incident at Kennedy Airport. I was waiting for my plane to be called, you see, and on the bench across from me was a Negro lady with her two children, two little boys. She looked like a St. Kitts Negro, big and strong but without the grace of the women of Trinidad and Barbados, or of the women of the French islands. One boy was, I'd say, about five and the other, in her arms, no more than a year or so old. The older boy had a most enchanting face—very large, very grave eyes, you see. He seemed so full of thought. I noticed him watching the baby in his mother's arms, and the baby was leaning back, you know, sound asleep. Every now and again he would smile. In his sleep, you see. The older boy watched the baby very close, very intent, and then he said to his mother, you know, in island talk, something such as: 'Tink you, Ma, Harvey be dreaming of something sweet?' The mother looked down at the baby and shrugged. Well, she didn't know. Then the boy moved over and without warning he punched the baby as hard as he could on the arm. The funny thing was—the interesting thing was—the baby woke up, opened his eyes and his mouth, and he started to cry, but he couldn't make any noise. The tears rolled down his face and his mouth was twisting and turning, but there was only silence. He was—how you say—a dumb mute. Fantastic, no? The boy resented his brother so much—that dumb baby—that he even resented his dreams."

31

Paris. 1938. The old comtesse, who'd been born in Toledo in 1852 and christened in Mozarabic rites in a chapel that was said to contain building stones of ancient Toletum, was dying in the brass bed in the flat in the Avenue d'Iéna, preparing for death as if for another voyage. She'd asked the nurse to fetch her suitcases from the basement. They sat on the floor on the far side of the room where she could see them, open and empty and ready to be packed. Charles's mother had put her foot down about the steamer trunk. She told the comtesse that her steamer trunk was in the adjoining dressing room. The old comtesse argued and then accepted the explanation. The prospect of a journey depressed her. When she was sixteen, her mother and father had uprooted the family to follow Isabella II into exile in France. She never returned to Spain, though she spent occasional winters in Portugal, traveling by ship from Liverpool. Over her bed there hung a small, cheap reproduction of a Fra Angelico *Mother and Child* that his grandmother had bought in Florence when she was a girl. Charles suspected she used it as an altar. When the old comtesse traveled, the *Mother and Child* traveled with her, wrapped in tissue paper scented with lavender. It was late afternoon. The day nurse was in the kitchen washing nightgowns and Charles and his mother were sitting by the bed when the old lady awoke. The eyes were fiercely intelligent while the rest of her face seemed to be dissolving into the pillow as they watched. There was hardly anything left except the eyes and some wisps of hair, white and streaked with yellow as if it had been washed in old plumbing. She had the manner of someone fallen among strangers. "I'm tired now," she said to Charles's mother. The old comtesse spoke in English, as she did when she traveled. "I'd like to rest and then, if you want, we shall start again."

32

Charles watched the fall of France as if it were the collapse of a tall building photographed by a stop-motion camera. As small pieces of the façade came loose, as the lower floors gave way and the upper walls fell inward, Charles was trying to fix events in time. To frame and comprehend them. He was seventeen and had been living in the old comtesse's flat in the Avenue d'Iéna for two years. Not long after his grandmother died, Charles left the university to work at the Studios Vincennes, a small unprofitable studio owned by a company in which his father held a minority interest. There had been no particular problem about experience. The joke at Vincennes was that it was staffed by retired concierges and mutilated veterans of the Franco-Prussian War. Within six months, Charles was a film editor. In a year, he was operating a camera. In eighteen months, he was writing and directing films, first advertising films and then propaganda films that ignored the war and concentrated on France's glories. In the last months there was no production of new material. There was little film stock available. There were scarcely any employees. No one wanted to be reported to. Charles made films like patchwork quilts. He took pieces out of old films and stuck them together to make new films. When he left the studio a week before the end, he was working on what was supposed to be a fifteen-minute history of Republican France. Among the films he'd been given to ransack were a historical film about Voltaire, in which the actor who played Voltaire looked like Fernandel, and a collection of educational films that explained taxation, conscription, suffrage, and the checks and balances within the Assembly, largely through animated graphs supported by dramatized incidents. He'd also been given a print of Abel Gance's *Napoléon,* a paean to France that became a kind of encyclopedia for Charles. He could open it anywhere and start to read. Charles had no script and no idea where to begin his film. At that point, nothing made sense but no one cared what he was doing anyway. He spent his days rerunning the Gance film through the editing machine, making small marks on the film that were meaningless since he knew he could never cut it. Finally he realized he was out of touch with any time whatsoever.

On his last afternoon at Vincennes he received a telephone call from his father saying that he was driving his mother and his brother Guy that night to the farm in Provence. His father had not asked Charles if he wanted to come. He said, "We're taking only a few things but the car is full. I'm told there are desperate people on the roads. Jacqueline and Serge do not want to leave Paris, so I suppose your mother will have to find help in the South." When he paused, Charles said nothing. "Jacqueline and Serge will stay in the house. With us gone, they will have nobody to complain about except each other. They'll probably be better off than we are."

Some days later Charles awoke, aware that it was all over though not sure what or how. He awoke in pain in the old comtesse's brass bed with the bowl-shaped mattress, his right arm under a pillow on which rested the head of a handsome, middle-aged Montparnasse whore called Diane-the-Wolf. His right arm was asleep. Charles was still out of touch with time. On the left wall were dozens of photographs of all sizes, shapes, and eras, in frames of silver for members of the family who were the old comtesse's contemporaries and of less expensive materials for the generations that came after. Isabella II, painted in miniature at age three when she ascended the throne, was framed with gold. She looked like an elderly Nazarene angel. Through the open door he could see the white wicker seat that sat atop the toilet and turned the water closet into something that had the air of a royal reception room. Such eccentricities fascinated the streetwalkers Charles brought home, and also convinced them that Charles was only a visitor, that there'd be little point in coming to call on him later, as some might have wanted to do, for money or for pleasure. On the wall to the right of the bed there was a poor copy of the David portrait of Charles's great-great-grandfather, the apprenticed blacksmith from Dôme who'd pulled Bonaparte's irons out of the fire during the last days of the Convention and had later been the architect of various banking reforms, for which he was rewarded with a title but no estate. Charles tried to put things in sequence. On the far side of the room the balcony windows were open and the shutters closed. It was day but the hour was missing. He turned his head to look at his watch and felt something like a frozen knife go from his right ear down the side of his neck into his shoulder. His watch had stopped. He tried to think and it was as if he were pouring water into sand. Fragments of memories were glimpsed and then disappeared. His head didn't ache. It was filled with asbestos.

The stiffness in his neck suddenly frightened him. He wondered if he might be coming down with poliomyelitis. Because he couldn't move the fingers in his right hand, he began carefully to pull the arm back and then push it forward under the pillow on which Diane-the-Wolf slept. The fingers tingled and his immediate panic subsided. He pulled his arm from under the pillow roughly but Diane-the-Wolf did not awaken. Her mouth dropped open and there was lipstick on her two upper front teeth. Without particular emotion he wondered if possibly she could be dead. He knew she took morphine. It was one of the things that made her so pliable and gentle. Nothing he suggested ever startled her. She had such a sweet, vague way about her that she sometimes left without remembering her payment. Who would one call to remove the body? Could he do it himself? As if he were a patient who'd had a radical stomach operation, he sat up in bed in a series of small, precise movements, put his feet to the floor, and then stood. He felt as if he'd erected a tower of reeds a hundred feet high. When he stopped swaying, he walked over to the marble-topped commode and poured a glass of brandy from a crystal decanter engraved with the seal of the Spanish Bourbons. One morning he'd felt so unsteady that instead of walking to the w.c. he'd pissed into the then empty decanter, which had been on the floor by the bed. That memory and the brandy revived him, and he heard the noise, the hum, like the flapping of a million batwings. He walked to the windows, carefully placed his brandy on a table, and raised the shutters. The noon sunlight and the feeling of cold almost sobered him. He stepped onto the balcony and turned his body to the left to look over the treetops up the Avenue d'Iéna toward the Étoile. Only the top third of the Arc was visible, but he could see part of a huge red banner that had been hung inside the Arc. He went back into the room to get his brandy. The brilliance of the banner's red fascinated him. It was a triumphant red. A red that accepted no opposition. He stood on the balcony quite naked, his face and shoulders warmed by the sun but the rest of him in shadow. He was aware of color, aware of the stiffness in his neck so painful that he had to turn his entire body to turn his head. He wondered whether this day would be considered some sort of holiday, whether he would be able to find a masseur. He was aware of the defeat of others.

33

Myrna came with the Liberation. Like the PX privileges and the jeep he was given when the Americans hired him as a consultant on captured German film materials. Myrna was a Wren. She was attached to the British Embassy and living with a married English colonel old enough to be her father. Charles's first impression of Myrna was one of organizational command. She was someone who straightened things out, rearranged schedules, effected short cuts, made telephone calls to the right people. It was, oddly, something that made her seem sexy. No matter how efficient she acted, she gave the impression that she was ready to drop every-thing for the reckless experience. She always had two things on her mind: what she wanted done and what she wanted to do. Myrna was tiny, almost flat-chested, and pretty in a pale blond way he had never before considered especially appealing. They met over the telephone in the bar of the George V and were married six weeks later, with Myrna's colonel as best man. It was less a marriage than the acquisition of an exotic import, a foreign mecha-nism that was more efficient than the domestic equivalent. Neither Charles's mother nor his father attended the civil ceremony at the Mairie. They were still in Provence. Charles's brother Guy, who wanted to become an actor, came to the reception that was held at the British officers' club in the Saint-James et d'Albany. Guy and Jacques Isserot, who had worked with Charles throughout the Occupation at Vincennes, were the only Frenchmen there. The rest of the guests were English and American officers. When the Comte and the Comtesse finally returned to Paris, they were polite to Myrna but not particularly interested without being rude. Myrna's father wrote them a long letter about how happy he was and how he had always known that Myrna, his only child, a motherless one for most of her life, would be successful. He said he was proud of them both, without explaining why he should be proud. It was a very long and sentimental letter to have been written by a newspaperman. Newspapermen usually hoard their words and write with lots of dashes. This letter was composed, worked over, then copied. Myrna's father was not typical. He was a retired drama critic who wrote occasional nature articles for pub-lications otherwise devoted to trades (*Coffee Wholesaler,*

Wine Importers Monthly) or professions (*Modern Dentistry*). He was very good at describing landscapes. "*Sans pareil,*" said Myrna, which was the sum and substance of her French. They spent a weekend with her father, the summer before V-J Day, in a small, ordinary nineteen-twenties house in a run-down London suburb as devoid of spirit or idiosyncrasy as he was. He was a wraithlike man who talked a lot that weekend about Family, which, it turned out, meant connections to Edward the Confessor. "Yes," said Myrna's father, tight on gin after supper, "we favor the French." They continued to live in the Avenue d'Iéna flat. The war receded. The armies left or, at least, became less evident. Charles worked for a while at the Brilliancourt Studios as an assistant editor before he became chief editor for a company that made short films for newsreel theaters. Myrna joined an American friend of theirs in setting up a firm to represent American companies seeking to establish outlets in postwar France. It was called public relations, a term that amused Charles's mother, who would have been shocked if she'd known that when Myrna was introduced to clients, she was introduced as Myrna the Countess du Chaudrun. Charles didn't care. He rather liked her but he didn't love her. Her ambitions didn't touch him. He watched her write, telephone, greet, plan. He monitored her enthusiasms, but vaguely, and he wished her well. It was through a job offered Myrna by a New York advertising agency that Charles and Myrna were able to emigrate to America in the autumn of 1949. They were not talking much to each other by then. On the flight across the ocean she did not speak to him between Reykjavik and New York.

34

There is an underground explosion. A discus separates from the bed of the street and flies the length of a city block. Someone on the thirtieth floor of an office building drops a typewriter from a window. (Charles had read this in the *Daily News.*) He steps between two parked cars onto Sixth Avenue, in the Forties, and is run over by a taxi that doesn't stop. A man and a woman, both black, both well dressed, are arguing in front of a Chinese restaurant on West Forty-seventh Street. It is Saturday night. The man puts his hand on the woman's arm. She brushes it away. The man steps back, waits, then he hits her in the face with his fist. Charles goes to help. As he picks up the woman, the man stabs him with a penknife. The blade is so short and dull it might even be a letter opener. It goes neatly between the ribs into the aorta. He rides in a cab. He doesn't know where he's going. As the cab turns a corner, the door suddenly flies open and he is thrown to the pavement. His skull is cracked. Killed instantly. There is a leak in the gas line to the stove. Charles is (1) peacefully asphyxiated as he sleeps, (2) killed when a spark from the refrigerator ignites the accumulated gas and the entire apartment blows up. Charles is not sure whether he is killed in the explosion or burned to death. He won't worry about that. He might only be badly injured. There is also the possibility that he suffers irreparable brain damage because of the lack of oxygen, which turns him into a living cauliflower for the rest of his days. In an Italian restaurant on Third Avenue he eats manicotti. It is cheap and good, though one should not order it four days in a row as he has done. This time he chews and is gradually aware that it has a peculiar, rough texture. It crunches. He swallows. Later in the night he awakes, hemorrhaging. The intern at the hospital tells him there is little that can be done. The intern has to be frank. Charles's intestines have been turned into hamburger. He has consumed enough ground glass to kill a horse. Charles faces death with resolution. Things to watch out for:

Botulism (canned tomatoes).
Rabid squirrels.
A bomb in a subway car, trash can, letter box, public toilet, movie theater. Bombs can be anywhere.
Policemen who don't listen.
Mayonnaise in summer if not properly refrigerated.
Paint with a lead base.
Sidewalk gratings.
Children in packs.

For more than a year after Myrna left, Charles remained in their tiny furnished apartment on West Forty-ninth Street. It was on the first floor in the front of a gray brick structure that had never seen better days. It overlooked the sidewalk where children who should have been in school played from sunup to midnight, often with firecrackers. The warm, sunny days of spring were the worst, the noisiest. God only records the sunny hours. Had he read that? The children were mean—to animals, to an old man in a wheelchair, to each other. There was one exception, a little girl with a square-cut Dutch bob who, on even the hottest days, wore an aged overcoat that reached her ankles and could once have belonged to the wife of a proper shopkeeper in Lyons. The coat was threadbare tweed, blue-gray, with ratty-looking gray fur at the collar and cuffs. Hour after hour, the little girl practiced riding an ancient bicycle that was more outsized for her than the overcoat. It was a man's bicycle with a bar between the seat and the handlebar shaft. To reach a pedal when it was at the bottom of its circle, the little girl had to throw herself recklessly to one side, at the same time letting the bicycle lean to the other side. She pedaled back and forth in front of the house with happiness others might have seen only as determination. With her voluminous coat flapping around to complicate the operation, she looked like a very queer midget.

Charles slept most of the day, though the children made sleeping difficult. On bad days when it was cold and rainy he would revive for a while. Full of purpose he would leave the apartment to look for a job, to call a friend, or to go to a movie, but he seldom succeeded in anything. He did regularly buy coffee, milk that would eventually go sour, and liquor. When Scotch came to upset his stomach, he switched to gin. Then he began to smell gin everywhere. There were juniper berries in the closet, in his clothes, in the refrigerator, in the toothpaste, in the drafts that came under the door to the hall, on his pillow and in the sheets and blankets on the bed, in the gray rubber-base paint that Myrna had slopped onto the already paint-caked walls, woodwork, and radiators of the apartment. Myrna had painted the apartment instead of cleaning it and when the paint peeled, it came off in such big fat strips that an archaeologist could have reassembled the apartment from this one coat of Fast-Dri E-Z-On. Charles finally switched to vodka. He drank it in combinations with other things that seemed to be food. Tomato juice, orange juice, carrot juice, cranberry juice, bouillon, clam juice, prune juice. Myrna had loved America for the juices it supplied, and had stocked them by the carton. He sometimes put vodka into Campbell's vegetable soup and sloshed it onto eggs as they were frying.

At last, in desperation, since he was aware that he was losing weight and he did not want to die of malnutrition (better death by manhole cover), he began to spend his afternoons in the Automat on Broadway at Forty-seventh Street.

His day officially began around six in the morning. He

would awaken, pour himself a straight vodka, and read for an hour or so until he was sleepy again. He quickly finished the Simenons he bought when they first arrived. He went through Myrna's collections of *Reader's Digest* condensations. He then read whatever magazines had been put into the garbage cans in the hall. Because the tenants in his building threw out magazines at irregular intervals, everything had been turned into history for him. He kept remarkably well informed about what had happened weeks and months earlier. For Charles, indecisions were often frozen. Matters of life and death remained suspended. He would awaken at noon, drink some more, eat Ritz crackers, sleep again, awaken again at about 3:30, shave, brush his teeth, perhaps sew a button onto a shirt. He prepared himself for the Automat on Broadway at Forty-seventh Street the way his father prepared himself for a rendezvous at Fouquet's. There were afternoons in the Automat when Charles returned to the dining room in the Cecil at Alexandria. Other times it was teatime in the dining room of the Hôtel des Bains on the Lido. Most often he thought of the dining room of the Majestic in Baden-Baden, so oddly lit that there were never any shadows. If Myrna had sent some money, he would dine on roast beef or baked ham. If not, baked beans, of which he was extremely fond, or halibut, of which America had a limitless supply. Charles assumed himself to be a regular, although, unlike most of the other regulars, he kept to himself. He felt he qualified because of the peculiarity of his habits, his narrowing absorption in his own physical movements. Most of the regulars sat at separate tables but held conversations with friends at other tables. Some gathered in clumps of four or six and always as if by chance, the way pigeons seem to do to an outsider. They would talk at but seldom to one another. They argued and agreed and then grew peevish since, much of the time, they weren't talking about the same things.

They reminded Charles of the people who would turn up at the Hôtel Jérome each May 5th. His grandmother, who had no sympathy for the Bonapartes in history, never failed to attend the annual celebrations, which were designed as charity teas but lost money that Charles's father and several friends had to make up. The teas were the reunions of survivors of some dimly remembered disaster. The spinster Princesse Anne de Verdado, whose great-great-great-grandfather had been the military governor of Cairo for three months and then secretary to Joseph Bonaparte during Joseph's brief reign in Naples, always attended, but one never saw a Bernadotte or a Murat. These were mostly the withered remains of families without title or fortune or function in the reconstituted Republics. Only tenuous attachments to pasts seen fuzzily through cataracts. At the Automat, Charles especially liked watching a small, neatly dressed old man who had the face of a family priest suddenly removed from his parish when the château had been sold to rich Bolivians. He, like Charles, was a loner, and he often moved four or five times in the space of the hour he took to drink his cup of tea. His elegantly shaped head, with its close-cropped gray hair, was every forty-five seconds twisted to the right in a kind of one-two double-time tic. He could have been complaining to God, but politely. These boozy reveries in the Automat were abruptly terminated the afternoon the Duchesse de l'Ouest made her suprising scene.

The Duchesse had been a favorite character at the parties at the Hôtel Jérome. She had been ancient for as long as Charles could remember, and she remained in perfect stasis between life and death as he grew up. Her costumes became increasingly bizarre, especially the things she put on her hair and, occasionally, through it, but she did not change. Only once did she speak, at one of the first reunions Charles had attended as a boy. Why, the Duchesse asked, in the quiet that followed the initial toast, had Achille Murat emi-

grated to Florida? Charles and Guy had thought her a witch
and named her the Duchesse de l'Ouest. She once came to
the Hôtel Jérome with her gray hair, which she wore in a
pompadour, spiked with thin steel knitting needles. She came
to none of the postwar parties and there was some speculation that she had been put away. It is singular that no one
thought her dead. Then, suddenly, Charles began to see her
again at the Automat, usually carrying two worn shopping
bags that advertised a savings-and-loan association on Third
Avenue. The shopping bags contained old newspapers she
clipped at random: news stories, advertisements, recipes,
obituaries, cartoons, editorials. She acknowledged no one
and no one acknowledged her until that last afternoon.

Charles arrived at the Automat at exactly 3:30, wearing a
new blue shirt that Myrna had sent him for no particular
reason he cared to think about. The Automat was without
shadows, in the lull between people on coffee breaks and
those who ate their evening meals in the late afternoon. The
former Archbishop of Reims, very seedy in unpressed gray
pants and black cardigan that didn't meet kindly around his
belly, was sharing a table with a stranger, an old man who
once might have been successful in trade and who now,
Charles could hear, was forced to live with an uncaring
daughter who dictated policy to the telephone company.
Charles chose a bowl of vegetable soup, a piece of apple pie,
and a cup of coffee, and sat down near a window at a table
on which someone had left yesterday's *New York Times*.
Charles had just finished his soup when the ancient
Duchesse confronted him.

The Duchesse, carrying a cup of coffee with a paper napkin
placed between the cup and the saucer, made her way directly from the coffee urn to Charles's table. He thought
she was passing by him, but instead she stopped in front of
him. She stared into his eyes with fury of the sort that can

be as transporting as joy. Her lips trembled. Then: "You're thitting at my table." The open mouth was toothless and the tongue shot softly against the gums. "You're thitting at my table!" It was the angriest lisp Charles had ever heard. "You dirty Dew bathtard." The voice was pure American. Charles was as startled by this and by the lack of teeth as by anything else. She picked the cup from the napkined saucer and threw its contents at Charles. The coffee was scalding hot. Some went on his new shirt, but most went into his lap. The physical pain was real. More intense was the realization that he was being thrown out of the club. The Duchesse had acted on impulse, on her own, but with the approval of everyone else. He did not belong. A week later, Charles answered an ad for a position with Mary Bargains, Incorporated. "The travel agency," said the letterhead, "specializing in tours for people who don't like to tour." Said the young man: "A travel agency for people who don't like to travel."

35

"I'm quitting," the young man, who was named Al, told Charles the first morning. "I'm staying on to help the old bitch until you learn the ropes." Charles said, "How long should that be?" "About three hours," said Al. "I have a lunch date at twelve-thirty."

Later Al took Charles out for a cup of coffee. Charles longed for a drink. He wanted to go home. He was bored. He didn't know where anything was. Al explained that he had been planning to leave for some time. He and his father-in-law had bought a Laundromat franchise in Bay Ridge. "I've had this travel game," said Al. "In three years, I've been to England, France, Spain, Portugal, Andorra, Italy,

Germany, Switzerland, the fjords, Majorca, Mexico, Yugo-
slavia, Puerto Rico, Guatemala, India, Hong Kong, Taiwan,
Japan, Sweden, Iceland, Bermuda, and Honolulu. I've also
been to Williamsburg, Las Vegas, the Carlsbad Caverns, and
San Francisco. There's nothing more I want to see. When
you've been around the world once, where else can you
go?"

36

The rotten poetess was one of several women Charles occasionally slept with during that early period in New York.
He met her as they stood in line outside the Art Theater on
Eighth Street waiting to see *The Magnificent Ambersons.*
She was munching sesame seeds and reading Fanon. In as
long as it takes to smoke three cigarettes she told him that
she wrote, that she had gone to Barnard, that she lived alone,
that she worked in a bookstore on Bleecker Street, and that
she usually spent her weekends with her family in Wantagh
where her father was a building contractor. She wasn't
pretty but she had a good robust figure that, most of the
time, she gave the impression of merely tolerating. She
covered it as awkwardly as possible, with oversized shirts,
with denim jackets, with peasant skirts or ski pants with
baggy crotches. She was thirty-four. She told Charles that
he looked more like a blond Italian or a blond Jew than a
blond Frenchman, which pleased him. He was also pleased
when she told him he had an American accent while most
Frenchmen she'd met had English accents. She talked a
great deal in bed, which did not please him. In sex we affirm
life, she once said, and then bit the lobe of his ear so sharply
that it bled on the pillowcase. Three small blots. Whenever

that pillowcase came back from the wash and turned up on their bed, the brownish stains each time a little less apparent, she wept. Once, in the morning after a night when Charles had been too drunk, she brought him an Alka-Seltzer and coffee. She wore the wan, distant expression she wore when she was writing. She'd been up since four, she said, looking for herself. When Charles apologized for the way he had behaved the night before, she ran the palm of her hand across his chest and searched for atoms in the air some distance behind his head. "Love," she said, "is a continuing process of recognition and denial." He didn't see much of her after that.

37

Charles met Daisianna on a Friday night in May in the bar of the Auberge Française in Rockefeller Center after the departure of the last of the end-of-the-week celebrants. She was the only customer at the bar when Charles entered feeling very clean-cut, very American, for the moment not without prospects. He liked the American word. Prospects. The nearest French equivalent, *l'avenir,* was without the mad optimism he associated with prospects. Gold miners not only lived on prospects but when they worked they were prospecting. Charles had been paid that day, and after returning to the apartment on West Forty-ninth Street for a shower and a change of clothes, he walked to Rockefeller Center where he knew he could get his check cashed. Louis, the bartender, had his back to the room, filing his nails in the light reflected from the cash register. The girl exhibited the poise particular to barflies. She sat very erect on the barstool, her chin high, in the midst of silent conversation with someone standing above her. In her right hand she held a cigarette as if it were an instructor's pointer. With her left hand she occasionally adjusted her dark glasses, which had a way of slipping down on her nose when she looked at her drink. She was both elegant and comic.

"Well," said Louis, in French, "how goes it?"

"Shit," said Charles. "The same old thing. I spent all day at B.O.A.C. trying to get some tickets changed. They are idiots."

Daisianna turned toward Charles. She did not smile. Her manner was that of someone in the habit of dispensing calm to the panic-stricken. She said, in French, "Perhaps I could help you. I have a friend who works at B.O.A.C. in the reservations department. Well, truly, she doesn't work there any longer but I know some of her friends." Charles looked at her with pleasure. He glanced at Louis, who shrugged and turned his back to make a drink. Charles said, "Thank you, but it is finished." Then: "You are French?" "No," Daisianna said, in English. "I went to school in Switzerland." Charles continued to speak in French. "You are not from Paris?" Daisianna shook her head with delight. The poise vanished. "I'm from Chicago originally." Charles: "You speak French so well. Very few Americans do." The girl spoke French with a kind of upper-class affectation that many Americans and English assume to be a Parisian accent. "I also had a French governess," Daisianna said. Charles was charmed: trollops who have had governesses. It was all part of the land he loved. He offered to buy Daisianna a drink, which she accepted even though she said she must leave soon. She had to work the next day. "Work?" said Charles. "But tomorrow is Saturday. No American works on Saturday. That is in the Bill of Rights, I believe." Daisianna laughed. It was not an especially good joke but it was French. She asked him what sort of work he did. "I work in a travel agency." Daisianna: "How fascinating. I love to travel." Charles: "I believe you love people too, and good music." Daisianna turned back to her drink. Charles, in English: "That wasn't very funny. I'm in a bad mood." Daisianna: "You sounded as if you were in a very good mood." "I was paid today. That's all." Daisianna: "So was I. And tonight I went to school. Two nights a week I go to the Madigan School of Design. It's in the Associated Press Building." Charles asked her if she had been meeting someone in the bar. "No," said Daisianna, "but I didn't want to go home right away."

Several hours later they went to Charles's apartment where, at four in the morning, they sat in bed drinking vodka on the rocks and eating vanilla ice cream from a single dish. "You are skinny," said Charles. "You should eat more." Daisianna, seriously: "I don't think I'm skinny." Charles: "I like skinny girls." He leaned down and, with his mouth full of ice cream, kissed her right nipple. Daisianna screamed and giggled and said, "Now it's all sticky." Charles: "That's all right. I'll clean it off." Daisianna, later: "When you came into the bar tonight, you thought I was a prostitute, didn't you?" "No. I thought you were a very beautiful woman." Daisianna: "Girls sitting by themselves in bars are usually prostitutes, aren't they?"

"No. Sometimes."

"Often."

"Now and then. Depends on which bars you go to." Charles paused, looked at her with amusement. "You really aren't, are you? If you are, you're the strangest one I've ever met."

Daisianna told him the story of the Los Angeles plainclothes detective. She told it as if it were a parable, something that she'd been taught and then memorized for her own edification. It was a tale she might have told to a group of assorted travelers, brought together by fate and stranded at a country inn during a thunderstorm.

"In Hollywood there's a bar called Nino's, on the Strip. I went there with friends first. Then, when I was lonely, I went several times by myself. It was called Nino's but it was decorated like an old English tavern. A lot of movie actors used to go there. I saw Bruce Cabot there twice. At least, I'm sure it was Bruce Cabot, though the bartender said he was a salesman from Sacramento. One night a man kept buying me drinks. He was a tall man, quite handsome, though he seemed a little bit like a farmer. He had a red neck and his suit didn't fit him properly. Around the neck and shoulders. His hair was cut very short, as if he'd just gotten out of the Army or something. He reminded me of three brothers I grew up with in Chicago. They're so alike it's impossible to tell them apart. Not the way he acted, but something about his expression, something sort of shy but mean, possibly. I felt sorry for him. He tried to sound at ease and debonair, but he was awfully corny. It turned out he was from Oklahoma, he said, and he didn't know anything about Hollywood. He offered me fifty dollars to spend the evening with him. I took it." Pause. "At that time I was very broke. I took it because I would have gone with him anyway, but I needed the money. That isn't being a whore, is it? I mean I was perfectly willing to go with him for nothing. He just happened to give me the money.

"As soon as he gave me the money the roof caved in. He had a partner who'd been sitting next to us watching and listening to the whole thing. They suddenly pulled out badges and said all those things about being under arrest and what my rights were and never even looked at me as they were doing it. They literally hauled me out of the restaurant into their car. I spent four nights in jail. They took pictures of me, fingerprinted me, and asked me who I worked for. At first I was so embarrassed I didn't call anybody. Then I got hold of a friend who called my father in Chicago. The rest is very complicated. My father was able to pay somebody who was able to pay somebody else and I was let out without ever having to go through a trial. The funny thing was after. The important thing.

"A week after it happened, when I was living in a room in Santa Monica, the detective called me up. He said he wanted to see me. He said he had something to discuss with me and I thought it had something to do with the records. That night he came to my room. His neck was still red. He said it was from working in his garden. He had a house in the Valley, he said, and he and his father ran a truck farm. He was wearing the same peculiar-looking suit he'd been wearing the night I met him. When he arrived he was carrying a bottle of whiskey and a box of cheese crackers. He said he wanted to apologize, that he'd been thinking about me and about what had happened and he could understand my position. He wanted to come in. He was very insistent, and I let him. In spite of everything, I liked him. He told me about his family, about how they'd all come out to California from Oklahoma when he was a little boy. How they hadn't had any money and had lived for a year on a kind of Poor Farm. He cried when he told me the story, and I cried. We drank the whiskey and he suggested that we go to bed. He said, after all, that was what we had planned before we'd been so rudely interrupted. He had an odd sense of humor but I thought I liked him. I suppose I was just feeling sorry for him. Well, we went to bed and then in the middle of the night he woke up and started beating me. He called me all sorts of terrible names and slapped me. He didn't hit me with his fists but with his open hands. I was screaming and the man who owned the rooming house called the police but, of course, he was gone by the time they arrived. I guess I didn't make much sense. I was afraid to tell anybody who it was. The police threatened to arrest me for disturbing the peace. I guess that sort of finished me for a while."

Daisianna went to work at Corduroy Incorporated that morning with no sleep but extremely happy. In the evening she returned to the apartment on West Forty-ninth Street, having promised she would cook supper for Charles. She brought more vanilla ice cream and two TV dinners. Roast beef.

38

"Why did you want to leave Paris?"

"I didn't want to. At first. Myrna did. She was offered a big salary and a bonus to come to New York. Myrna wants to be successful more than anything else." Pause. "Myrna is a bitch but I still admire her. She has *courage*. Also, when she puts her mind to it, she is a fantastic lay."

"Oh, Charles."

"She is."

"But you had a good job in Paris."

"It wasn't a good job. I'm a good editor and sometimes I had good things to work on. But there weren't that many. You don't have to be very good to make films about Les Frères Lissac, for Christ's sakes." Pause. "Then, too, I began to think that if I came to New York I would contact some of the Americans I met during the Occupation. You know. The fliers who stayed in my apartment. Maybe one of them would have some influence in films or television here."

"Have you?"

"Not really."

"Why not?"

"All that is over. Or it should be. Calling on those people is like asking for a tip. I did write to one man. He lives in Atlanta. When he came to New York six months ago he took me to lunch at '21.' We didn't have anything to talk about. He's in the Coca-Cola bottling business."

"Do you want to go back?"

"There's nothing for me in Paris. Nothing that interests me, except maybe a few old whores and a couple of good restaurants. It's too bad you aren't a better cook." Pause. "I like New York now. The first few months were terrible, but now the city doesn't bother me. I keep thinking that perhaps I'll strike it rich. I'll win a prize. I like hamburgers and the *Daily News* and television. There's nothing secret here. I like Americans."

"But we're so vulgar."

"I like vulgar people."

"You don't."

"I do. Americans are sincerely vulgar. They take pride in vulgarity. The French are just as vulgar when they have the opportunity, though they never admit it. Someday I'll take you to the Côte d'Azur in August."

"We're moneygrubbing."

"What's wrong with that?"

"We don't care about culture. We have none."

"What's culture?"

Pause, then: "Literature. Painting. Versailles. Yves Allegret."

Charles laughed and kissed her. They lay side by side in bed on a Sunday morning. He said, "There's never been anything like it. This place. It's like being inside a bubble that's getting bigger and bigger. It's also like being drunk. Everything is possible." Pause. "At least, that's the way I feel right now, at this minute."

"What about me?"

"What about you?"

"You haven't said anything about me."

"I love you."

"It's about time."

"It *is* about time. Little dear."

Several weeks after they moved into the apartment on Bank Street, Daisianna arranged the luncheon at Sardi's with Jimmy Barnes on Washington's Birthday. From the manner of Jimmy Barnes when he left them, it was obvious he thought the luncheon had been a disaster. It was obvious he could not place Charles in any familiar scheme of things. He asked Charles about the war, the Occupation, de Gaulle, and he told Charles a long story about a friend who'd changed five hundred dollars into francs on the Paris black market only to find he'd received counterfeit notes. Charles thought it a funny story. A moral story. It made Daisianna sad. It was clear that Jimmy Barnes was full of uncertainty and disapproval. He disapproved of the three cocktails that Charles and Daisianna had before lunch. He disapproved of the wine that would make him sleepy. He disapproved of the brandies after lunch. He disapproved of Charles, and Charles approved of his disapproval, though it worried Daisianna. Jimmy Barnes was the first Taft Republican Charles had met in America. After Jimmy paid the enormous check and departed, Charles and Daisianna stayed on to have several more drinks. By the time they returned to Bank Street Daisianna was well into a crying jag. When she'd begun to cry in the taxicab, Charles held her and laughed happily. It seemed a classic crying jag. An outpouring of tears for the world's misbegotten. She wept for Jimmy Barnes, who'd married a plush horse, for Jimmy's father, who had no tongue and had hanged himself, for the middle-aged lady butcher who'd been shot by the Germans in a courtyard in Saint-Cloud. She wept for the Little Lord Jesus.

The next morning before they got out of bed Charles asked her how she felt. "Fine. Why?" "You were very drunk last night." "So were you." "I didn't have a crying fit." "Did I? I don't remember." "You were feeling sorry for everyone. Jimmy Barnes, Madame Rouxelles, Jimmy's father, the Little Lord Jesus. For a while I thought He might have returned."

Daisianna frowned. "No," she said. "I promised I would tell you."

39

In those early days on Bank Street there were echoes of the old boredom and fears Charles had known on West Forty-ninth Street. There were times he wore the same shirt four days in a row because Daisianna couldn't remember to go to the laundry that was next door to Corduroy Incorporated. There were times he came home from the office at noon, shaved at midnight, and went to bed at three in the morning. They would make love at six in the evening and have supper at ten. It was at this time that Daisianna bought the sewing machine advertised on television for $26.95. In the first six weeks she had it, she made new slipcovers for the couch and two dresses for herself. Then she left a lighted cigarette on the machine's plastic hood. The hood exploded. It burned for a moment, as if made of magnesium, and went slowly out. The separate parts of the machine inside were fused together like pottery fragments found at Saint-Pierre. In the following months the company threatened to sue Daisianna for nonpayment of the $2.25 monthly installments. Daisianna wanted to make them. Charles would not allow it. He said the machine had been a hazard to health. It should not have been sold. They fought, and Daisianna said that if that's the way he felt he should go back to France. Charles asked Jimmy to help him write a letter to the Attorney General's office, with copies to the television station and the sewing machine company, which no longer existed except as an account with a collection agency. Charles saw this as a validation of his position. Daisianna worried. In time she came to believe that it was Charles who had left the cigarette on top of the sewing machine, probably on purpose, risking injury and jail for them both. Whenever she was drunk.

Their first years together were very lean. Charles worked at Mary Bargains in an office next to the Dolly Fashion House (wholesale hose), on the second floor of a building at the corner of Fifth Avenue at Forty-second Street. His desk was by a window that looked down on Fifth Avenue. It was a perfect place to watch parades. He saw the St. Patrick's Day parade, the Columbus Day parade, the Veterans Day parade. He saw the parade that welcomed General Mac-Arthur to New York after he'd been relieved of his command by President Truman. MacArthur sat in the back of an open limousine scarcely acknowledging the crowds of secretaries. He had the manner of a man who had become his own wax effigy. Charles's time was devoted to the making and canceling of airplane reservations to and from places like Boston, Hartford, Albany, and sometimes Miami. Daisianna worked six days a week in the Village as a saleswoman in the shop that specialized in clothes made of corduroy. Her hours were long and her salary small. Most of the clothes she sold she sold to herself. For a while she dressed entirely in corduroy. She wore corduroy skirts and slacks and jackets. She had corduroy hats, corduroy purses, corduroy gloves, corduroy handkerchiefs. She even owned a corduroy evening dress. Her favorite outfit was a suit and cap made of matching dark blue corduroy. Charles said she looked like a coal miner, that all she needed to complete the effect was a lamp on her hat, which prompted Daisianna to burst into tears and sulk through an entire Ed Sullivan show.

They lived in a shabbily renovated Federal house in a furnished apartment with a tiny bedroom, a Pullman kitchen, and a bath in the hall, which they shared with a pretty girl who taught at the Little Red School House and always seemed to be in a state of abstraction. It turned out she was also an actress and was often learning lines for plays that were never reviewed in the *New York Times*. Charles heard once every month from his mother who complained about the cost of living in Paris, the general strikes, the C.G.T., his father's increasing senility, his brother's unproductive interest in the theater, and the weather. She longed to get away to Deauville in the summer and to Juan-les-Pins in the winter, and she did, though, she explained, she depended upon the courtesies of friends, not family. Charles wrote her regularly, and occasionally he sent her money, which she acknowledged by asking for more. Leola wrote Daisianna once that first year. It was a reluctant sort of birthday greeting ("A year older! With love, ever, Mummy") on the top of a clipping from the society column of the Chicago *Journal-American*. Circled was an item about Dodie and Ida's having bought a house in Tangier.

They had no real social life. Their poverty was a kind of quarantine. It sometimes bored and depressed Charles but Daisianna accepted it as if it were something that had always been. In matters of this sort she was infinitely adaptable. It wasn't that she had a strong character or believed that things would one day be better. She seldom looked far enough ahead to be either optimistic or pessimistic. It was enough to plan for a Sunday. When she looked back, she looked back to birthdays or Christmases as a child, and she recalled events with no greater or lesser emphasis on the happy times than on the horrors. Her memory was a kind of album. It was someone else's life that had been placed in her keeping. The recollections were picture postcards sent from private places. Daisianna's tenth birthday: Dodie had left the house in Lake Forest to drive to Libertyville to play golf and was reported missing and perhaps dead by the police. They'd found the wreckage of his car strewn alongside the Chicago & North Western railroad tracks. The car had stalled on a crossing and had been hit by the *City of Milwaukee*. Leola had become hysterical. Daisianna had wondered if she were at least technically an orphan, and the birthday party was canceled. Several hours later, Dodie was brought home in a taxi by some new friends he'd met in a local tavern.

In those years, as Daisianna told of them, Dodie was always being brought home by strangers. Once he was brought home by the police who had arrested him and two other men for shooting at pheasants from a moving car out of season. They'd been taken to the Lake Forest jail where, according to one of the policemen, Dodie had tried to attack the game warden, who'd been forced to protect himself. Dodie, who was five feet five, was still so drunk when he was brought home that he did not know that his nose and two ribs were broken. Daisianna to Charles: "Mother refused to talk to him but I used to sneak into the room to look at him. He would have nothing but raw filet mignon for his black eye. He was always spoiled."

Daisianna did not fret about the past or future and Charles found her very easy to live with after certain adjustments were made. She was a terrible housekeeper. She refused to wash a dish. She preferred to wipe things off with linen towels, which she threw out every few months. She never put anything away. Plates, clothes, bills, laundry, make-up.

She handled tubes of toothpaste as a chimpanzee might. She seldom associated the tube with its top, with the result that the toothpaste was always as thick as old peanut butter. It had to be mashed onto the bristles of the toothbrush between the thumb and forefinger. She took no interest in cooking. If left to her own ways, she would have fed them nothing but TV dinners. Though she could never resist buying something that had been newly processed as an instant food, like Instant Tacos, she seldom found the time to prepare them. She took no interest in cooking but she insisted that whatever they ate be served on carefully warmed plates, which, very often, still bore the remainders of earlier meals. She was, however, enchanted by Charles. She was responsive to his moods in ways that no other woman had ever been, without seeming to be either servile or imbecilic. If Charles awoke at three in the morning, hungry, she was awake and hungry too. When he wanted to read most of the night, she would read for an hour and then fall asleep, the magazine in her hands, not moving until he turned off the light and put his arms around her. She was always surprised when he wanted to make love, then eternally grateful.

40

It was a Sunday in mid-March. The city was exhausted and stiff, as if inhabited by people who had spent all their lives in bed without stirring for fear of the cold. In the afternoon the sun appeared, and Charles suggested they take a walk, which was his alternative to going back to bed with a bottle of vodka and staring at the ceiling. They walked up Fifth Avenue to Fifty-eighth Street, around the fountain in front of the Plaza. They looked up into the windows of the Edwardian Room and saw the tops of the heads of people having tea. Daisianna's red corduroy coat was bright but not warm. In the gulleys of Central Park, out of the sun, she shivered. Her lips turned blue and Charles tried not to notice. Behind a bench near the skating rink Daisianna found the handbag, a big, functional, old-lady's pocketbook of fake black leather with the initials "F.R.M." on the side. Inside were a dozen pieces of Kleenex, separately folded, a key ring with five keys on it, a set of New York State divorce papers dated 1936, and a change purse. Inside the change purse were sixty-five dollars in tens, fives, and ones, plus several dollars in coins. Also a card requesting that the purse, if found, be returned to Mrs. Fritzie Morton at the Pickwick Residential Hotel for Women, on West Sixty-fifth Street.

"I suppose I should telephone her," said Daisianna.

"Yes," said Charles.

"She'll want her keys," said Daisianna.

"And her divorce papers," said Charles.

Daisianna laughed and put her arms around his neck and hugged him. They posted the purse in a mailbox on Fifth Avenue and walked to Madison, where, in a drugstore near the Westbury, Daisianna bought $32.80 worth of cosmetics, as well as some dental floss. Afterward they took a taxi to the Village. They dined at an expensive restaurant and grew very happy over the food and the wine. When they arrived home, Daisianna decided to telephone her mother. They hadn't talked in over a year. Leola, however, was either out or not picking up.

41

Three nights after Christmas, the twelve Christmas trees that had been set up on the islands dividing Park Avenue between 68th Street and 79th Street were incinerated by persons unknown on behalf of a cause that was never to be revealed. According to almost a dozen witnesses, the perpetrators were young white men who wore blue jeans, windbreakers, and ski masks. The trees, whose lower branches had been soaked in gasoline, went up in one big simultaneous whoosh of flames at exactly 2:35 a.m. For a moment Park Avenue looked like a firey seam splitting the city in two. Then it went dim again. The first reactions were mostly of comic disbelief, followed by anger and fear. A furious editorial in the *Daily News* asked what else one might expect in a society that could seriously debate God's death. The *Times* advised its readers not to lose their heads. The *Times* thought it might be a prank, though not a funny one.

42

That was the winter they went to the New Year's Day eggnog party given by Naomi Harte, who had grown up in Chicago with both Dodie and Leola. Naomi was a sculptor of nymphs and cupids that decorated formal gardens and swimming pools from Florida to southern Maine. She was successful in a field in which, admittedly, there wasn't much competition, but her vast income was derived from a railroad-car coupling that had been invented by her grandfather. When Daisianna was a child, she and her mother often stayed in Naomi's house on East Seventy-fourth

Street, a fine large old city house that was always full of people who didn't seem to have been expected. In the middle of the night, Daisianna was frequently moved from one bedroom to another to make way for new guests. One night two men she did not know had a fight on the twin bed next to hers. She also remembered a wastebasket made from an elephant's leg that had been hollowed out. "She's one of the kindest, dearest people in the world," Daisianna told Charles on a Lexington Avenue subway. "She speaks perfect French. She lived in Paris in the twenties and knew everybody." "Who?" said Charles. Daisianna couldn't remember.

It took Daisianna and Charles ten minutes to push their way from the front door up one flight to the bar that had been set up in the library. They knew nobody and nobody wanted to know them. Daisianna drank the drinks Charles fetched for her and adopted the moony smile meant to be welcoming to friends she couldn't see when she wasn't wearing her glasses. Charles had drunk three drinks and Daisianna two when Daisianna recognized Naomi's voice coming from the hall. "Gallagher and Shean," said a husky voice that cut a rough, mean-edged hole through all the other voices. "Gallagher and Shean. I don't know which one it was, but one of them tried to make me in the lobby of the Muehlebach Hotel in Kansas City in 1919." "That's Naomi," said Daisianna. She took Charles by the arm and pulled him into the hall. Naomi stood halfway up the stairs leading to the third floor, holding court. Her old face was a mask of white powder defined by crimson lipstick and black eye-liner. "It doesn't make any difference," she said, "I had them both." A young man dressed in black suède said: "Is there anybody you haven't had, Naomi?" He sat on the steps at Naomi's feet carelessly holding the hand of a girl who was asleep. "You, darling," Naomi said. She wore what looked to be a long sable dress, a sable turban, and eyelashes so thick they seemed to be sable, too. Charles watched Daisianna work her way up the stairs where Naomi kissed her and wept, as did Daisianna. He went back into the library and sometime later found himself talking to a slim, pretty, ageless woman who said she had known him in Paris. She called him by name and teased him about not remembering her. She said her name was Elena Noilles. "Actually, the Marquise Noilles." She said her husband was Henri Noilles but that Charles probably didn't know him, although Henri was a friend of Charles's father. Then: "I saw Guy not three weeks ago."

"My brother?"

"Your evil brother," said the Marquise. "Such a charming boy."

She laughed more fully than the statement seemed to warrant. "You still do not remember me? I thought not."

Her accent, when she spoke English, was unlike any he'd ever heard. Then, when she abruptly switched to French, it was still terrible, full of superfluous vowels and syllables, with accents over the wrong e's and with g's as blunt as old stone axes.

"We met in Paris soon after the war," she said. "I was then newly married to José Villa Santos-Wilson. My father-in-law was the Brazilian Ambassador to France. You and José used to play tennis at the British Embassy."

"Of course," said Charles.

"And you were married to a very sweet little English girl."

"Yes," said Charles.

The Marquise switched back to English: "She had very thing blond hair. I remember thinging that she would one day be bold. Is she?"

Charles said he didn't understand.

"Yore wife," said the Marquise. "I'm sorry but these days

my accents are completely hopeless. I've lived too long in too many countries. I mean, yore wife had thing hair, like some men."

Charles said yes, that Myrna had had very thin hair.

"Is she bold?" the Marquise said. The idea amused her greatly, and the picture of a bald Myrna began to seem funny to Charles also.

"I don't know," said Charles. "We're divorced. She's living in San Francisco."

He remembered: the young German girl had come to Paris during the Occupation to act in German-made French films. Instead she'd married the oldest du Plessix son and his family had been so outraged they'd never talked to him again, even when he was dying of tuberculosis. The German girl had kept the title but the courts saw to it that she received none of his fortune. She was subsequently made acceptable (receivable) by a Brazilian millionaire.

"You were always very kind to me," said the Marquise, "even when everyone else ignored me."

Charles had difficulty attaching this extremely chic-looking woman to the shy, fragile wife of José.

"Where is José now?"

"In Rio," said the Marquise. "Where else, my God. Living in that dreadful house with his father and mother and all of his brothers and sisters and their husbands and wives and their children. My son, too. The little José. He's now seven and wants to become a priest."

"What happened?"

"I couldn't stand it," said the Marquise. "I'm afraid I do not have an excellent character. I'm quite evil, really." She rattled on about Brazilians ("Brazilians are marvelous in Paris and ghastly in Brazil"), about her son ("I think I will one day be more fond of him. When he is older. Now he is a little saint"), about Rio ("I hated the poverty even though

we were very rich"), about the tribal living of Brazilian
aristocrats:

"I could not leave the house alone. Never. I was always
chaperoned by a widowed aunt or some servant with a de-
formed arm or leg."

"It sounds like a convent," said Charles.

"No such luck. A monkery, or whatever it is. For men."

"A monastery," said Charles.

"Yes," said the Marquise. "I speak five languages and I
am horrible in all of them."

They sat on big, soft red-and-white striped cushions facing a marble fireplace in a walnut-paneled room from which
all other furniture had been removed. He was later aware
that he was tight for a short while and then heavily drunk
for a much longer while. Elena did most of the talking while
Charles went through little locks of consciousness as she
pulled him back to Paris. She spoke an extraordinary mixture of French and English, full of German and Portuguese
and Spanish pronunciations that often turned meanings and
emotions upside down. There was too much animation, too
much laughter. There were too many confidences. "I am an
adventuress," she announced at one point as if she were
telling him she had her pilot's license. Later: "José was very
naughty. We had a very bad time. When I told him I wanted
a divorce, he obtained an annulment. He loves his son but
he hated me more, so he turned little José into a bastard.
Of course, all of that last year in Rio José was having an
affair with a mulatto girl. I didn't realize it until later. She
was at the university. I must admit she was very beautiful.
I could have fallen in love with her myself." The Marquise
laughed in a way that was approximately twenty years too
young for her. "But, as I told you, I am evil." Charles said:
"You are most frank." "I'm staying at the Nassau, room 407,"
she told him in the middle of a story about Paris. There was the

possibility, he realized, that she had been in love with him for years, all that time he was playing tennis with José in Paris and seeing her out of the corner of his eye, a pretty, pale girl, very thin, dressed more simply than the women around her. If they could, most rich Brazilian women would put everything they own on their backs at one time. "When you are next in Paris," said the Marquise, "you must come to see me. We live in the Fourth, on the Île Saint Louis. It's a small but fantastic Louis XIII house. Henri spends most of his time in the country and I join him on weekends. The weekdays are mine." Charles put his hand in the Marquise's lap and she giggled prettily. "I should explain," she said, "that although Henri is much older than I, he is my one true love. I love him dearly. I'm very serious. When I first came to Paris from Germany, during the war, long before I ever met Paul du Plessix, Henri was in love with me and asked me to marry him. It was the worst mistake of my life that I didn't. It would have saved a great deal of time." She patted Charles's hand. "On Tuesdays I have marvelous parties and do a lot of naughty things. I have a lamp that is shaped like a big penis. I put it in the drawing room on Tuesday nights. Once I forgot it and one of the maids, a sweet old lady from Brittany, found it. She was horrified, and when she woke me to tell me about it, she couldn't bring herself to use the word for penis. She kept calling it a gentleman's utensil. But Thursday nights are the gayest."

Charles looked at her solemnly. She caressed his hand. "Henri knows all about it. All about Thursdays, too. Black boots and leather helmets and garter belts. You know the sort of thing. I told you I was very naughty." Charles said: "You are magnificent. When can we go to bed together?" The Marquise assumed the manner of a coquette. "I'm not sure," she said. "I am not in New York alone. I have a friend with me." She nodded across the room to a young, plain-looking woman wearing a tweed skirt and a sweater. "Ann-Marie is a sculptor. Very talented. I brought her over to help arrange a show. I'm hoping Naomi will help, but I don't know. Naomi doesn't find Ann-Marie attractive."

"There must be times when Ann-Marie goes out," said Charles, "to buy stone or something. I can come to the Nassau then." "I'm not sure," said the Marquise. "You are a most attractive man and I've always liked you though you don't remember me. You see, I don't often sleep with men anymore. I'm a lesbian." She squeezed his hand. "I've always been, primarily. I do like men, but I usually prefer very young, very gay boys. I like to be their first experience with a woman. I like to teach them how beautiful a woman can be. How sweet. How gentle. They're all scared to death, poor things." "Do you cure them?" Charles asked. "Infrequently," said the Marquise. "That is not the point. I don't care about curing people. I only want everyone to have more fun." "You are magnificent," said Charles, "and I would like to fuck you and Ann-Marie in the same bed at the same time." "Mercy me," said the Marquise, "I would love that too, my God. But Ann-Marie would object. She's very jealous. She's very young still and I cannot be too evil."

Much later Charles fell asleep on the cushion, but when he awoke he remembered having been introduced to Ann-Marie and receiving the Marquise's telephone number in Paris. He also remembered Elena's saying that Guy occasionally came to her Thursday nights, although he was not a regular: "He's very strange, very shy but most eager. He's evil, too." The room was empty and Daisianna was standing over him talking in the carefully unemphatic way she had when she didn't care to seem drunk. "Charles," she said, "I want to go home. I don't feel well." He heard music and laughter from other rooms on other floors. She was wearing a coat of what appeared to be leopard skin and carrying her red corduroy coat over her arm. He stood up and ran his hand over the fur, which felt rather like a horse's flank. Daisianna said, "Naomi gave it to me. She didn't want me to go out in this corduroy thing." "She *gave* it to you?" "Yes," said Daisianna, "to keep." They went to the cloakroom to get Charles's coat, and then down the stairs and out of the house. "Tell me again," Charles said when they were on the sidewalk, "tell me once again. That old bitch gave you that coat?" "Yes," said Daisianna, "and I'm going to keep it." "For old times' sake?" said Charles. "She's one of Mummy's closest friends," said Daisianna. Said Charles: "She's an old lesbian. What did you have to do for it?" "Nothing," said Daisianna, "and don't call her a lesbian." It was cold and quiet on the sidewalk and there were no taxis. "She's one of the dearest, sweetest people in the world. Mummy says so too. I won't have you saying things about her."

With some shock, Charles understood that Daisianna was trying to sidetrack him by being prissy. He said, "Shit." When he said it again, his carefully cultivated American accent had gone. "Sheeeet," he said, "where'd you do it?" "Where'd we do what?" said Daisianna. "We! We!" said Charles. "Then you did go to bed with her! My God! Where in that house, with all those people crawling all over the place?" "I didn't do anything," said Daisianna, and she began to sob. Big tears engulfed her eyes and rolled down her face and off her chin in rivulets. She shuddered with unhappiness. "I didn't do anything. Not really. And I didn't do anything for the coat. She gave it to me later, just when I was leaving. It's Indian leopard." She looked as if she were about to faint and Charles put his arms around her and around the Indian leopard. They stood together as Charles blocked the wind from her face. Daisianna said, "If someone likes me very much, I find it very difficult not to like them back."

In the cab going home Daisianna put her head on his chest and before going to sleep said, "But I won't have to return it, will I? I do need a heavy winter coat, after all." Charles looked at the stalks of the incinerated Christmas trees that still accused Park Avenue. He loved her as he had never loved anyone else. And she loved him. She depended upon him. He was her entire life. There was nothing else. He was also aware that he could leave at any time and that her life would not change substantially. She'd continue to do whatever she'd been doing when he left. She had no power to alter her own course. She was an object in space.

43

Three years later Charles found a job as a film editor with Micro Entertainments, a small, disorganized company that produced television commercials and a fifteen-minute adventure series about a private eye named Hugo Colt, played by an actor whose suits reminded Charles of the one worn by Daisianna's Los Angeles detective. They didn't fit properly around the neck. Charles was hired because he was nonunion and would accept a good deal less than union scale, though it was still more than he made at Mary Bargains. His hours were from seven in the evening until three in the morning and his offices were in a large ugly building on Ninth Avenue in the Thirties. The building was called Cinema City and was occupied mostly by one-man production and distribution companies and semi-legitimate entrepreneurs, some of whom supplemented their incomes by making pornographic films on the premises after regular business hours. The conversations in the elevators were always about futures, about possible deals, about possible financing, about possible thirty-nine-week commitments, about possibly not having to go out of business. The celebrity of Cinema City was Gerald Lipofsky, a well-tailored, portly, gray-haired man, who rented the entire twelfth floor where he wrote, photographed, edited, and scored soft-core pornographic features with titles such as *Little Red Riding and the Hood, The Girls in the Back Room Will, Moll Flanders Returns,* and *From Petticoats to Panties,* which was his only musical revue. It lost money. His most successful film was *Frankenstein's Ugly Sisters,* which, Charles heard a number of times in the elevator and in the Cinema City coffee shop, had grossed $168,000 on a production investment of $33,000.

Before joining Micro Entertainments, Charles took two weeks off to fly to Paris to see his father, who—his mother had been saying for several months—was dying. She had said that even before his father entered the hospital. Charles did not have the money to take Daisianna, even on the reduced fares the agency obtained for him. Daisianna, in fact, did not seem especially interested in going. She couldn't leave Corduroy Incorporated, she said, and there was her school. She became increasingly vague as the time for Charles's departure approached. In bed the night before he left, he held her and tried to reassure her. "I don't really want to go," he said, "but I should." "I know," said Daisianna. "I'll be back in two weeks." "Yes," said Daisianna.

"Everything will be better, you'll see."

"What's wrong with it now?"

The Comte was in an oxygen tent at the American Hospital in Neuilly when Charles arrived, and though the hospital was only a five-minute walk from their house, his mother insisted that they go by taxicab. "Where's Guy?" said Charles. "Doesn't he still have his car?" "Yes," said his mother, "but he had an audition this morning. He's been having a lot of auditions these days. Last week he auditioned for Jean-Louis Barrault." "Has he worked?" "Just that television program last winter. The one in which he played a gangster." His mother smiled and patted Charles on the back. "He was really quite good as a gangster. And then he had a tiny part in Viviane Romance's last film." "I didn't know that," said Charles. "You didn't write me that." His mother sighed. She was putting on gloves, which required pulling the glove an inch onto each finger, stretching the fingers, pulling again, smoothing the material, pulling again, gestures once associated with his abandonment. Said his mother: "It wasn't actually a part. He sat at a table in a café with a very pretty girl while Viviane Romance and whoever it was she was then living with played the scene. Your father found it very good. I thought she looked cheap. Guy looked very handsome but most of the time you couldn't see much more than his hands."

At the age of seventy-five, his mother was still an exceedingly good-looking, vigorous woman. She dressed for the hospital as if she were going to the Ritz for afternoon tea, but she carried the style without effort. She was also able to talk to Charles about his father and their finances without using the vocabulary of resentment and self-pity she employed in her letters. Although Guy was living in the Avenue d'Iéna flat, she kept all the rooms of the Neuilly house open with only Serge to help her. "Once a week Serge and I clean," she said. "It does us both good, though we never get through a day without a few tears. He always comes across something that reminds him of Jacqueline. He no longer remembers that they had not spoken for years at the time she died. He was very hateful to her. Now that she's gone, she is the saint he worships."

His father lay on a high white bed, enclosed in a clear plastic tent, in a private room that overlooked the hospital gardens. Except for his pallor, he seemed in good health.

"Remember," his mother said earlier, "he is senile." The Comte often smiled, which was not his custom, and he seemed genuinely fond of the young American doctor who was taking care of him. His mother sat by the bed, holding his father's hand through the plastic, and talked to Charles as if his father were unconscious. "He's a good patient," said his mother, "but the birds have come home to the roost." Said the doctor to Charles in the hallway later: "He's a very good patient, but the chickens have come home to their nest." "What precisely is wrong with him?" The doctor smiled benignly. "It would be easier to tell you what isn't. His kidneys are shot. He's had at least three strokes that I know of, each one a little more serious, and his heart is exhausted. Our most immediate concern now is the lungs. How to keep them clear. Our problem is that we can hardly treat one thing properly without aggravating another organ. It's very tricky but it's also a challenge. We must always beware of the atrocious assault."

They dined that night in the dining room of the Neuilly house. Charles, Guy, and their mother, their mother in a champagne-colored evening gown that she had had ever since the thirties, Guy in slacks, open-neck shirt, and an English tweed sport jacket that he draped over his shoulders. Charles wore a conventional suit and tie. Their mother sat at the head of the table, Charles on her right, Guy on her left, the way it had been at family dinners when the boys were growing up. The emptiness at the foot of the table acknowledged that the Comte was already dead. Guy looked awful. He was essentially a somewhat taller, prettier version of Charles. He had the same dark reddish-blond hair and dark skin, but the features were more lean, more like their mother's. Guy looked worn out. The eyes were puffy. Charles felt censorious. He wondered if he should mention Elena. They dined by candlelight, as his mother said she was in the habit of doing now to save money, but the dining room was ablaze with illumination. The room looked like a grotto at Lourdes. There were candles burning everywhere, on the table, on the mantelpiece, on the sideboard, on the floor. "Serge makes them, don't you, Serge?" his mother said as the old man, wearing a soiled white jacket and black trousers in need of pressing, served the soup. "It's his hobby," said the Comtesse. "My difficulty is finding enough candlesticks. You see, I have to put them on plates."

Guy talked about his career in terms of social life: a dinner party given in honor of Marais and Cocteau, a weekend at a house near Dieppe attended by Gérard Philippe and Michèle Morgan. Sometimes it was only in terms of shared public places. He often had cocktails at the George V when Dietrich was there with Gabin, whose usual costume was green United States Army fatigue clothes. He'd met Roberto Rossellini's brother, Marie Bell's niece, Clouzot's lawyer, and had once been mentioned in an American newspaper story by Elsa Maxwell as "that handsome young French actor Guy du Chaudrun," or so he had been told by an American girl from Denver with whom he corresponded. He'd practically been promised a job with the Barrault company when there was an opening. "By whom?" said Charles. "By Barrault?" "By one of his assistants," said Guy. "I'm supposed to go to a party with him tonight in Saint-Germain." Guy became bored when Charles talked about money. His mother became defensive.

"How much is there from the sale of the farm in Provence?" Charles said. "Is there anything?"

"What do you think we're living on?" said his mother. "If we hadn't sold the farm, we'd have been in the street years ago. There's enough for another two years, if I'm careful and if the prices don't continue to go up. And if you can give me dollars from time to time. I can still get a good exchange on the black market. Serge and I are very good at that sort of thing."

"And this house?" said Charles.

"There is very little left," said his mother. "Your father has borrowed on it. He has never told me how much."

"Didn't you ask him?"

"No," said the Comtesse.

"What does Guy give you?"

"What do you expect me to give her?" said Guy. "I've taken over the rent on the Avenue d'Iéna flat. She'll have that if she ever has to move out of here."

Said Charles: "What are you paying? Six hundred a month? That's nothing."

Said Guy: "But I'm not working."

"Maybe you should."

Guy laughed. "You know, Charles, you are not in a very strong position to tell us what we should do. You moved to America. You left Mother and Father alone. You took no interest in their affairs for six years, and now you return and criticize what's been done."

"I'm not criticizing what they've done. I'm criticizing you. I think you are a fool."

"Mother," said Guy as if nothing unpleasant had been mentioned, "I must go or I shall be late."

He kissed his mother on both cheeks and left the room. The Comtesse and Charles remained at table while Serge served the cheese, fruit, and terrible coffee. "Serge buys Swiss instantaneous," said the Comtesse. "It's more expensive than chicory but he says its saves on fuel costs."

His mother did not like to talk about money directly, although she did not hesitate to devote entire letters to the subject when Charles was in New York. The interest from his father's various investments, which, before the war, had given them more than a comfortable annual income, now paid the expenses for no more than a month.

"All those grand projects in Indochina have vanished," said the Comtesse.

"So," said Charles, "have a lot of lives."

Said the Comtesse: "Your father always thought you were a secret Communist."

"No," said Charles. "I trust in nothing."

"What do you say of de Gaulle?"

"*Vive de Gaulle*," said Charles. "How are we going to pay the hospital bills?"

"I still have some jewelry. And the six Daumiers."

"Six? There were twelve."

"I've already sold six. I had to, to be able to move your father to a private room at the American Hospital. At first he was in a clinic in Passy, in a room with five other men. I thought he was going to die there. He had no peace. They didn't know who he was. They made jokes about his silver walking stick. He had a stroke, right there in the clinic."

"How did you sell the Daumiers?"

"Through the Galerie Ubis. They obtained a very good price." The Comtesse rose from the table and began to snuff out the candles. "I know what you're thinking," she said. "The Daumiers were promised to you."

After his mother had gone to bed, Charles telephoned the Marquise.

"Mercy me," she said. "Monsieur le Comte. Fantastic. You must come over immediately."

"It's not possible," said Charles. "I'm very tired. I arrived just this morning."

"Of course," said Elena. "And it *is* Thursday night. You remember what I told you about Thursdays? Perhaps it is *not* a good night to see you."

"Tomorrow night?"

"No, my dear boy. I go to the country tomorrow. To be with Henri. I must rest sometime. Are you free Monday night? I think Monday night would be an ideal night. I'm supposed to dine with some horrible friends but I will put them off. I'm always very respectable on Monday nights. Respectable and rested. Sometimes I even go to the Opéra. Come on Monday night and dine with me here. I promise you no wickedness. Monday night at eight. Understood?" She hung up the telephone before he could answer.

44

"You are looking at what is virtually a brand-new Elena," the Marquise said when Charles was shown into her sitting room. Said Charles: "A weekend in the country does extraordinary things, I believe." The Marquise giggled. "Dear boy, there is no weekend in the country that could do what I'm talking about. Mercy me, no. I've been reconstituted. I'm just one month back from Zurich. I had everything done. Even my buttocks. Everything except my breasts. I drew my line at that. If you are nice to me, I'll show you my scars later. They're practically invisible. Of course, they should be, considering what Henri had to pay. Every morning when I wake up, I reach for the mirror to see if anything has yet fallen. I feel like Chartres."

After dinner Charles called Serge and told him to tell the Comtesse he would not be home until morning. He gave Serge the telephone number where he could be reached in case there was any change in his father's condition. "You are a very good boy," said Elena. Said Charles, in English: "Let's fuck." Elena had the body of a sprinter but without extravagant muscles or stringy tendons. She was so slim Charles found he could put an arm around her waist and scratch himself with the same hand. She was also remarkably limber. When he said something about this, she answered, "Being evil is hard work. I have to practice." At another point she said, "You are naughty. You are undoing the habits of years. I love it." They were served breakfast in bed by a vacant-eyed Basque girl with insect bites on her legs. "Henri hired her," said Elena. "He knew she would be safe." Before he departed, she made him promise to come to dine Wednesday night. She said, "Perhaps I'll have a surprise for you."

The surprise was Ann-Marie, the sculptor. The Marquise laughed with pleasure at Charles's initial confusion. "I had thought that I would have to argue with her," said Elena. "I thought I would have to twist her arm, maybe handcuff her. But no, unhappily. She was delighted, the naughty girl." Ann-Marie smiled at Charles, then shrugged like a Paris taxi driver. After supper they went up to Elena's sitting room where Elena gave each a marijuana cigarette, though she did not take one herself. "Oh, no," she said. "I don't smoke. I don't need it. I am evil enough without smoking." Charles was not fond of marijuana, but he smoked in hopes that something would help him. He felt very foolish, very old. Later he wasn't certain whether the marijuana had worked—there were times when it seemed to have no effect whatsoever—or whether his own curiosity had carried the night. Elena made love to Ann-Marie, at first with all the seriousness of an amateur magician performing in front of family and friends. She was nervous and just the least bit irritable when a movement or a change of position was executed awkwardly. Then, as Charles watched and as Ann-Marie began to respond, Elena finally lost herself in her own enthusiasm. Later Charles worked very hard, tenaciously. He'd forgotten how much attention was required to see that everyone was properly taken care of. Somehow Elena's enthusiasm was so structured that such thoughtfulness was natural to her. Charles kept having to think what he should do next. Because he had no particular desire to watch, he found little rest, although both Elena and Ann-

Marie took periodic respites. At the end he was exhausted without being finished. "Well," said Elena while Ann-Marie was in the dressing room getting ready to go home, "what do you think? I told you I was evil." They were lying side by side on the bed, naked except for the pillow Elena had put over his lap. Charles smiled sleepily. "She's a very nice girl. She has a good figure. She's amiable." "What else?" said Elena. Charles took a cigarette from a box by the bed and lit it. He thought. He put a hand on the back of Elena's neck. "I think," he said carefully, "that after Ann-Marie leaves I would like to fuck you just for the fun of it." "Mercy me," said the Marquise. "The thing is," said Charles, "with three, after a while one might as well simply masturbate." Later in the night, Charles asked Elena about Guy: "What does *he* do?"

"He's a performer. He likes an audience. He can take care of four at one time."

Charles: "Four what?"

"Oh, my dear boy, you sound so American now."

"I'm curious, that's all."

Elena laughed at him. "Actually he doesn't visit me that frequently, only when he thinks there might be some film or theater people here. Guy should be a performer in blue movies. He loves to show off and there are people who love to watch him. The poor boy. He thinks he will get ahead in this world by doing in front of others."

45

Two nights later, there was a sudden atrocious assault. The Comte gave up. Everything ceased to function at the same time, as if by carefully negotiated treaty, at midnight. He was seventy-five. To Charles's surprise, the Comtesse and Serge had already made most of the plans necessary for the announcement of the Comte's death and his funeral. It was only a matter of putting the plans into effect. Additional servants appeared the day before the funeral to clean the house and prepare it for the reception for members of the family and old friends. Three hundred people came, which seemed an extraordinary number to Charles, at least for a family that was at such loose ends. He thought of the recent evenings he and his mother had dined together, attended by one cross, forgetful old man, when it seemed as if they could all be swept away and no one would notice. This was the Automat in drag. A cousin of his father's on the Spanish side, a formidable old lady who wore the red and yellow royal sash across her breast, said to Charles, "You have no children. That's a pity. It's not an important title, of course, but it's a valid one. There is no one to carry it on if you don't do something. I understand that Guy is not serious." In Charles's family "not serious" also meant bad manners at the bridge table. Meanwhile Guy looked on the bright side. He pointed out to Charles that their mother had anticipated that their father would probably last through the rest of the spring and summer. The money they would save in hospital bills would allow the Comtesse more time to decide the disposition of the house and what other property there was.

Late that night Charles and his mother drank warm champagne in her bedroom, the Comtesse sitting up in bed wearing an old-fashioned nightshirt. Charles sat near her in a chair that felt too small for him. His mother's eyes periodically erupted with small tears, though it wasn't really weeping. She was getting drunk. Once the house had been sold, she said, and once Guy had found himself another suitable accommodation, she and Serge would move into the

Avenue d'Iéna flat. It would be more convenient for her and less work for Serge. "We will die there," she said. "Does the lift work?" Charles said he didn't know, that he hadn't been there recently. "I suppose it must," she said. "If it doesn't, Serge and I will move in and never leave." She suddenly put a hand in front of her face and sobbed. "I miss him so much." Said Charles: "Dear Mother . . ." Said the Comtesse: "I sometimes think that what was wrong with us— as a family, I mean—was that your father and I cared too much about each other. When we were first married, we were complete. That is why we did not have children until so late. We did not want the interruptions. I suppose that is why neither you nor Guy have ever been serious. You knew about your father and me very early. You were still a little boy when you moved out of the house. You had to think of yourself, but you survived. I worry about Guy. I know what he is. Which, I realize, is why each day I love him a little more."

46

On his last afternoon in Paris Charles walked through the Luxembourg Gardens, up the Boulevard Raspail, past the haunted Balzac, down the Boulevard Montparnasse to the Coupole. He sat at a sidewalk table, wearing the dark glasses he seldom wore in New York, his coat over his shoulders, drinking Pernods and smoking Chesters. He felt disconnected and depressed. It was as if the city had become a foreign territory. He was no longer truly French but not quite an American. He occupied the space between. At just that moment when he might have felt a tear, he was brought up short. Jacques Isserot, tall, gaunt, gray-haired, and gray-faced, sauntered toward the café in a small cluster of shorter people, three young men and a young woman who moved around him like tugboats. He gestured and shrugged and told his story without ever looking at the members of his escort. He looked over their heads. He always took the long view. They turned in to the café and were passing his table when Charles removed his glasses, stood up, and called to Jacques. Jacques stopped. He smiled. He took off *his* glasses. It was a knightly exchange. "My God. Monsieur le Comte!" He put his arms around Charles and kissed him on each cheek. "What a great pleasure. Truly, Charles, what happiness to see you. You have been in Indochina? Algeria? Jail?" Jacques turned to the lead tugboat and told him to seek a table inside. "No," said Charles. "In America. New York." "No, but that is incredible. What are you doing? Television?" Charles said yes, and then explained that he hadn't yet started, that he was returning the next morning. Jacques sat down at the table and let Charles order a drink for him without appearing to notice. "I say it is incredible because this afternoon, just one hour ago, I signed a contract with N.B.C. to make a film for them about New York. An absolutely ridiculous contract. Fifty thousand dollars. A budget of two hundred thousand. My own cameraman and my own crew from Paris, if I want them. And, as you know, I've never even seen New York. I've never wanted to." Isserot laughed at the idiocy of it. "That is why they ask me. They think a man who makes films about headhunters and aborigines is the perfect man to explore New York." "Perhaps you are," said Charles. Jacques stuck out his lower lip, grunted, and laughed again. He asked Charles how long he had been living in New York, what he thought of the possibilities of his (Isserot's) being able to shoot anything of interest in New York, whether he (Charles) would like to help him. "The money is somewhat better than Vincennes," said Jacques, "and I assume the working conditions are more calm. No Gestapo." They talked for an hour, at the end of which Isserot was calling Charles "Claude," which had been the name of another colleague at Vincennes during the Occupation. Nevertheless he took Charles's New York address and telephone number and promised to contact him when he arrived in New York at the end of the summer. "Be thinking about this thing, Claude," he said. "Put your mind to it. I'm not interested in things exotic. I'm interested in how people look to themselves. Not how they look to outsiders. I don't think they could have chosen a more unsuitable man for the job. It will be a disaster." He prepared to depart, sighing with mock dread. "I'm in the middle of an American interview. My first."

47

For everyone except Charles the project turned into the disaster Isserot continually predicted it would be. Jacques hated New York. He found it filthy, inhuman, ugly, dangerous, and physically exhausting, partially because he had not fulfilled his promise to learn English before he arrived. He had a terrible time getting around the city on public transport. He walked everywhere with a small city atlas. This enabled him to see a lot of the city, but as he came to know it his loathing grew. He was late for every appointment. He distrusted the network people with whom he had to deal either because they did not speak French or because they did. The ones who did speak French (there were only two) he feared as spies. The ones who didn't were invisible to him. People who could not talk to him did not exist. Charles once asked him how he could have been so successful making films in New Guinea and Borneo. Did the natives speak French? Jacques laughed and calmed down. There were problems with the unions. He was not allowed to use his own cameraman and he was forced to hire an eight-man crew, though he was planning to shoot in 16-millimeter without synchronized sound. One week into the eight-week shooting schedule, an American writer was hired to give some shape to the ideas that Jacques had dictated into a machine. Jacques said the writer was out to stab him in the back. Two weeks into the production, Jacques took to sneaking off by himself with his illegal French cameraman to shoot at random in Queens, Staten Island, and the upper West Side. When asked what yards and yards of footage of Queens garages meant, he said he wanted to describe the boredom that New Yorkers refused to acknowledge. Three weeks into production, he flew to Hollywood where his Borneo film was awarded the Oscar as the best feature-length documentary of the year. After that he stayed in his St. Regis suite watching television, drinking Scotch, and not answering the telephone. Charles, who had been in the middle, the bearer of messages between the kidnappers and their victim, was asked if he could possibly finish the film according to Isserot's original ideas as modified by the murderous American writer. With Jacques's approval, he did. The network was pleased, the sponsor was pleased, the critics were pleased, and months later Jacques accepted the invitation of the Academy of Television Arts and Sciences to attend their annual awards ceremonies. "Jacques Isserot's New York" had been nominated for an Emmy. It was a terrible night. By the time the film did not win, Jacques was very drunk, furious at the injustices done to his name if not to his film. Later Charles and Daisianna sat with him in his hotel room until four in the morning while he alternately criticized the film he had never seen and tried to persuade them to join him on a new expedition to New Guinea. "What innocence," he said. "Those people are my friends. The true headhunters are here."

48

Daisianna received Dodie's reappearance without question. As if she were a favorite Pomeranian that had been picked up at the kennel after the family had been on a long vacation. She had no memory of unanswered letters, of the years without contact. When Charles asked her if she'd ever told her father about Bellevue, Kings County, and the Veterans Hospital, she said she hadn't. It would just worry him, she said, and he had worries enough. Dodie gave no sign of this. After his initial grief at Ida's death, which lasted maybe ten days, he went again into society, always wearing the black armband that provided a point of departure for conversations with friends newly made at P. J. Clarke's and the other Third Avenue bars he liked. He sold the house in Princeton and moved into the Princeton Club while he made up his mind where he wanted to live permanently. He talked about Palm Beach and Palm Springs most often as it became increasingly clear he had no intention of leaving Daisianna and Charles, barring a new marriage. He had no friends to turn to, at least none he was sufficiently fond of to seek out. Two or three nights a week, he asked Daisianna and Charles to dine with him at the Pavillon, '21,' Côte Basque, sometimes at places in the Village Daisianna and Charles avoided but to which he was steered by his various companions—pretty, mostly foolish girls who liked to eat in restaurants lit by candles set in old wine bottles. Dodie spent money freely but he was a completely self-centered man, so self-centered that one evening when Charles, who was having a drink with him at the Princeton Club, told him about Daisianna's problems, Dodie became angry. He turned red in the face. His forehead perspired. His hands shook. "I don't want to hear things like that," he said. "That's what Ida did. Ida came between us. I'm shocked at you, Charles. Daisianna is your wife."

Dodie was so attached to Daisianna and Charles that he traveled to Chicago with them for Leola's funeral and cried as hard as Daisianna at the gravesite. He made them promise that if he ever died they would bury him next to Leola. It was a perpetual-care family plot at Rose Hill, one that had been given as a wedding present to him and Leola by his mother. Six months later, when Dodie died, Daisianna and Charles returned to Rose Hill, the only mourners.

Daisianna gave up her job at Corduroy Incorporated and her plans to become a dress designer without actually admitting that she had. She had taken a leave of absence to go to St. Constance and, on her return to New York, never got around to going back to work. While she was in St. Constance she had missed registering for the new semester at the Madigan School. She told Charles that she would make up the studies in the next semester. Before forgetting about that phase of her life, she gave a party for all her old friends at the shop and at the Madigan School when she and Charles moved into the Fifth Avenue apartment. She invited fifty people. Twelve came. An uneven assortment of earnest, tongue-tied Brooklyn girls, severe older women in harlequin glasses, young men who dressed fashionably but who became shy in the Fifth Avenue address and one instructor, a middle-aged man who had taught Daisianna's watercolor class and whom Daisianna had described as one of the most interesting men she had ever met. As a house present the instructor gave them a small, conventionally pretty Central Park landscape and was later sick to his stomach in the guest bathroom. "Well," said Daisianna when it was all over, "I'm glad I did it even if nobody came." When they bought the house in Greenwich, Daisianna used the Fifth Avenue apartment less and less frequently. She stayed in the country with her horse and a number of dogs and cats, mostly strays or pets that had been abandoned in their driveway. Charles used the Fifth Avenue apartment at least twice a week, when he worked late. Elena came to New York regularly, and there were other affairs that occupied him. Their social life, what there was of it, was entirely connected with network people: young, ambitious husbands and wives in whom Daisianna had no interest unless they had dogs, cats, or horses. Or unless they drank. She wanted to join Alcoholics Anonymous, not because she had a drinking problem herself but because she thought she could help others. She looked into the matter and was told that a donation would be preferred. The night Charles came home to find the emerald ring missing from her finger, he also found her in tears and tight. She'd tried to make onion soup, which had simmered away leaving a deep sludge of burned onions in the bottom of a kettle she had bought to make bouillabaisse for large dinner parties. She finally admitted having spent the afternoon at Sean's Pub and having given the ring to the bartender. "It's so sad," she said. "He's marrying a darling little Hungarian girl and he hasn't enough money to buy her a decent engagement ring."

"Oh, Christ."

"What's wrong with wanting to give people things?"

"Do you know how much that ring is worth?" Daisianna shook her head. "You shouldn't even be wearing it. It's crazy."

Daisianna: "I don't think it's crazy to be kind."

"Thirty-two thousand dollars," said Charles. "Do you

know that we now pay as much for insurance on your jewelry as you and I used to make together in one year?"

Daisianna was so impressed by that fact that she ceased her weeping, and Charles said he would get the ring back tomorrow unless it had been sold. "Sometimes I can't understand you," he said. "I don't like being rotten."

Said Daisianna: "Well, it wasn't the Little Lord Jesus, if that's what you're worried about. I would have told you if it had been something like that."

Less than six weeks later the Little Lord Jesus did reappear, in His role as Holy Redeemer.

49

Even though it was very expensive, Hickory Hollow looked like a run-down writers' colony, a place that might create blocks, not remove them. There were six one- and two-story clapboard houses facing a wintry, weedy common where last summer's lawn furniture still sat frozen to the ground. The compound was surrounded by Connecticut forest, a leafless tangle of hickory, oak, and birch trees, which, on one side, hid the highway a hundred yards away. The houses were old and weathered. Each sagged comfortably in the middle, as if sinking into a drain in the earth. The second-floor windows in one cottage were brilliant with cut-outs of Santa Clauses, reindeers, and Christmas trees, though this was late February. There were no fences, no bars. There was a parking lot for cars owned by patients and, somewhere in the woods, a tennis court. The office of Dr. Mandelbaum, who had been assigned to Daisianna, looked more like that of a rural practitioner than the office of a psychiatrist. There was a hot plate with a Silex coffeepot on it on the desk.

Medical journals overflowed the bookshelves and were stacked in high unsteady piles on the floor. A pair of ice skates, tied together with their laces, hung over the knob of a door leading to the interior of the cottage. Two soup dishes on Mandelbaum's desk were filled with cigarette stubs. The air was blue with cigarette smoke. Everytime Mandelbaum put out a cigarette, it started a fire among the earlier castoffs. "You're going to call me Jack and I'm going to call you Daisy," Mandelbaum said when they arrived. "And I'll call you Chuck." There was a portable electric heater on the floor near the chair where Daisianna sat facing the doctor at his desk, filling out her entrance form. It was Saturday. Charles thought Mandelbaum must have been interrupted in a game of touch football. The doctor, a tall, untidy man, was wearing the sort of sweat suit with a towel around the neck worn by coaches in prewar American films about open-faced American college students whose lives centered around their tournaments. He was also wearing gym shoes and a wristwatch with several interlocking dials that told him what time it was in London, Paris, Rome, Moscow, Calcutta, and Tokyo, as well as his altitude. Later Charles learned that this was Mandelbaum's usual costume. "Mandelbaum," a doctor at Payne Whitney told Charles, "has several bizarre mannerisms but he's one of the best."

Mandelbaum broke the silence. "Do you always wear dark glasses?"

"Yes," said Daisianna. She had been tranquilized into a state just this side of sleep.

"Take them off."

"I can't see without them."

"I'm not going to steal them from you," said Mandelbaum. "I only want to see the color of your eyes."

Daisianna removed the glasses as if she'd been asked to undress in a public place. She stared at them as she held them in her lap.

"You have beautiful eyes," said Mandelbaum. "Blue-gray." He leaned toward Daisianna. "I have one brown eye and one blue eye. See. Am I right?"

Daisianna, who couldn't see more than a blur of the doctor, said, "Yes."

Mandelbaum was pleased that she liked to paint. Perhaps she would paint his portrait. "How old do you think I am?" Daisianna shook her head. "Go on," the doctor insisted, "guess." "I can't," said Daisianna. "Of course you can," said the doctor.

"Forty-five?"

"Sixty-three," said the doctor. "Not bad for an old man, am I?"

Daisianna shook her head slowly. She asked a question, enunciating each word as if she were carving something out of soap. She hesitated to start the word, then it suddenly slipped away from her, finished. "How . . . long . . . do you . . . think . . . I'll have . . . to stay . . . here?"

"Only as long as you like," Mandelbaum said cheerfully. "It's up to you."

Daisianna turned her lazy attention back to the form. Charles, sitting on the couch behind her, was conscious of pockets of cold and warm air in the room. The walls radiated cold but his feet were hot. A wisp of warm air passed across his forehead and was gone. Daisianna looked exceedingly small and dear from the back. She was wearing ski pants and a thick turtleneck sweater of matching pale yellow. Her hair, which he had brushed and tied that morning, was soft and fine. The skin on the back of her left hand was no longer tan. It was an old-fashioned white. He was aware of Daisianna's struggling to find things in her mind. "How old did I say I was?" said Mandelbaum.

"Thirty-six."

"Sixty-three," the doctor said impatiently. "You aren't trying very hard."

Charles was desolate with love and loneliness. He would not have returned to the house except for having to feed the dogs, the cats, and the horse, a mean elderly mare Daisianna had bought thinking she was saving it from the glue factory.

50

The following Saturday morning Mandelbaum sat at his desk wearing his sweat suit, towel, sneakers, and multipurpose watch. Charles sat in the chair Daisianna had been sitting in.

"What can I tell you?" said Mandelbaum. "Daisy is a troubled girl, Chuck." He smiled, exposing feeble, old teeth. "But she always has been." He laughed in a way that was meant to be comforting. "Certainly ever since you've known her. There's no reason to be downhearted. She's the same girl you've always loved. That is, I assume that you do love her." Charles nodded. "She's sick, which of course, we all are, more or less. Daisy's case is somewhat more extreme. More complicated. To be blunt about it, she's psychotic. I'd say she is schizophrenic but I don't want to panic you. Does it?" Charles shook his head. "It shouldn't. We can do extraordinary things these days. There's no point in wasting your money on analysis. Daisy is unanalyzable. Some people are like that. I'll keep her here six or eight weeks. I'll give her all the therapy she can probably understand, but most importantly I'll be working with her chemicals. We can raise her up or bring her down with some nice little blue pills. Whatever needs to be done. Right now she needs rest and constant attention. She has to be able to feel that whenever things get out of hand for her, that whenever she feels the spirit world"—laughter—"is about to over-whelm her, she has a place where she can be safe. She must trust me and love me and understand me—or, at least, think that she does. That's why I'm asking you not to see her for several weeks."

"Is there any possibility of a cure?"

"What's a cure? What's normal? Do you really want her cured? Normal? She might be quite a different person."

"I want her to be happy," Charles said.

"What is happy?" said Mandelbaum. "Daisianna is pro-bably happier more often than either you or I. We worry a little bit all the time, which is supposed to be normal. Worry is a kind of protection system. Daisy goes for great stretches without worrying. Then she panics. She begins to despair. She sees signs of impending doom everywhere. She calls up the Little Lord Jesus." He laughed. "She's not at all sure she wants to trust her Little Lord Jesus with a Jewish psychiatrist. I had to tell her that my mother was an Irish Catholic."

"Was she?"

"Of course not," said Mandelbaum. "God rest her soul." Mandelbaum lit a fresh cigarette from the stub he had been smoking and tried unsuccessfully to blow several smoke rings. "It's my teeth," said Mandelbaum. "I can't whistle properly, either. You wonder if she's going to be like this all her life. Always prey to her demons. Maybe yes, maybe no. Some patients seem to grow out of it. As if they had become tired of all the trouble. Others live to a ripe old age, still swinging back and forth, keeping their Little Lord Jesuses in phantom court. Daisy is not that far gone, of course. She is, in fact, a very rare creature. I'm not talking about her illness, about her medical history, Christ knows. Daisy's case is common enough. It's just another cold in the head. It's that ordinary. I mean Daisy herself. She's gentle and sweet and fragile. She's one of God's blessed creatures. She's also as nutty as a fruitcake, and I like her. I like to like my patients. It can be a burden when you don't."

The next week when Charles went to Hickory Hollow, Mandelbaum reported that Daisianna was coming along beautifully. "She's great with the other patients, especially with our two teen-agers. It's too bad she can't have any children of her own."

"She's never wanted any," said Charles.

"Couldn't," said Mandelbaum. "Her father and step-mother apparently saw to that." Charles shook his head. "Don't tell me you didn't know? She never told you?"

"No," said Charles.

"Nipped right out, everything was," said Mandelbaum, "at that fancy abortion shop in the desert."

Charles told Mandelbaum about the elaborate birth-control precautions Daisianna took. Said Mandelbaum: "Well, that should be one less thing she'll have to kid herself about."

On Charles's next visit, Mandelbaum allowed him to take Daisianna to lunch at a roadhouse several miles away. "I might join you later," he said as they drove off. Daisianna looked beautiful and a little shy. Her hair was hanging loosely down her back. Under her mink she wore a painter's blue smock and blue jeans. "I'm afraid I look very artsy-craftsy," she said. "I'm also getting fat. I wasn't allowed to smoke until this week. I have three cigarettes a day. One after each meal." She asked about the dogs and cats and Precious, the mare, but she didn't ask about Charles. She talked mostly about the clinic, about the other patients, and about Mandelbaum. "He's an incredible man. I'm sure he's half crazy himself. He runs five miles before breakfast every morning." At the roadhouse, a country dance hall that served food in the daytime, they sat at a table in a large

otherwise empty dining room, staring across the dance floor
to a jukebox that had been unplugged and pulled away from
the wall for repairs. Charles ordered a Scotch and soda and
Daisianna a Dubonnet, which, she said, was allowed. She
had drunk about half of it when Mandelbaum arrived.
"What's this?" he said. He picked up the glass of Dubonnet
and drank it himself. He sat down at the table. "Your wife,"
he said to Charles, "sometimes presses her luck." "If I'd
finished it before you got here," said Daisianna, "you would
never have known the difference." "No," said the doctor,
"I would only have seen that you were walking as cockeyed
as a Chinese sailor and having some difficulty with your
consonants. You can't drink anything until I find out what
sort of medication you can tolerate." Daisianna giggled.
"Oh, Jack . . ." Daisianna, Charles realized, was in love.
He wasn't sure what he felt, but in it there was some measure
of relief.

Daisianna signed out of Hickory Hollow the first of May,
a week before Charles's thirty-seventh birthday, for which
she bought him a fawn-colored 1948 Rolls-Royce sedan with
brown leather upholstery, walnut paneling, and a television
set in the back seat. The first evening they had it, they went
to Sean's Pub to dine. Charles drove while Daisianna sat in
the back and complained about the snowy image on the television screen. "Have you got something turned on?" said
Daisianna. "The ignition," said Charles. "Well," said Daisianna, "I guess we'll have to hire a chauffeur. There's not
much point in sitting in the back alone if the television set
doesn't work." Daisianna also bought herself a bright red
M.G. in which to drive herself to and from Hickory Hollow
three days a week. She spent fifty minutes of each visit with
Mandelbaum and the rest of the morning assisting the instructor in the hobby shop. Charles continued to commute
to Manhattan in his old Renault. The Rolls stayed in the

garage most of the time under a huge chamois blanket that cost almost as much as the car. Daisianna made no secret of her love for and dependence upon Mandelbaum, but it had the effect of intensifying her feelings for Charles.

After much searching, they found a couple to live on the place so that Daisianna could travel with Charles. They were a retired Greenwich policeman and his wife, an exhausted-looking woman with pale blue eyes whose kleptomania had been a factor in her husband's early retirement. That fall Charles and Daisianna spent six weeks in Las Vegas, Reno, Tahoe, and San Juan while Charles was making a film about legalized gambling.

51

The next year they lived in Lausanne. Charles was producing two rather complicated special programs, one about de Gaulle and the other about the European money market whatever-that-is, as Daisianna put it when she got drunk. That was usually when Charles was away from Lausanne, which he was for five days of every week, and when Purity Mellon's Swedish lover, a ski instructor, had deserted Purity for a younger client. Early one Friday afternoon Charles returned to their apartment in Lausanne to learn that Purity Mellon was asleep in the guest room with a doctor from the Valois Clinic. Daisianna was in the kitchen baking bread, something she attempted once every two years. "Get her out of here," Charles said. "Purity Mellon is a vicious, foulmouthed bitch." "She is not," Daisianna said tearfully. "Purity Mellon is a real person."

"She's a tramp," Charles said.

"She has almost as much money as we do."

"That has nothing to do with it."

Purity Mellon had become a celebrity of the second rank during World War II. She was an exceptionally tall, unexceptionally pretty showgirl of the dumb-blonde school whose name was, surprisingly, real, as was her figure though not her hair. Purity had never been the waif some publicists would have preferred her to be. The Mellons were people of consequence in the tiny Georgia town where she was born. After three marriages, three divorces, two children, and one film, she lived in Lausanne under the care of the doctors at the Valois Clinic. The clinic accepted her most recent husband's money and supplied Purity with unlimited Seconals, which she used as stimulants.

The doctor, a small Greek man with no knowledge of English, heard the row in the kitchen, got up and dressed, and left without nodding to Daisianna and Charles as they stood in the kitchen door. A few minutes later, Purity came downstairs in nothing but her shoes and a mink coat.

She greeted Charles: "Welcome home, shithead, you scared the piss out of my guest. Thanks a lot."

"Was it necessary to bring him here? You have an apartment of your own."

Daisianna spoke up. "But it's being watched."

"Who's watching it?" said Charles. "The vice squad?"

"My ex-husband, shithead. My ex-husband Shithead." Purity laughed at her wit. "Be a darling," she said to Daisianna, "and get me a drink." While Daisianna was in the kitchen, Purity noticed that she hadn't finished dressing. "Oh, goodness, Charles, you made me forget myself." She stretched herself on the couch and closed her eyes. The body, even at forty-three, still retained its pneumatic shape. Daisianna returned to the room carrying Purity's drink.

"Really, Purity," said Daisianna, "you shouldn't go around that way."

Purity sat up to take the glass. "Why not?"

"Taxi drivers," said Daisianna. "They're very rude."

"Let them look," said Purity. "I started my career flashing. I'll probably die flashing. There are worse ways to go."

Several Sunday afternoons later, when Daisianna was at the clinic acting as prop woman for a French-language patient-doctor production of *The Rivals*, Purity telephoned Charles and asked him to come over immediately. Sven, the ski instructor, was threatening to kill her. Charles went, though he wasn't particularly worried. Purity had not sounded desperate, and she wasn't. She was lonely. Charles was bored with the European money market. He knew it was a mistake, but it was also an opportunity. It was as if he had found himself in Arizona and had seized the chance to go down into the Grand Canyon. On Monday, he returned to Paris and took Daisianna with him. It was time, he said, that Daisianna met his mother.

52

The Comtesse was charmed by Daisianna and Daisianna was instantly in love with the Comtesse. Neither could understand why Charles had made no earlier effort to bring them together. Separately each told him of her pleasure. Said Daisianna: "Your mother is one of the most beautiful women I've ever seen. She *looks* like a countess." Said the Comtesse: "I'm not sure what it is about Daisianna. She has the manner of someone in a fairy tale. Someone enchanted." On that first visit, Charles and Daisianna dined every evening with his mother in the Avenue d'Iéna flat, and on their last day in Paris before returning to Lausanne Daisianna invited the Comtesse to have lunch with her at Maxim's, without

Charles. The Comtesse accepted. It was a very long lunch for without Charles they had little to say to each other. The Comtesse was not especially interested in the subject of hospital theatricals and had never heard of Purity Mellon, the famous American film star who was Daisianna's oldest and dearest friend. Daisianna's mind wandered when the Comtesse, prompted by the menu, discussed the differences between prewar and postwar prices. For the last hour of the lunch, the Comtesse told the story of Charles's great-great-grandfather, the first Comte du Chaudrun, and how he came by his title, a story demanding a certain understanding of and interest in French banking procedures before 1789.

53

In the spring of 1964, while Charles was in Egypt working on his Khrushchev show, Purity Mellon telephoned Daisianna at the house in Greenwich. Purity had brought her two children, a boy seventeen and a girl sixteen, back to their father from Lausanne where they'd been visiting her. "It was bloody exciting, I can tell you," said Purity. "Sven took one look at them and caught the first plane to Stockholm to see a sick friend. Did you read the piece Earl Wilson did about me today? Fabulous. Of course the picture he ran was from 1902. I've already had an offer to do *The Seven-Year Itch* in Texas and somebody in New Jersey wants me to attend the opening of a bowling alley. In Teaneck. What do you think? I'm bored. I can't stand these New York creeps. They either want to lay you immediately or go out with them and their boyfriends. Come in to the Plaza. We'll have an old-fashioned pajama party. I have a suite but all of the expenses are being paid by

Daddy, and I don't think that even if I try I can run up as many bills as I'd like. To make the bastard mad. If Charles is in the Congo, he need never know. Come on, baby. I'll dig up some men and we'll have a ball." For one reason and another, no men showed up. Daisianna and Purity had several drinks in the suite and then walked over to the Colony where, when the headwaiter failed to remember Purity, she said, very loud, "Go fuck yourself." In the taxi to '21,' Purity said, "If there's one thing I cannot stand, it's a phony frog." Daisianna laughed. She said, "I've missed you." "So have I," said Purity. "Missed me, I mean. Christ."

Said Daisianna: "You know, I probably shouldn't tell you this, but . . ."

"But what?"

"Well, one of the reasons I've always liked you—"

"Is my good manners."

"No. It's silly. . . ."

"What is it, darling? Make me feel good."

"Well," said Daisianna, "you've always reminded me of my mother."

"Oh my God!" said Purity. She said it with such force that the driver thought he'd hit someone and slammed on the brakes. "Thanks a lot. Your mother!" The cabdriver started up again but did not go over twenty miles an hour the rest of the way to the restaurant. "Your mother," Purity said at every stoplight. "Jesus." The people at '21' were delighted to see Purity, which took her mind off things for a while. She kissed the headwaiter and the hat-check girl, both of whom had read the Wilson item, and, before sitting down, she went to the bar to kiss the bartenders. When Purity joined Daisianna at the table she said, "Old-home week. The first time I ever ate at '21' was with the Aga Khan. They remember things like that here. That's why it's a good restaurant." They had two more drinks each and Purity took a red capsule because she was depressed. "Why am I depressed? Are you serious?"

"Yes," said Daisianna.

"You mean to tell me you have no idea why I'm depressed?"

"You were sorry to leave your children?"

"Jesus, Daisianna," Purity said, "you can't be as dumb as everybody says you are."

"What do you mean?"

"You have no memory at all of what you said to me in the cab?"

"Yes."

"Not one half-hour ago?"

"Yes," said Daisianna.

"You sat there in that idiot fun fur, in the corner of that taxicab, and you told me, in all seriousness, that I—that I reminded you of your mother. Didn't you?"

"Yes," said Daisianna. "You do."

"Jesus Kay-ryste, Daisianna."

"She was one of the wittiest people I ever knew," said Daisianna. "That's what I meant."

Purity's eyelids had slipped halfway down her eyeballs. Daisianna could not be sure that Purity could see her or that she could see anything. Purity was rapidly sinking into one of those moods that weren't fun at all.

"I think we should order something to eat," said Daisianna. She would have asked Purity what she suggested but that would have been a dangerous question. Daisianna, who was not wearing her dark glasses, studied the menu as if she were reading it.

"Put that goddamn thing down," said Purity. "I'm talking to you." Her eyes blinked in slow motion. She turned her head from the left to the right and back, as if she were testing the feel of a sixty-pound tiara. She focused on Daisianna.

She aimed at Daisianna. "Some people have said some shitty things to me in my time," said Purity. "Most of them women. But tonight, in that taxicab, I think you took the cake. Can you possibly understand?"

"No," said Daisianna. ". . . I think we should order."

"We'll order, darling, when I'm goddamn good and ready to order. I'm going to pick up the check, anyway."

"You don't have to," said Daisianna.

"Well, I want to. After all, you're my best friend, aren't you? That's why I can't understand why you wanted to hurt me the way you did. You stupid cunt." The word, at least its articulation, terrified Daisianna more than anything Purity had said earlier. People at nearby tables listened.

"I didn't want to hurt you," said Daisianna.

"You said that I reminded you of your mother. I don't have to point out to you that you have told me on more than one occasion that your mother was a lush. That she had bad breath. That her feet were swollen to the size of watermelons. That's beside the point. I'd be just as hurt if your mother had been Eleanor Roosevelt. What you said would have been just as insulting. What you said to me was to deny my entire life. My career. I may not be Nazimova, but I am an actress. I have a talent. You have no conception of what that means, do you? You've sat on your ass all your life, letting people wait on you hand and foot. Well, honey, I've had to work to get where I am. I studied. I trained. When I was a little girl, I took ballet and ballroom and tap until I thought my teeth were going to come loose, and when I got older, they did." She grunted with amusement and bared her perfect teeth to Daisianna. "Every goddamn one of them capped," she said. "On top of that, you seem to consider me some kind of duenna. You act as if you thought I were one hundred and five. I can take a certain amount of kidding about my age, but let's get one thing straight, baby doll, I'm no older than you are."

"I'm so sorry," said Daisianna. "You're my best friend."

"Cunt," said Purity. "The people one meets in loony bins. Even the fancy ones. You know, Daisianna, you may possibly be the dumbest cunt I have ever known, and I've known some dumb ones. You're so goddamn dumb you didn't even know that I was fucking Charles, did you?"

"No," said Daisianna. These were matters she preferred not to think about.

"Sure," said Purity. "All that winter in Lausanne. Whenever he could sneak away."

"Charles doesn't like you," said Daisianna.

"Honey," said Purity, "Charles would divorce you and marry me in a minute, if I gave him the least encouragement."

"That's not true."

"If you want, I can describe his cock. Shall I?"

"No," said Daisianna. "Please don't." She pushed the table away to be able to stand. "I've got to go." Purity was suddenly cheerful. "It's around the corner to the right. Do you need some change?" Daisianna said she didn't. She left her coat on the chair. She walked down the stairs, out the front door, and asked the doorman to find her a taxi. The cabbie charged her a flat rate of forty-five dollars to drive her to the Greenwich Station, where she picked up her car. Instead of going home to the cats, dogs, and Precious, she checked into the Yankee Clipper Motel. Several months later Purity was found dead in her Lausanne apartment. An accidental overdose of barbiturates. Daisianna wept over the loss of another dear one and Mandelbaum told her she was nuts, that she should have her head examined. Daisianna finally smiled.

54

*"The pyramids are piles of shit.
This dam is more important."*

—NIKITA S. KHRUSHCHEV,

departing from the prepared text of a speech delivered in Aswan

In May, 1964, Charles flew to Egypt to cover the Khrushchev state visit on the occasion of the opening of the first stage of the new high dam at Aswan. He was working on a documentary to be called "Khrushchev: The Man Outside His Country, Conspirator or Clown?" Charles had had a special fondness for Khrushchev ever since the Soviet leader had taken off his shoe at the United Nations and thwacked it on his desk. He suspected that Khrushchev was the last American frontiersman, a nineteenth-century circuit stumper who'd arrived on the wrong scene a hundred and fifty years too late, which was the point of the proposal he'd made to the network. Charles was accompanied to Egypt by a freelance cameraman he'd hired in London, a capable but illtempered Norwegian who'd immediately understood the sort of material Charles wanted and grew increasingly irritable every time Charles made suggestions. On the press plane from Cairo to Aswan, the Norwegian turned on Charles and said, "Please don't follow me around anymore. You make me nervous." In their first three days in Aswan, attending lethargic official ceremonies, the Norwegian became so nervous that his ulcer returned. One morning Charles found the Norwegian breakfasting on spaghetti with butter sauce. "See," he said to Charles, "this is what you've done to me." The Norwegian also ate spaghetti with butter sauce at luncheon and dinner, looking up from time to time to glare at Charles, who always sat alone on the other side of the press dining room. Charles stopped attending the functions that were announced each morning in bulletins written in Arabic, Russian, French, German, and English. He spent one day sightseeing at Abu Simbel. He spent other afternoons lying on the sun deck of the Nile steamer *Isis,* moored along the Aswan quay. He ate hamburgers and drank Scotch, and the day before the Russian and Arab parties were to leave Aswan, he flew to Luxor to await the press party there.

That afternoon Charles accepted the invitation of an Egyptian reporter he'd met on the plane to visit the necropolis on the west bank of the Nile with the reporter and his young friend, an assistant curator at the temple of Karnak. They went first to the Valley of the Kings, to the tomb of Seti I, with its unfinished wall paintings that seem to have been outlined with lipstick, and to the tomb of Tutankhamen, which was filled with people from Cleveland. It was early evening by the time they reached the great terraced temple of Queen Hatshepsut. The curator parked the jeep at the foot of the ramp that leads up to the temple's second stage, and they were in shadow. The sun was behind the oatmeal mountains. The air was cool and the sky seemed floodlit, the way it is in the desert at evening. Charles and the two Egyptians were the only people at the site. They walked up the ramp and stood looking past the colonnade into the temple's dark interior. "Another temple," said the Egyptian reporter. "Either temples or tombs. No habitations. What a curious people." He spoke with an elaborate English accent that sounded colonial. On the plane he had told Charles that he was thirty, that he was married and had four children, and that he had studied at the London School of Economics. "I am a radical conservative," he had said, "one hundred per cent in the corner of our President." The young curator, who supplemented his income by acting as a tour guide, waited for his friend to stop speaking and then began at the beginning: "This temple is dedicated to the cult of the beautiful and gifted Hatshepsut, and to her family, and it differs in plan, architecture, and decoration from all other temples in Egypt." The young man did not look at the temple or at Charles or even at the reporter, with whom he had locked little fingers in friendship in the Arab fashion. He stared upriver, toward the heart of Africa, his manner being that of schoolboy in a class pageant. "There are few buildings remaining anywhere in Egypt," he was saying, "in which the struggle for power within one family can be so clearly traced. The temple was built by Queen Hatshepsut in the Eighteenth Dynasty, but in every place on its walls and pillars where her lineaments and appellations appear, her lineaments and appellations have been chiseled out, effaced. . . ." A small yellow dog appeared at the top of the second ramp, sniffed the air, and came loping down the incline toward them, a bit off-center like a sailboat without a centerboard. The lope was even, nonchalant, revealing neither curiosity nor territorial resentment. His gaze went beyond them to the river in the distance. When he reached the bottom of the ramp he went to Charles, raised his right hind leg, and urinated on Charles's shoe and trousers. Automatically Charles kicked at but did not hit the dog, which, still in no great hurry, turned and loped back up the ramp in the direction of the Hall of Punt. The Egyptian reporter smiled and the curator looked uncomfortable. "He obviously knew I was not Egyptian," Charles said. "It is only pee," said the reporter. The curator seemed bored or angry. ("When Arabs are embarrassed," an English newspaperman had said in Cairo, "they can appear to be frightfully rude.") The curator continued his narrative, which had moved on to Tutmosis III, "who now gave full range to his campaign for revenge. . . ." When Charles returned to the Winter Palace, there was a telephone call from Jimmy Barnes. The owner of the Connecticut Yankee Clipper Motel, outside

Darien, had threatened to have Daisianna arrested. She'd signed into the motel three days ago, alone, and when she'd left, the motel owner had found she'd thrown a gin bottle through the screen of the color television set, had ripped the telephone wires from the wall, and had smashed every lamp in the room. In addition she'd tried to set the mattresses on fire, without complete success. She'd been drinking, said Jimmy, but she'd managed to drive herself to the clinic. The motel owner had demanded six thousand dollars in damages and Jimmy had settled the matter by giving him his own check for three thousand. There was a long pause; then Jimmy's voice again rolled across ocean bottoms and through the air. "Mandelbaum has her under sedation," he said. Under sedation. Daisianna slept peacefully with her right cheek turned to the pillow, her left hand made into a soft fist that rested a few inches from her forehead. She was out of it. "She's all right." It was apparent that Jimmy was yelling but space absorbed all urgency. "You needn't worry." Charles laughed, but the connection at his end was so poor that the laugh didn't even reach the operator monitoring the call in Cairo.

Charles should have returned to New York immediately. Instead he remained in Luxor until the state visit was over. In the compound of the temple at Karnak, in the confusion of Secret Service men, Arab reporters, and foreign secretaries of various degrees of importance, he approached Mrs. Khrushchev, who was smiling at everyone and looked ready to faint in the African sun. On behalf of the people of the United States, Charles thanked Mme. Khrushchev for having personally expressed her condolences so movingly at the United States Embassy in Moscow after John F. Kennedy was assassinated. Mrs. Khrushchev was bewildered but continued to smile as Charles tottered away into the crowd. When it came time for the official party to leave the temple compound, all discipline had broken down. The thousands of fellaheen outside pushed against the gates so that they couldn't be opened. Nasser and Khrushchev stood in the rear of their open limousine waving to the people, which increased their excitement and made departure even more difficult. After fifteen minutes of this, Khrushchev, his face turning gray in the heat, abruptly sat down. A moment later, he reached up and grabbed Nasser's coattail, pulling him roughly back onto the seat beside him. The Norwegian, standing six feet from the car, called something to Khrushchev, who turned and frowned. Nasser turned and gave his movie-star smile. In the afternoon, Charles flew to Cairo, changed planes, and went on to Alexandria for a holiday. He had spent two vacations there before the war with his father and mother and Guy and the old Comtesse. When he registered at the Cecil he said he would be there a week but he stayed only two days. The city had been reoccupied by the Egyptians, each of whom owned his own transistor radio. He could not escape the sound of transistor radios, in the park in front of the Cecil, along the Corniche, on the beach, in the corridor outside his room, where the tall Nubian attendant in a gown of pale blue mattress ticking sat on a straightback chair holding a radio to his ear, though the radio was so loud Charles could continue to hear it even when he was running a bath. On Charles's second and last night a taxi driver brought him a souvenir of Farouk's Egypt, an elderly Greek whore who, before she left, showed Charles pictures of her Egyptian grandchildren. The flight back to Cairo arrived at 7:30 in the morning. Being at that time still drunk, Charles was hugely amused by the sight outside his window: a wheel had swung gravely down from the plane's overhead wing and, for a moment as they circled the approach to the Cairo airfield, the wheel described a perfect arc above the tombs of Giza. When the nose of the plane dipped down, it was as if a dog were lifting its hind leg.

55

Daisianna had written her lists in longhand on sheets of lined yellow paper torn from a legal pad. There were lists of people to whom she wanted to send Christmas cards, of records she wanted to buy, of colors she didn't like and of colors she did like, a list of words she didn't understand ("arcane," "solipsism," "id"), of canned and frozen foods she planned to stock, of magazines to be subscribed to, and a list headed "People Who Have Been Kind to Me:"

Dr. Mandelbaum
Charles
Purity Mellon
Mother
Dodie
Jimmy Barnes
Sheila (at shop)
Sheila (at Dobbs)
Bobby & Eunice
Mother du Chaudrun
the man at Bohack's
the man at the bank
Cleo (?)
the girl on the telephone
the woman at Dior's
Judy
Precious
Pip
Pétain
No-Name

The last five names on the list belonged to animals.

The night Charles returned from Cairo, Dr. Mandelbaum called at the farm near Greenwich. When Charles showed him the lists, Mandelbaum laughed and threw the papers onto the sofa cushion at his side. "Is there anybody she knows who isn't mentioned?" The doctor stood up and walked around Charles's study as if it were a store. He pointed to an English hunting print. "How much did you pay for this?" "I don't know," said Charles. "Daisianna bought it." Said Mandelbaum: "It's not a very good one." He poured himself another drink and lit a new cigarette from an old one. "You shouldn't have done that, Chuck." "What?" "Play around with that Mellon broad." "I know," said Charles. Mandelbaum: "Lay down with dogs, you get up with fleas, as my mother used to say." "Your Irish Catholic mother?" "Yes," said Mandelbaum. "Chuck, you're a nice guy for a foreigner." Mandelbaum abruptly sat down on the sofa again. He seemed ill. The body inside the sweat suit was skeletal. He wiped his face with the towel around his neck. "I got a house as good as this near Putney," said Mandelbaum. "My wife lives there. I live down here at the hospital. In two rooms. I don't know what to tell you."

56

In Paris, late one afternoon in December, Charles took the Métro to the Château de Vincennes. He walked past the walls of the fourteenth-century château, past the entrance to the street that led to the Studios Vincennes, up the Rue de Fontenay that later became the Rue Défrance, toward Fontenay. It was the most uninteresting walk in Paris. Through a petit-bourgeois world of one- and two-story buildings that housed appliance dealers, dairy distributors, cloth merchants, barbershop-equipment representatives. At certain points in the street, he would automatically cross to the other side to have a longer view of the way ahead. The street curved around the hill in such a manner that it was often difficult to see more than fifty yards ahead or behind. He had taken this walk so many times during the Occupation that he was familiar with the cracks in the sidewalk, with the doorways that could be stood in, with the gates that led to back alleys. At times he made notes. The store that had once been Mme. Rouxelles's butcher shop now sold sheet music and recordings. A Citroën salesroom and garage had filled up a vacant lot. It was dark by the time he reached the Place Fontenay, so small that the autobuses could barely make their turnarounds. The square had not changed. It still looked like a tacky stage set of failed picturesque. The light from the street lamps was so dim that he felt as if blindness might be coming on. He turned right and walked two blocks down the other side of the hill, down the Rue Herbert, which was lined on the high side with tiny two-story, pink stucco villas, each fronted by a minuscule garden and protected by an iron picket fence. On the other side of the street the hill sloped away into blackness. In daylight it sloped away toward the Marne, toward factories and railroad yards in the valley, and, in the far distance, green hills. Charles stopped at the gate of No. 14 and rang the bell. The lights in the kitchen and dining-sitting room were burning. A dog barked. A baby began to cry. He rang again. A young dark-haired man opened the door and called to ask who was at the gate. Charles walked into the garden. The young man was polite but impatient. Charles asked if this was still the home of M. Robineau and his family. The young man said the Robineau family had moved but that he was a grandson of M. Robineau.

"You are Paul?" said Charles. The young man said he was. "I am Jean-Pierre," said Charles, "from the old days." The young man looked incredulous. "Jean-Pierre," he said. "Jean-Pierre?" He smiled with pleasure. Said Charles: "You were only four or five when I last saw you." "Seven," said Paul. "Come in, Jean-Pierre." Paul called his wife from the kitchen. "What good fortune, Jean-Pierre. You will have supper with us." He introduced Charles to his wife, who looked no more than a fatigued sixteen, and to the two oldest of his four sons. "One each year," said Paul. "These are three years old and four." Charles explained that he was most interested in locating Paul's grandfather. "But that is simple," said Paul. "They live in the Rue Beckett, just the other side of the square, two houses beyond the café." He told Charles that his grandfather was well, that he continued to sell his ices in the summer when the weather was fine. Also going well were Paul's mother and father. "They all live together," said Paul, "all except Antoine. You remember Antoine? The baby?" "Yes," said Charles. Said Paul: "He is now twenty-six. In the merchant marine." Charles: "And your grandmother?" Paul slapped the three-year-old, who was putting greasy fingers on Charles's camel's-hair coat. The little boy screamed. "Unhappily, we lost her. It is three years now. You know, Jean-Pierre, she was never in good health." Charles could see beyond the small entrance hall into the kitchen where Père Robineau had installed bars, waist-high, along the walls so that Mme. Robineau could pull herself around the kitchen. She had had polio as a young girl and had lost the use of one leg and had only partial use of the other with the help of braces. "It was after Grandmother died that they moved to the house in the Rue Beckett and gave me this one." The child continued to scream and was slapping Paul's leg in fury. The father looked down and laughed. "Shut your mouth," he said, and made a grotesque face. "Little prick."

Père Robineau, code name Eustache, opened the door of

the house in the Rue Beckett. The old man was shrinking into age, but otherwise he seemed to have resisted major change. He embraced Charles, holding on to him for a long moment with his forearms. "Madeleine, Julian." He called to his daughter and son-in-law, who were watching television in the dining room. "Jean-Pierre has returned." Père Robineau released Charles. He held his left hand, which had been shattered in the '14–'18 war, cupped in his right. Charles pointed to the Legion of Honor ribbon in the buttonhole of the old man's lapel. Père Robineau shrugged. He said, "In 1954 they remembered me. Unfortunately it doesn't sell many ices."

At the age of forty-four, Madeleine had the blushing prettiness she had had in her twenties, but she had become very fat, something that her mother would not have allowed. Charles had never before met Julian, who had been a prisoner of war all the time Charles had known the Robineaus. Julian was an auto mechanic, a giant of a man, his hands big and muscular with the grime of years worked into the skin. He smiled all the time, like someone deaf or blind. Each in turn embraced Charles again. "At just this minute," said Charles, "I saw Paul. He is so tall." Said Père Robineau: "Four sons, Jean-Pierre. What do you think of that?" Said Madeleine: "I think they should stop." They escorted Charles into the sitting room. Not until that minute had Charles considered the possibility that the old lady would still be alive. In the blue light reflected from the television screen, huddled in a chair and wearing a type of black wool shawl he remembered from earlier times, sat Père Robineau's mother-in-law. "Grandmother," Madeleine shouted to the old lady, who was sleeping, "look who's here." Madeleine turned on a light. The old lady stared up without seeing. "I'm not hungry," she said. "Just a little wine with water, please." Said Madeleine: "Grandmother, it's Jean-

Pierre." "Jean-Pierre who?" Said Charles: "She won't remember me." Said Père Robineau: "Nonsense. She is an elephant. Grandmother. It's Jean-Pierre. Your lover from the Sixteenth." The old lady's face cleared. She smiled. "Jean-Pierre?" She held out her hand for him to kiss. "Là, là, là."

Said Père Robineau: "Là, là, là is correct. What a scandal you two were."

Said the grandmother: "A scandal beyond explanation by war. Isn't that true, Jean-Pierre?"

At table they talked about America, about crime in New York, about John Kennedy and Indochina and Algeria, about Mme. Robineau, about children, about film stars, about food and the cost of it. At last Charles spoke of the project he planned, to commemorate the twenty-fifth anniversary of the fall of France.

Père Robineau listened to Charles politely and then said, "It was a very long time ago, Jean-Pierre. Time and memory distort things. Sad events become merely sentimental."

"That need not be," said Charles.

"But I am not an actor," said the old man. "Who would tell me what to say?"

"No one," said Charles. "You and I will talk, the way we're talking now. I promise you that after five minutes you'll forget all about the camera. You will be a grand *vedette*."

"My Lord," said Père Robineau.

Julian clapped his hands. "The new Belmondo. Here he is."

"You must do it, Papa," said Madeleine.

"Why?"

"It will give you an interest." Madeleine turned to Charles. "Since Mama died, he just sits around the house all winter, arguing with me, arguing with Grandmother, arguing with the television."

"He has become a vegetable," said Julian.

Said Madeleine: "He has become a vegetable with a very big mouth."

57

Charles shot all of the material in Paris in January and February and saw a first rough assembly on March 15th in the company of the programing vice-president, the sales vice-president, six agency representatives, his cameraman, his editor, his soundman, and the woman who was going to write and direct the English dialogue translation. "Charlie," said the programing man, "this is going to be your first Emmy." An agency man wondered whether the voice-over narration and English dubbing could be properly completed in time for the June 17th show date. The dubbing lady said it could. "What kind of voices are you hiring?" said the programing vice-president. "Middle Atlantic," said the woman, "with just a soupçon of accent." The editor was worried about the interviews with the American fliers. "You've never seen four more square idiots. They're so square they're almost anti-American. They're going to ruin the rhythm of the thing." Said the sales vice-president: "Beautiful. Absolutely beautiful. I'm still crying. Charlie, where'd you ever find them?" "For Christ's sake, Frank," said the programing man, "where've you been? Charlie was a Resistance fighter, weren't you, Charlie?" Charles said no, but no one took him seriously. Someone from the agency suggested that it was too bad Charles hadn't thought to film Eustache doing his Cyrano schtick. "Is it too late?" Charles said it was. "I mean he's so goddamn real," said another agency representative, "just like the old actor in those great prewar French movies.

Old what's-his-name. You know the guy I mean." Said
Charles: "You mean the one who fucks nine-year-old boys?"

58

EUSTACHE

Synopsized transcript of initial rough assembly. Footage to
be picked up as indicated.

(1) Silent. Voice-over to be added. Camera pans across
the view of the Marne Valley as seen from the gate to the
Robineaus' former house, the one now occupied by Paul
Robineau and his family. Camera pans 180° to show the
exterior of the house, which is small and pinched. It looks
like a miniature. It seems out of proportion to the rest of the
landscape, like a toy house one might put beside the track
of an electric train. The camera passes through the gate,
moves over the flagstone walk, and goes up the steps into
the house. The kitchen. There are short zooms to the stove,
coffee grinder, sink, a newspaper photo of Mendès-France
tacked to the wall, other details. The camera moves on to
the tiny sitting-dining room. There is a large dining table
in the middle of the room. A TV set in one corner and a
day bed along the wall. The water closet, just big enough for
the toilet. Zoom to a pile of *France-Soirs* on the floor. Up
steep steps to the second floor. Two small bedrooms, each
with two single beds. Periodic zooms into wall railings once
used by Mme. Robineau. In the hall, the camera pans up to
the ceiling. A hand pulls down a ceiling door. Cut to attic,
so small it is possible to stand only in the center where the
roof peaks. Three mattresses on the floor. Cut to long shot
of Marne Valley. Slow zoom back. We have been looking

through a small round window, the only window in the attic.

(2) Sync sound. The interior of the Café Brillant on the Place Fontenay. Sunday afternoon. Père Robineau sits at a table with three of his former comrades. Père Robineau wears his beret, slacks, shirt, and a cardigan sweater with a pocket on the left, where he shields his withered hand. Père Robineau introduces his comrades, each of whom is his age or older. They are shy at first but a continuing supply of brandies puts them at ease. One man begins to tell a story about the First World War and is told to shut up by his friends. Another man, a former baker with a face that looks like the aged Buster Keaton, tells about the troubles he had in supplying bread to the Robineau household during the Occupation when it included a great-grandmother, a grand-mother and grandfather, the mother, two small children, and usually two or three fliers in the attic. "That little villa con-sumed almost as much bread as the garrison at the château." On film the story isn't as funny or as moving as it is to the people in the bar. They laugh so hard and so foolishly that the scene abruptly stops. The actors have got drunk.

(3) Sync sound. Day. Père Robineau stands across the street from the towering walls of the Château de Vincennes. He talks to Charles, who is outside camera range. Then, as now, he explains, he was a vendor of ices. This has been his daily post since 1933. It was on this very spot, he recalls, that he was first approached in the spring of 1941 by Colonel Nallième, who had been his commander in World War I, about the possibility of helping the English and Canadian airmen who'd been shot down and had found their way to the safety of Paris. Charles asks why Père Robineau empha-sizes the safety of Paris. Père Robineau shrugs. He lights a cigarette. He shrugs again. The French farmers, he says, were sometimes as eager as the members of the Gestapo in track-

ing down Allied airmen. There were bounties on them. Père Robineau walks up the street to a tobacconist's shop and introduces the proprietor, a short, round-faced man who never stops looking directly into the camera and never stops grinning. With some irritation Père Robineau instructs the tobacconist to look at him, not the camera. They talk about the tobacconist's son, who died early in 1944 in Ravensbrück, where he had been sent after he'd been arrested for escorting an American airman who had been assigned to Père Robineau.

(4) Sync sound. Day. Père Robineau sits on the day bed in the living room of the house in the Rue Herbert. Madeleine sits on his right and Julian on the left, holding his two youngest grandsons. Paul and his wife sit next to his mother with their two other children. The sequence begins with a self-conscious group shot; then the camera zooms in on Père Robineau as he describes the smallness of the house, the difficulties of living with strangers under such cramped conditions. "There were occasions when it was like the Bourse," he says. Some of their guests stayed only two or three nights. Some stayed for months. Were there ever problems? Père Robineau laughs, looks at Madeleine. They were good boys, most of them, he remembers. One of them fell in love with Madeleine, which was difficult. He tells about one boy who had a nervous breakdown. He couldn't stand being enclosed in the attic. He wouldn't eat. He cried all day. At night, when Père Robineau would sometimes take the other two airmen for walks through the quarter, the boy would not go. He was afraid to leave the attic and afraid to stay. What happened? One night he hanged himself. Luckily the cord broke and he simply had a sore neck. He was so frightened at the thought he might have been successful that he changed after that. He became very nice. Later he escaped to Spain. Does Père Robineau ever hear

from any of the men today? Have any visited him and his family? Père Robineau takes some letters from his pocket, perhaps a dozen. "We heard from five, right after the war. We haven't heard recently." Most of the men, he explains, never cared to know where they were hidden. Some were in a kind of shock all the time. And you must remember, he says, smiling, that most of them didn't speak French. One young American taught himself to speak French with the help of Madeleine and Mme. Robineau. Another studied botany. At that point, botany books were the only books in English Père Robineau could obtain.

(5) Sync sound. Day. Madeleine, dressed in a pale blue cloth coat that is cut to hide her figure, stands at the gate to the house in the Rue Herbert. She remembers coming home one afternoon and hearing a terrible fight in progress. It was so violent she could hear the sounds half a block away. The two guests in the attic were having a fist fight and wrestling match. She ran to the café to seek aid from M. Lutierri, the *patron*. By the time they returned, the two men were playing cards. They had not been angry. They had been bored.

(6), (7), (8), (9) Footage to be developed and inserted, including an interview with M. Rouxelles, shots of Charles's flat in the Avenue d'Iéna, which was one of the staging areas for airmen being sent on to Fontenay and other, more permanent hiding places.

(10), (11), (12), (13) Interviews with four fliers who stayed with Père Robineau's family between May, 1941, and June, 1944. One of these men is remembered by Père Robineau in (16).

(14) Sync sound. Day. Interview with Colonel Nallième in his apartment near the Trocadéro. Colonel Nallième, who speaks English, explains the system of underground railroad stations, of which the Robineau home was one of two dozen

he supervised. He refers to Eustache as a man of patriotism, valor, wit, and poetry. "Ask him to recite Cyrano's speech for Christian," he says. "He's frightfully good, really."

(15) Sync sound. Day. Interview with Guillaume Taisse, who had been the chief of the Fontenay gendarmerie during the first two and one half years of the Occupation. He is a typical French functionary. Yes, he remembers searching houses in which Allied airmen were reportedly hidden. Yes, he remembers searching the Robineau house. Did he purposely not search the attic? The question is repeated. Of course not, he says indignantly. He did not search the attic because he believed it impossible that anyone could be successfully hidden in such a small, mean cavern. If he had found any airmen, he would, of course, have done his duty as he saw it at that time. In point of fact, he had found three during his two years in the gendarmerie. What happened? He never asked about the disposition of the cases. The men were prisoners of war. The people who helped them were traitors. That's all. He had eventually resigned because of poor health. Frankly, he did not like the job, but while he had it he carried it out to the best of his abilities.

(16) Sync sound. Day. Père Robineau walks from the Church of the Madeleine, down the Rue Royale to the Place de la Concorde. This, he remembers, was the Paris inhabited by the Germans. Only occasionally did one ever see them in places like Fontenay. He pauses in front of Maxim's. He mentions *The Merry Widow*. He is reminded of a curious story: in 1947 a lady from Cincinnati wrote him that she'd learned that he had saved the life of her nephew. The lady was coming to Paris, accompanying her husband who was on a business trip. She would like to meet Père Robineau (or should she call him Eustache?) to thank him personally. He met the lady at the Crillon, Père Robineau remembers. She looked very rich, very handsome. Very fine clothes. As

a present, she brought Père Robineau a pound of bacon
("Sweeftsss Premiuuum") wrapped in cellophane. Perhaps
because the bacon had been in her suitcase, it smelled of
perfume. She told Eustache of her husband's sister, an American woman married to a French viscount whose château in
Normandy had been confiscated by the Nazis, forcing the
American lady and her husband to spend the rest of the war in
the gardener's cottage. "*Les boches!*" Père Robineau remembers the lady's saying as they walked along the Rue Royale
together. "Oh, Eustache, how could you bear seeing our be-
loved Paris occupied by those dreadful men?" The true
French, Père Robineau comments, such Americans.

(17) Sync sound. Day. The grandmother sits in her old
chair in the sitting room of the house in the Rue Herbert.
When the scene starts, she is covering her mouth with one
hand, as if embarrassed by her teeth, and laughing at something said by Charles, who remains offscreen. Her silver
hair is drawn up in a Breton topknot tied with a black
ribbon. She is a small, delicately boned old lady. Though
frail, she is also firm. She: "You made the promise to me."
He: "What?" She: "That one day you would take me to the
Côte d'Azur." He: "I don't remember." She: "You do. You
just want me to tell the story." He: "What story?" She:
"About that terrible night." He: "You tell me about it." She:
"The night I thought we were going to be arrested." She
pauses, then continues. "I don't want to remember it. I don't
think of such things anymore." He: "When was it?" She: "It
was winter. Was it January or February? I've forgotten, but
it was very cold. Jean-Pierre had brought two new Americans
to the house. About nine o'clock. They went upstairs, the
Americans. Jean-Pierre sat in the kitchen talking to my
daughter, son-in-law, and my granddaughter. He was preparing to leave when we heard the police van." The camera
zooms in onto the old lady's hands. She has a tic in the left

one. "It parked at the end of the street, just down there. They searched the first two houses. We were certain that Jean-Pierre had been followed from Vincennes, or that someone here in the quarter had informed." She pauses, almost angry that she remembers the night as vividly as she does. Camera goes into a tight close-up of her face. "We put the children to bed and we sat in the kitchen in the dark. The van stayed there all night and the gendarmes patrolled the street. About two in the morning, my daughter and son-in-law and my granddaughter went to bed upstairs. I lay down in my bed here. It was very cold. The stove had gone out a long time ago. Jean-Pierre lay on the floor by my bed. I could feel him shivering with the cold. He was shaking the bed. I asked him to come up on the bed with me. The next morning he thanked me like a prince. When it was all over, he said, he would take me to the Côte d'Azur. We would never be cold again." He: "Grandmother, if you had it to do all over again, would you?" She (quietly): "Never, never, never. It was not worth it. I would not again risk my family to save strangers. You know, they were always strangers. If there is another war, I shall collaborate. . . ."

(18) Sync sound. Day. Père Robineau stands in his attic near the small round window that looks toward the Marne Valley. The light from the window makes his outline fuzzy. Only his gestures and his voice are distinct. He tells about the morning early in 1943 when the gendarmes searched the house. By the grace of God, he says, the three men who had been hiding here had been sent on to Limoges the night before, and he had not yet received any new fliers. Also by the grace of God, he notes, his mother-in-law, daughter, and grandsons were away. "I think it would have killed my mother-in-law. She's a brave woman but there are some things that bravery cannot protect against. The only persons in the house were myself and my wife, my Janine who

is no longer with us. Janine opened the door to them. There were three. . . ." As Père Robineau talks on the sound track, the camera searches the rooms as the gendarmes did. "Janine and I followed. Janine holding on to the bars that you have seen. She'd had polio, you know, and to walk was difficult for her. She was stalwart, Janine. She never complained. She was very pretty, even then, and I remember . . . I remember thinking as we followed those three men through our house, I remember thinking how even fear did not diminish her beauty. . . ." Cut back to Père Robineau in the attic. "For no reason I could think of, they did not search the attic. A good thing it was. It was very dirty. I speak now not only of—you understand—they had no facilities in the attic. They used chamber pots that I emptied. I speak not of that. I cannot tell you the things we found. The men had been living here for two and a half months. They were not clean. It is curious how some of them were clean and some did not mind if they lived like animals. It had nothing to do with the sort of men they were. It was something else entirely. . . ."

(19) Sync sound. Night. Interior of the house in the Rue Herbert. A party is in progress. Very crowded. Very gay. We see all the members of the Robineau family, Colonel Nallième (looking very formal—very English, really, and out of place), the tobacconist, the comrades from the café, M. Rouxelles. Wine, brandy, and Scotch whisky are being served. Père Robineau sits at the kitchen table with Madeleine on one side of him and M. Taisse, the former gendarme chief, on the other. Père Robineau holds his three-year-old grandson on his lap. Guests press around the table. As he talks, Père Robineau is unaware that his grandson is playing with his withered hand, examining it, bending the fingers back and forth as if they were the appendages on a doll. ". . . Who can say?" Père Robineau says. "I was much

younger then. I had strength and vigor, and I had my Janine. I believed very strongly in the cause, in France, and because I believed, she believed, or at least she said she did. And she did. No woman could have stood up the way she did if she had not believed. When France surrendered, it was as if a part of me had been rendered useless. Worse, disgraced. They were very dark days. At first I was almost willing to believe that the thousand-year Reich was to be a reality. I waited for the fall of Britain the way a sick man waits for death. But"—he shrugs—"it did not come. Instead we received an opportunity to help." He smiles. "What can one say about lives already lived? One says, 'They were that way. That is what happened.' Anything else is speculation." He laughs, holds his glass up. "Ah, come, Jean-Pierre. Let us drink a toast to the Allies, to all Americans, to all Englishmen, all Canadians, all Frenchmen, then and now. . . ." Offscreen someone says, "The Russians?" which prompts general laughter. Père Robineau says, "All Russians, all Chinese. . . ."

59

Charles had liked "Eustache" at that first screening. It had turned out as he had hoped it would, but in the weeks that followed, as they edited and dubbed, as they timed sequences for the commercial breaks, as they attached stock newsreel footage and still pictures (Hitler's seeming to dance on one foot at Compiègne) to set the story of Eustache in its proper context, Charles began to have intimations that something was going wrong. It was hardly more than a kind of sensitivity, the first hint that a tooth is about to ache. Yet, he realized, things were not about to go wrong. As with the tooth, they already had gone wrong. The more he looked at the footage, the more remote the people and the events became. More remote and meaningless and commonplace. The film had been intended as a tribute to a rare sort of heroism, sustained and intellectual as well as instinctive in its strength, as opposed to the heroism of the moment when reflexes of love or panic direct a man to enter a burning building or throw himself on a live hand grenade. Instead he had transformed the Robineaus into figures of entertainment. They had joined with him to promote a reputation for America's second largest petroleum refiner as the Western world's major defense against poverty, disease, malnutrition, overpopulation, bigotry, boredom, and Communism.

He left the laboratory early one afternoon in late April and drove home to Connecticut to find that Daisianna had decided to paint the old white clapboard barn a blazing magenta color. Mrs. Kolbach, the kleptomaniac, met him as he parked his car. She was sinister with pleasure. "I think it's going to be very pretty," Mrs. Kolbach said. "But it takes a little getting used to." Mrs. Kolbach's face had turned blue in the spring cold. She had apparently been outside all day monitoring the operation. She nodded in the direction of the barn, one side of which was already newly painted. Daisianna, watching from the ground and wrapped in her mink coat, was directing two painters who stood on a scaffold near the roof. Charles walked over to the barn. Five-gallon cans of blue paint, red paint, white paint, and black paint were standing nearby. The lower portion of the barn door was a sampler of colors ranging from various shades of pink to deep purple. Daisianna ran to him wearing the happily vague look he recognized with anger. She carried a can of beer and the right sleeve of her mink had been freshly dipped in red paint. Daisianna asked what he thought. "I wanted to surprise you," she said. "I knew you'd think the idea was awful unless you could see it."

"Oh, shit," he said.

"What's wrong?"

"It looks ridiculous."

"I like brightly painted barns," she said.

"But it doesn't go with the color of the brick foundation."

"We can paint that too."

"Why? I thought one of the reasons you liked this place was the old brick. You said you liked the color old brick gets."

"Well," said Daisianna, "I'm tired of it now."

Charles studied her face for clues. "Have you been taking your pills?"

"Yes," said Daisianna.

"When?"

"I've forgotten. This morning, I think."

"Shit," said Charles. He turned away from her and walked to the house. He went up to their bedroom and lay down on their bed that had not been made for two days. Daisianna followed several minutes later. She had a fresh can of beer in her hand and moved as if on roller skates. She was gay. "I've asked Bill and Angelo to have supper with us," she said.

"Who are Bill and Angelo?"

"The painters," said Daisianna. "But Angelo has to call his wife to see if it's all right. He's terribly sexy-looking, don't you think?"

"What?" said Charles.

"Angelo," said Daisianna. "If I were younger, I'd call him cute."

"Well," said Charles, "you better tell Angelo not to bother telephoning his wife. He's not having supper here."

"Why not?"

"Because I said so."

"I can invite them if I want," said Daisianna. "After all, I paid for this house."

"You may have paid for this house," said Charles, "but I pay all the bills. If you want to put it that way. You didn't know that, did you?"

Daisianna looked at the floor.

"Do you know how much money I made last year? Over sixty thousand dollars. Do you know how much I have in my savings account at this minute? Do you? About four hundred and eighty dollars, plus interest. Do you know why? Because I pay all the bloody bills around here, all the bloody bills on the Fifth Avenue apartment and all your bloody bills with that quack Mandelbaum."

Daisianna sank down on the foot of the bed, her eyes filling with tears. "What's wrong?"

"What's wrong! Are you asking me? Do you honestly want to know? It isn't often you seem to notice. You're too busy playing princess among the bartenders, clerks, and stable-boys. What's wrong? I'm bored, goddamn it. I'm bored with my job. I'm bored with New York. I'm bored with you. Jesus, am I bored! For Christ's sakes, hold back the tears until I finish talking. Or go cry on Mandelbaum's shoulder. I've had it, little dear. I've had it up to here. The moods, the pills, the booze, the tears. Sometimes I wonder how I could ever have gotten into this mess. I think I'm going out of my mind."

Daisianna stopped crying. She stared at him as if she'd been physically assaulted. She looked terribly vulnerable, but even this angered him. It had recently occurred to him that Daisianna was quite capable of acting the part assigned to her by life and by her doctors. She said, "Do you want a divorce?"

He hesitated a moment, aware that his hesitation was part of the game he'd initiated. "I don't know."

She walked from the room, leaving her can of beer and her mink coat with the one red cuff on the floor by the bed.

A minute later he watched her from the bedroom window as she crossed the driveway, walked past the garage over to the barn. He saw her speaking to Bill and Angelo, who were sitting on the running board of their truck drinking beer. They didn't bother to stand while she spoke to them. She turned and came slowly back toward the house, and his anger vanished. Later he took her out to dinner to apologize. He tried to explain about the film, what he saw happening to it, about his feelings for the Robineaus. "It's strange," said Daisianna. "You'd hardly mentioned them until you went to Paris in December." He found himself sinking easily into alcohol while Daisianna seemed to surface into unexpected sobriety. "That was a very important time in my life," he said. "The most important. It was the only time in my life when I was something more than a witness." He took her hand. He examined the texture of her skin. He stroked the absurdly big emerald. "I love you very much, little dear, but there are times when I feel I'm just a witness to your life. I'm not a part of it. At most, I'm a kind of caretaker." He was so drunk that he couldn't be sure she understood what he was saying or that she was even listening to him. Whatever he had said, however, seemed to have brought her down from her high or up from her low. She drove them home from Sean's Pub and put him to bed, the only time that ever happened.

The next morning at seven, while he was shaving, Dr. Neilen, the director of Hickory Hollow, telephoned Charles. Jack Mandelbaum, he said, had been killed on the Merritt Parkway about 3 a.m. He had been driving alone, coming out from Manhattan, and had gone off the road traveling, according to the police, between eighty and ninety miles an hour. Even the license plates were unrecognizable. The car seemed to have flown off the road, up an embankment, and into a tree. "I don't know how to advise you to tell your wife," said the doctor. "This is going to be most difficult for her. Perhaps you'd like to bring her here. But perhaps not. All her associations with Hickory Hollow are through Mandelbaum. What kind of sedation do you have there? What is her daily dosage? I wish I could tell you something that would make it easier. Jack Mandelbaum was not just a good doctor, he was a very good, very selfless man. You know, he himself was a schizo for years. He fought his way out. Some can. Recently he had been drinking too much. I assume that may be what happened last night. He hadn't been well. He was having trouble with his prostate. Nothing serious. Nothing that required surgical procedure, but he allowed it to worry him. He was a compulsive worrier about unimportant things."

Daisianna was sitting up in bed looking puzzled when Charles came in from the bathroom. He lay down beside her and pulled her to him. At first she did not react to the news. "Hang on to me, little dear," he said. She began to moan and whimper. Like an Arab mourner she wailed but didn't cry. "Hang on to me, little dear. Hang on to me. I'm here. I'll never leave." She did hang on to him. She clutched him so desperately he could feel blood pulsing in his neck. "Hang on, hang on, hang on."

That afternoon he cabled Mary Magnuson in St. Constance and asked if she would consider renting her house to them for the summer. They wanted to get away as soon as possible. He talked to the people at the network. "Eustache" was complete except for some opticals, which could be overseen by someone else. He needed a rest, he said. Five shows in eighteen months were two more than his contract called for. He explained that there had been a death in the family and they were considerate.

60

Jane Maria Barrett Ridgely, Daisianna's great-grandmother on her mother's side, was born in Island Grove, Sangamon County, Illinois, on April 1, 1840, and died in Palm Beach, Florida, on March 15, 1922. Among the family papers Daisianna inherited from Leola was a fifty-page, handwritten memoir addressed to Mrs. Ridgely by her brother and attached to some suspect genealogies designed to certify the old lady's eligibility for membership in the Mayflower Society. One study carried the family all the way back to the Wars of the Roses. The Barretts were identified as Plantagenets. When Daisianna had mentioned this to Dodie, he had said, "That's funny, I always thought they were Dandelions."

The following are excerpts from the memoir entitled "Recollections of William Theodosius Barrett, Written in His 80th Year for His Sister, Mrs. Jane Maria Barrett Ridgely":

Robert Allen Barrett was our great-grandfather and a Miss Lewis our great-grandmother. This much I know to be true. He was rector of St. Martin's Parish, Hanover County, Virginia, during the Revolutionary War. There are letters I have seen that state he represented his parish at the General Convention of the Episcopal Church in 1785, called for the purpose of reorganizing under the new state laws of the Union.

In one of our father's trips to Virginia he brought a copy of the will of Robert Barrett and I read it when I was a boy but I have no distinct recollection of its contents except that in one place it alludes to "My Eldest Son William," who was our grandfather, and in another place it says "By the grace of God, Amen."

Robert Allen Barrett belonged to a land company which

was not wound up until after his death and he was entitled to a considerable sum of money which neither he nor his heirs ever got. That was why Father got a copy of the will. Aunt Fanny, our old negro cook, used to tell me that she had a good recollection of our great-grandfather. Said she saw him seal a letter with sealing wax and a lighted candle and how his hands shook when he sealed it. Aunt Fanny said she was very small when she knew him and it was after our grandparents were married, for she said he called to Dolly to send him a candle and that our grandmother sent the candle to him by her to melt the wax to seal the letter.

Captain Merriwether Lewis, who commanded the expedition over the Rocky Mountains with Captain Clark and extended our possessions to the Pacific Ocean in 1806, was an own cousin to our grandfather. Father had an old negro man by the name of George who came from the estate of Robert Barrett and I got a good many items from him. He always called our grandfather Master.

He also told me that Master (Captain Wm. Barrett) was vaccinated for the smallpox at the Soldiers Hospital at Williamsburg while he was serving with General Thomas Nelson (by looking at your Encyclopaedia you will find all about General Nelson and about Merriwether Lewis, our grandfather's cousin on his mother's side). In the night our grandfather told George to bring him a drink of water and he said to him the doctor forbid giving him any and Master was so big and strong he got out of bed and went to the barrel of water and took it by the chimb and turned it up and took a good drink and spilt water down his bosom and improved fast after that. George was the body servant of the Master and attended him as such during the war. He told me a great many tales of adventure.

In this connection I must tell you the story of our great-grandmother Barrett as told to me by Aunt Fanny. When I was a little boy I sat on the floor one warm day in front of her, she in her rocking chair, and she told me the following tale about Miss Lewis:

"Your great-grandmother when she was a little girl lived with a man who made her work and when she got big enough he sent her to the mill with sacks of corn and wheat to get meal and flour ground for the use of the family. So at one time she met a man who asked her what her name was and when she told him, he said to her: You own all this farm and all the negroes where you live and they have no right to make you work.

"And after that she did not work any more but came into possession of a fine estate and was so smart that when she grew up she married a fine gentleman, your great-grandfather Robert Barrett."

Our mother and father lived after they were married at the old Barrett plantation near Greensburg, Kentucky, and our oldest brother Smith and myself were born there, then they lived in the town of Greensburg about two years and our brother James was born there. They then went to Meadow Creek farm in the fall of 1820. At this place all the rest of the children were born down to you and you were born at Island Grove, Sangamon County, Illinois.

During the time we lived at Meadow Creek farm our father frequently took droves of horses and mules to the south to sell to the cotton planters. He also had an agency to collect two estates in Virginia on which accounts he made several trips to that state and by which he made about six-thousand dollars which was considered a very large sum of money in those days. He also represented Green County in the Legislature several times.

On the Meadow Creek farm the negroes worked their own way and everything was run by Aunt Fanny and Uncle as we called Aunt Fanny's husband. They were both honest and good as could be and worshipped "Mister Jimmy" and "Miss Maria," but they did not manage to get much work out of the rest of the negroes and a large portion of what our father made went to support his negroes and about 1832 our negroes got something like typhoid fever and between then and 1835 when we moved to Illinois, a great many of them died which made us much poorer, as negroes were valuable and the doctors' bills were large. I think this had much to do with our moving to Illinois. When we were ready to move from Kentucky to Illinois, I was sent with our brother Robert in the spring and we lived at the old Sangamon County place and cooked for ourselves and made a fine crop of corn and oats and got two good milch cows and some nice hogs to fatten, so when the family came in the fall, they came to a land of plenty. The family rode in a nice covered spring wagon and the plunder was hauled in a large ox cart and a large horse wagon. Six hound dogs and three fine thoroughbred mares and a good assortment of guns was brought along and the old Sangamon County farm was a place of hospitality and high living as long as the Barretts lived there.

We had not lived in Illinois long till our father was nominated for the Legislature by the Democrats and such men as Lincoln, Baker, Logan, and N. W. Edwards were run by the Whigs and I have heard our father on the stump with all these men at different times and I have never had occasion to feel ashamed of the outcome. Sangamon was then a Whig county, full of Kentucky men that admired Henry Clay and our father a Democrat and an admirer of Clay. Our father was the first Democrat that carried Sangamon County. When our first railroads were built, it was done by the state (about 1839) and our father was agent for the state to receive iron (which came from England) at New Orleans and reship it to Illinois. In 1841 our father was made Register of the Land

Offices at Springfield, which place he held for eight years.

I have said but little about our mother as you were with her so many years yourself and, with me, I know that you can always be consoled with that pleasing thought that we were children of a being too good ever to have lived on this earth.

I will now tell you of my pioneer work in this country, hoping the tales will amuse you some, when you have nothing else to do.

My first recollections are living in the town of Greensburg and our moving from there to the Meadow Creek farm. The first school I ever attended I had to go and stay at Uncle William's as there was no school near our place at Meadow Creek. I was quite a large boy never to have gone to school but I was in some respects further advanced than most boys my age. Our mother had done a good job in teaching me at home and by the time I was 17, when I came to Illinois in 1833 to do business with Uncle Richard, I had read all the historical works common in those days, nearly all the British poets, Shakespeare's plays, and nearly all of Scott's novels.

The first job Uncle Richard had for me was to take a man and an ox team and go to Burlington to fence a large number of lots he had in that place. In the fall of 1837 Uncle Richard formed a partnership with Mr. Nicholas Ridgely (and probably others) which I think was called the Illinois Land Company. It was for the settlers who had no money to enter their land with and land sales were to come off in November. Mr. Ridgely was then cashier of the State Bank of Illinois and our brother Jim was clerking in the same bank. So I was sent for and Mr. Ridgely loaded me up with fifty or sixty thousand dollars which I took to Burlington on horseback. A good many of the lands which Uncle Richard entered for the settlers were not paid for when the notes were due and I spent part of my time for several years collecting these notes and selling the forfeited lands.

On these trips, which I made on horseback, I frequently went through country that was unsettled for miles and saw hundreds of deer and wolves and saw a man shoot a panther one day when I stopped to get some dinner. I worked for low wages and never got more than I bargained for as Uncle Richard was not generous but he paid all my expenses and what little I got was made clear. I must say for Uncle Richard that he always put the greatest confidence in me and would trust me with thousands. He always addressed me in a most affectionate manner as "my son" which made me love him very much.

In the winter of 1837 I came back from taking the money to Uncle Richard at Burlington for Mr. Ridgely and took school and taught that winter and Ellen Butler was then 15 years old and came to school to me and in the spring when she was 16 I made her the first visit as a lover. She had no finery of any kind but I noticed a bright new pair of slippers on her feet and she was always the cleanest person I ever saw and made the greatest use of wildflowers.

In 1846 and 1847 I served as a lieutenant in the Mexican War. I have seen General Jackson and General Scott, General Taylor and many other famous men. I was well acquainted with Lincoln who always called me Billy Barrett. I was well acquainted with Douglas and have danced with him in the same set at cotillion parties. I have seen old Black Hawk and slept in the same room with him. I was present at the first meeting of the first legislature that ever met in Iowa.

I am now in my 80th year and very little of what I have written is known to any other living human on earth. I might say that I am now in sight of the open gate that leads into that Silent Land and through which I will soon pass and that what little I have known and seen will pass with me and be forgotten forever. To this I am perfectly reconciled for the God that I have always worshipped is the God of Mercy.

As I have given you my pioneer life, the rest is not worth relating.

> *Your affectionate brother,*
> *William T. Barrett*

Villa Oleo

Mackinac Island, Michigan, 1896

61

Home movie: a lawn in summer many years ago. In the background a large, pseudo-Georgian house. Oak trees in full leaf. A squat, very fat black woman in a nurse's uniform and cap leads a little girl of about two across the lawn. The girl wears a short organdy dress. Her hair is corkscrew curls. The black woman points to the camera and laughs, but the little girl is too intent on negotiating the lawn's hillocks to notice. Are her shoes too big? Too stiff? Cut to close-up of little girl. She sits astride a four-wheeled toy horse and tries to push it over the grass. She becomes stuck. She rocks forward and back but the horse will not move. It topples onto its side. The little girl screams silently with surprise and fright. She holds out her hand to the black woman and to a pretty-faced buxom woman with bobbed platinum hair. The nurse and the mother laugh and point to the camera. The little girl stares at the camera. She attempts to get up but can't. Her mouth is contorted with fury. She looks like a baby bird that hasn't yet found its voice.

Every time Dodie and Leola showed these films to Daisi-anna when she was growing up, they made her cry again. It was a family joke. The films had been taken at Grandmother Caffrey's Lake Forest house where, in the kitchen, there was

a large table covered with yellow oilcloth, under which
Daisianna would play while Mo, her nurse, helped the cook
in the preparations for evening meals. It was dark and comfortable under the table. And safe. It was a small house.
Daisianna liked to play there with her friends Mary and
Joseph and the Little Lord Jesus. Joseph never had much
to say. He was always napping, as if it were Sunday afternoon. Mary would comfort her when she skinned a knee or
twisted an ankle or if she was simply lonely. The Little
Lord Jesus told her to say she had a stomach ache when
she didn't. He taught her how to play with matches, how to
steal change from a large black purse that Mo carried with
her, though she always left it unattended in the kitchen. Mo
said that the Little Lord Jesus was a Blessed Redeemer and
she gave Daisianna pictures of him. They showed a fat-
thighed, cherry-lipped baby whose thing was covered by a
piece of cloth that seemed always floating by at the time the
picture was made. Sometimes there were gold plates above
his head. Sometimes rings.

62

When Daisianna left Jimmy Barnes's apartment in Chicago
and moved to New York, she took a room in an apartment
shared by three girls on Park Avenue. It was a lovely old
apartment, though there wasn't much furniture. Two of the
girls were airline stewardesses, away much of the time. The
other was studying to be a dental technician and was neither
attractive nor interesting. She was also ill-tempered and
marked the containers of yogurt she kept in the refrigerator
and suspected Daisianna of picking at. Daisianna had no
job. She lived on the remainder of the money Dodie had

given her. Instead of looking for a job she stayed home all day sketching dress designs. She still remembers some. The more she sketched, the more ideas she had. She didn't want to sleep for fear she'd forget the ideas. When she did sleep, she'd dream new designs and wake herself to put them down on paper. She went for almost a week without sleeping. That's what she was told later. One Sunday she left the apartment at dawn. It turned into a fine bright winter morning with no one about except people walking dogs. No garbage trucks. An occasional taxi. She walked to Fifth Avenue and down Fifth toward Rockefeller Center. As she walked by St. Patrick's she was suddenly filled with a most marvelous sensation. Every nerve shook with pleasure. The Little Lord Jesus appeared and more or less floated at her side. She had thought she was going into the cathedral but she exchanged purpose for ecstasy. Though surprised, she questioned nothing. He had chosen her, as it should be. They were on Madison Avenue. They stopped to look into the windows of Brooks Brothers. The street was being torn up and chunks of concrete had been placed in a pile near the sidewalk. She later told the doctors that the Little Lord Jesus had suggested she throw a piece of concrete through a Brooks window, and she did. That is, she tried. For some time she tried as people collected to watch. The driver of a cruising taxi said, "Keep it up, honey. You show them bastards." When she told Charles about it she said, "I suppose I shouldn't admit this but I still have the memory of it and it's as real as anything that's ever happened to me. What I miss most is the feeling of happiness. I've never been as happy before or since. Of course, I was out of my mind. I know it couldn't have been the Little Lord Jesus. I don't even believe in God."

63

Their first weeks in St. Constance were like a string of perfect mornings all day. Daisianna lay by the pool and quickly turned dark gold. Charles read in the shade or swam in the sea, which, in May, was as calm as a lake. He bought a spear gun and a snorkel outfit, and one day he shot a Moray eel in the grotto under the point. The mortally wounded eel fought lazily on the axis of the arrow. It pulled one way and then the other and bit at the water as blood trailed from its jaws. The blood attracted a large grouper and hundreds of small nervous snappers, which would have been transparent except for their yellow fins. As Charles swam sidestroke back around the point where Daisianna lay by the pool, he let more and more line out so that any fish going after the eel would not confuse him with the bait. His arms ached. He saw tiny fins breaking the water where he judged the eel to be. He called up to Daisianna by the pool, but she couldn't hear him. She lay on her back, staring directly into the sun through closed eyelids. He could have been drowning. The experience so unsettled him that he never again used the spear gun in the grotto.

One moonlight night he persuaded Daisianna to swim in the sea with him before going to bed. The sea was absolutely flat and the horizon as distinct as it was during the day. The light was not the light of night but of a total eclipse. Though it was dark, one could see with perfect clarity. Even colors. At one point Charles looked down into the water and saw a shape following them. Very calmly he told Daisianna to swim toward the beach. Slowly, without fuss. When they reached the shallow water he realized he had been watching his own shadow on the sea floor. They dined two or three nights a week with Mary Magnuson in

Marigot at the old island house she was restoring, a grace-ful, two-story West Indian house with a second-floor gallery overlooking a center court full of tropical plants that no one tended and that had become a small jungle. Through Mary they met M. Bouché, the mayor of Marigot and its richest citizen, a white, fat-faced Frenchman with an Oliver Hardy mustache and a wife who, instead of talking, raised her eyebrows in a kind of personal Morse code. Most of the time she seemed to be spelling out variations on SOS. They met Maitland Jaegger, the Mr. Big of the Dutch side, the chief of the Oranjestad Town Council, a mulatto with white cousins and black cousins. He was the representative through whom foreign hotel interests negotiated construction rights and casino privileges. He was rapidly becoming very wealthy. One night, smiling through his anger, Maitland Jaegger told Mary Magnuson that she couldn't possibly un-derstand these things when she asked him how much of the money being made on St. Constance was remaining on the island. She passed Maitland Jaegger his demitasse. "You people are so short-sighted," she said. Maitland Jaegger smiled even more broadly. "You should mind your own business. You are a troublemaker, Mary Magnuson." She said she was also concerned about the free influx of Haitians, Santo Domingans, Dominicans, and St. Lucians coming to the island to find work when so many local people were not working. Said Maitland Jaegger: "They do not want to work. We know what we are doing." Said Mary Magnuson: "You are making a lot of money." One afternoon Mary ar-ranged for Charles to meet Peabody Prince, an old black man of eighty-four who, thirty years before, had founded the St. Constance Democratical Party, which had been instru-mental in gaining independence for the Dutch side. When Peabody Prince had retired from the political scene, he had been given a sinecure as the film censor on the Dutch side.

He also ran a small grocery store built of corrugated iron in the hills behind Oranjestad. Charles and Peabody Prince spent a long rainy afternoon sitting in the grocery store drinking tins of warm Pepsi-Cola, but Peabody Prince was no longer interested in politics. He preferred to talk about the films he was censoring. He shook his head mournfully. "Almost every one I see these days is full of what we here call fucking and sucking."

"Eustache" was televised on June 17th and received excellent reviews, which made Charles restless. He considered the possibility of doing a film about St. Constance. It was clearly going through extraordinary social and economic changes. It would be possible to record them as they happened. Fonse Devanner was enthusiastic about the project, but as soon as Charles had described it he saw all the difficulties. It would require at least one or two years of the time of the film maker. No one would finance it. He put it out of his mind.

The days rolled into each other slowly, like puddles of syrup. Charles made notes for a series of films about the great men of American history: Franklin, Jefferson, Burr, Hamilton, Adams, Jackson, Lincoln, Johnson. He was not interested in biography but in the events of the times that shaped their ideas. The political pressures and compromises that resulted. Charles wrote: "We devote too much of our programing to publicizing the opinions of the stupid, which become self-perpetuating. This is not our function." Three afternoons a week he and Daisianna took scuba-diving lessons at the new Naked Boy Beach Hotel. Daisianna was not pleased, but she did not like to be left alone in strange places, even if it was only the side of the Naked Boy Beach Hotel pool while Charles was inside it.

At the end of June there was an international crisis of sorts when Marigot's full gendarmerie of six men, one of whom was ill with pneumonia, was unable to stop a sit-down demonstration by the French side's eighty Algerian refugees. The Algerians, who had been delivered to St. Constance two years earlier, had refused to leave their squatters' camp on the Marigot beach and take up residence in houses that had been constructed for them in the mountains. After delaying as long as he could with honor, M. Bouché went to the squatters' camp at sunset. The Algerians held up their scrawny babies for him to see and laughed at him. De Gaulle, they said, had promised them houses not shacks, jobs not welfare, food not rations. They'd sent a delegation to inspect their new quarters and had decided to remain where they were. The new compound was seven miles from Marigot. There would be no transportation to and from Marigot for those of them who had jobs. There were no sanitary facilities. They said they'd rather shit on the beach. M. Bouché stood on the running board of an abandoned truck. He tried to look confident and cheerful, but the more he tried, the more aware he was that the fat face was melting into the mask of a buffoon. Someone shouted, "Prick!" Another shouted, "Communist!" "Arab!" shouted another, which broke the tension with laughter. They began to lob things at the mayor. Nothing dangerous, mostly soft garbage. M. Bouché stood it out until he was hit on the shoulder by a small empty can of Heinz's tomato purée. So wounded, he retreated. That night the Algerians—husbands, wives, and children—moved their camp onto the highway that was the only direct route between Marigot and Oranjestad. The seven hundred other residents of Marigot, black and white, were furious. They loathed the Algerian pieds noirs, who pretended to be more patriotic, more French, more sophisticated than they. In a panic M. Bouché telephoned Guadeloupe, and the next afternoon three hundred troops arrived in two transport planes to put down the insurrection. Because the military planes were too big to land on the Marigot airstrip, they were forced to use Wilhelmina Airport, on the Dutch side, where the authorities insisted that every French soldier pass individually through immigration as if he were a tourist. "How long do you plan to stay?" each soldier was asked. "What will be your residence?" "At what telephone number can you be reached?" "Do you have a return ticket?" "Proof of citizenship?" The Algerians finally moved to their new camp on the promise of further help. The troops were evacuated five days later by ship.

On the Fourth of July Daisianna gave an all-day party in honor of the second anniversary of Charles's United States citizenship. She hired a rock group from San Juan to alternate with a local steel band. The food, drink, and service were provided by the Naked Boy Beach Hotel, starting at eleven in the morning. The guests began arriving at noon and continued to arrive all day. The politicians came dressed as if for an evening party. Their wives wore long dresses, hats, and white gloves. The Americans—the residents as well as the tourists—came in slacks, shorts, jeans, bathing suits. At the height of the party there were two hundred people in and around the house, the rocks, the pool, and the beach. At 8 p.m. only a handful of people remained, including Mary Magnuson and Fonse Devanner. There was also a homosexual couple from Detroit who demonstrated the tango accompanied by the rock group's uncertain fox trot. Lyman Rainwater, who had taken off all his clothes early in the day, watched the dancers with haggard lust. Sometime after eight Daisianna woke up. She had fallen asleep in the guest bedroom in the late afternoon. She rushed onto the terrace like someone in a fever dream. She screamed at the party. "Get out of here! All of you. This is my house. Get out. Leave." She caught her breath, turned to Charles and began to cry. "Please," she said. "Get rid of them."

64

From "Two Island Boys," an irregular feature in the *St. Constance Island Light House* ("The People Will Conquer All Things"), published weekly in Oranjestad:

WILLY: *Morning there Bo. Where you be these past few weeks?*

BO: *I been by Aruba working for the oilmen fellas. What's new on de island since I be gone?*

WILLY: *Oh, Bo, these are happy days on de island. We got love hereabouts all over. French side, Dutch side, front-side, backside. Aint no cause to fly KLM to Curaçao for the jig-jig.*

BO: *Why, Willy, who's responsible for all this joy? When I leave to Aruba, the island is as quiet as a sweet summer night. Wife ladies and husbinds and those acknowledged, they be the only ones having such joys, except maybe a few rascal boys and girls down by Guana Bay on dark nights.*

WILLY: *Bo, we got a great government Man here now. A Curaçao fella, he named Minister Shefanner.*

BO: *He same fella that ministers de Inter-Island Affairs, Willy?*

WILLY: *You got it, Bo. Minister Shefanner he all de time now fly up from Curaçao to minister de she-fairs on de island. Mostly a big blond American lady who likes to be as tall as he.*

BO: *But, Willy, this Minister Shefanner, he has got hisself a wife on Curaçao.*

WILLY: *Yes he do, Bo, but she is not so clear. Minister man now a Big Man and has got hisself a Big White Woman. Last month they be riding horseback down Front Street and minister fella he had a rude time. He so sick for two days he could not take de government plane to Curaçao. The horse made his bottom hurt but at de airport, it was he eyes dat was making water. It was sad to see, Bo. But minister fella, he come back de next week and we all is happy again.*

BO: *Minister fella, he makes de boys happy too, dey say.*

WILLY: *No, Bo, that's idol gossip. Minister fella aint no backside boy. He's frontside by the splittails. But by he example and by he rule, de backside boys going on top with love.*

BO: *Explain me, Willy.*

WILLY: *On the Fourth of July I be walking up Rouge Beach in de Low Lands, night fishing for gar, when I come upon de house of de big blond American Lady. There was music and there was Minister Shefanner and the aunty men, they was dancing together a dance I aint never seen even at a bullfight. Minister fella and Lady they be laughing and laughing, spreading joy.*

BO: *Minister fella, he work hard in Curaçao, Willy. He needs the relaction.*

WILLY: *Okay, Bo, but he don't have to fly in government plane just to minister one she-fair. When he has businesses here on de island, he should let them accumulate a pile, then service all at de same time.*

BO: *Willy, you sure are one dumb island boy. Don't you know you cant accumulate a pile of love?*

65

The second week in July the winds slackened. The temperatures rose and the island began to parch without rain. Daisianna continued to spend her days by the pool, but now she had a gin and tonic instead of orange juice for breakfast. Charles, who had taken to sleeping in the library where it was cooler, would hear her getting ice from the refrigerator at six in the morning. When he joined her, she would be sweating in her bikini, looking tan but exhausted. At the height of the summer the island's green foliage turned autumnal, the leaves of the banana trees and lime trees and beach-plum trees went pale yellow or red or brown. A precious cycle had been broken. The island was in a fever that everyone said would pass. The kamms were not due until late September or October. They never arrived in July. This was unheard of. July was one of the loveliest months. Still the island sweltered. Tourists came for two weeks, stayed one week, and departed. Daisianna and Charles, often accompanied by Mary Magnuson, dined almost every night at the Casino, which was one of the few places on the island then air-conditioned. One night they ran into Dinny Murdock, whom Daisianna introduced to Charles as an old friend from Lake Forest, though he was apparently some years younger than Daisianna. Dinny was a tall, lean, towheaded man who looked to be about twenty, though Daisianna said he was at least thirty-eight. He wasn't tan. He was one large accumulation of freckles. His eyebrows and eyelashes were white from the sun. Dinny was a collection of freckles and of twitches. He picked at his nose, his ears. He was always brushing back a lock of hair that had not fallen into his eye. When they met him at the Casino, he told them he had stopped overnight in St. Constance en route to visit friends in Antigua, but when Daisianna suggested he come stay with them for several days, he immediately accepted. As far as Charles could tell, he did not bother to cable anyone in Antigua that he was being delayed. He had no job, no income. He was a professional guest. Daisianna told Charles about the time that she, Dinny, and Jay Bixby had tried to drive to Hollywood only to be arrested in Omaha. "It was all very mixed up," said Daisianna. "Dinny was in love with Jay, and Jay was in love with me, and I wasn't in love with anybody." "He's a fag?" said Charles. "No," said Daisianna. "I don't think he's anything." At first Charles didn't mind Dinny's presence. He was company for Daisianna in the sun. They could lie in it for hours without talking, without swimming, without moving an inch. Like lizards. Then Dinny began to get on Charles's nerves. He borrowed clothes without asking. He'd walk into the bathroom unannounced. They had no privacy. Without telling Daisianna Charles gave Dinny two hundred dollars to continue his travels. Dinny accepted it as a loan and moved on. Daisianna barely missed him. The heat and the sun continued. Except to dine in the evening, they seldom left the house. The landscape around them shriveled. The flowers were all dead. When the cistern ran low on water, they began to bathe in the sea. One night they were told that an elderly American woman who was spending the summer with her son in a house at Anse Rouge, on the Atlantic side of the island, had been found that morning tied up and raped. The son was on a business trip in New York and the mother had been staying in their house alone. She was alive but in shock, they were told, incapable of answering questions. The news frightened Daisianna. The woman had been at their Fourth of July party. That night Charles woke up hearing Daisianna crying in the bedroom. When he went in he discovered a land crab partially squashed on the tile floor. "He was on the bed," Daisianna said. "I woke up and found him on me." Said Charles: "Land crabs don't usually get onto beds." Another night, Daisianna screamed for Charles to come, that there was something trying to get in. Charles laughed. "There isn't much way to keep anybody out of this house if he wants to get in. Just see that your door is locked." Several nights later Mary Magnuson admitted that her house sometimes made her nervous. "One night not long after Mark died, I was staying out there alone. I woke up at about three because I thought I heard something. I looked through the bedroom shutters into the garden and saw a tall, quite well-dressed black man. He had been in the drawing room and was coming down the steps to the bedroom. I began screaming that I had a gun and the poor man said not to shoot, that he was looking for the Hagen house."

"Was he?" said Daisianna.

"It turned out that he really was," said Mary. "He was a taxi driver and he was lost. People down here have no conception of trespassing. I don't think he was going to steal anything. He was just looking around, since he was already there."

That evening Mary went out to the house in the Low Lands with them and took Mark Magnuson's elephant gun out of a closet where it had been wrapped in oil rags. There were five boxes of shells, also neatly wrapped against the damp and mildew. She said that Mark had brought the gun down to the island to shoot sharks. "But, of course, after we had the gun here, we never saw any more sharks. One summer we used to see them all the time. Now I haven't seen one in years." She showed them how to load the gun, how to remove the elaborate safety catches, and then how to unload it. "It might make you feel better to keep it in the bedroom."

66

They had rented the house until September 15th but the first week of August Charles suggested that they leave. He said he was fed up with the heat, with the house, with the island, with the people. "It's like an endless cruise," he said. "I find myself getting bored too early in the day." "I want to stay," said Daisianna. "I have nothing to go home to. All my friends are here." Daisianna never mentioned Mandelbaum, and the thought of finding a new Mandelbaum for her prompted Charles to put off any more talk about leaving. Then the heat also got to Daisianna. She began to sleep most of the day and to stay up most of the night, though Charles was never sure what she was doing locked in the bedroom by herself, all the lights burning. Sometimes she sorted laundry. Sometimes she indexed books from Mary Magnuson's library. She asked him one morning why he thought Mary Magnuson would have three copies of *Les Misérables*. Charles said he hadn't any idea. "She has three copies of *Les Misérables*," said Daisianna, "and two copies of *The Oxford Companion to English Literature*." Daisianna ate very little. She took no interest in the running of the house, leaving him to argue with Fernande and Reuban, who materialized and disappeared according to schedules he never understood. The second week in August the trade winds returned. There were rains at night and sun showers during the day, and the island that looked like a winter battleground became green again within several days. Charles's spirits revived but Daisianna did not want to abandon her upside-down schedule. He pushed her, bullied her, bribed her, and frightened her. "I'm fed up," he said several times. "I'm leaving. If you want to live like this, you can. But I'm leaving." It was largely through threats of that sort that he persuaded her to go scuba diving with him that last afternoon.

67

"What is it?" Charles asked. He had pulled his tank onto his back and turned to see where she was. He stood at the water's edge, the horizon line between sea and sky passing through his just-beginning-to-spread waist. "What's taking you so long?" Everything about him was arrogant, even the casual way he wore his brief swimming trunks as if to advertise his unsupported genitals. She sat on the bank and tried to adjust the strap of her face mask. "What the hell are you doing?"

"The strap was too tight. I'm trying to loosen it."

"For Christ's sake. It was all right this morning."

"It was too tight this morning. I told you."

He took a step toward her and the toe of his flipper caught in the sand, almost throwing him to the ground. "Shit." With great care he walked to her, lifting each foot slowly and putting it down again with caution, as if he were wearing snowshoes and crossing a possible crevasse. "Give it me," he said. She handed the mask to him, then looked away with disgust. His sunburn was uneven. His shoulders were burned red, his back was dark brown, his nose pink and peeling and raw. He smelled of sweat, like someone in a subway.

She said, "I'm not going."

"Now, little dear . . ."

"I don't think it's safe."

He said nothing as he worked to push and pull the strap through the clamp at the side of the mask.

She said, "We should have one of the boys from the hotel with us."

"They know less about this equipment than I do."

"I don't care," said Daisianna. She looked up and down the

deserted beach, then out to sea. There were no clouds. The only life was a pelican, which would circle for seconds, suddenly plummet into the sea, emerge a few seconds later and repeat the procedure. Then the pelican was gone too. Pelicans eat fish. Fish eat pelicans. From somewhere across the landscape came the smell of burning garbage. She was not imagining it.

"There," said Charles, handing her the mask. "Try that on."

"I'm not going," Daisianna said. "Please don't make me."

He said nothing. He shrugged and turned back toward the water. He carried the spear from the spear gun but not the gun itself. "It doesn't make any difference. Me, I'll go by myself." He stopped at the waterline and pulled his mask over his face and gripped the air hose in his mouth. He was up to his waist when Daisianna called to him to wait. Slowly he returned to the beach to help her on with her tank and flippers.

Thirty feet out, with the water up to Daisianna's chest, they submerged. At first they stayed close to the surface; then, as the sea floor gradually fell away, they descended to a depth of about 20 feet, permitting them a good view of the bottom that was never more than 35 to 45 feet deep. Charles's goal was 100 yards off shore, an old fishing boat that had sunk fifty years ago after striking a reef. Charles moved easily through the viscous green haze. Above him the bottom of the gentle sky looked like thousands of small, agitated mirrors. The sandy bottom was rippled, marcel-waved. They passed over a huge starfish. A conch inched along leaving a trail of disturbed sand. They saw no fish and Daisianna's panic began to stir. It was not a silent world. It was a world of limited vision, measured by noise. The sound of the oxygen was the sound of an anesthetic being administered when one was fighting unconsciousness. Every breath became accountable. One held it as long as possible and then gulped more air to stay awake. It wasn't even fresh air. It was air that some unknown person had pumped into the tank in San Juan weeks or months ago. It was old air. Ahead of her, Charles looked like an armored Peter Pan forcing his way through melted lime Jell-O. His strokes were strong and regular. Daisianna followed doing an underwater dog-paddle, trying to remember to keep her fingers together. She later had no memory of the school of manta rays. Like great black kites, the manta rays swept around them, above them and below, diving, soaring, turning back and charging them, feinting away at the last minute, and then moving on like mischievous children, having disoriented her and separated her from Charles. She had no memory of the fact that in eighteen minutes she had used up forty-five minutes of air. The terror, while unforgivable, was out of her immediate reach.

When they returned to the house, Charles gave her a shot of Scotch and a Valium. He said, "I'm so sorry, little dear." He said it a number of times. He helped her off with her bikini and they took a shower together. He held her in the shower. He soaped her back, her arms, her legs, her feet. He soaped her buttocks and her vagina. He caressed her with soap and made jokes about his excitement. He apologized. He kissed her. She wept, then smiled. Instead of rubbing themselves with towels, they sat on the terrace above the sea and let the evening winds dry them. They watched the Anguilla lights come on as the sun set and Charles made more drinks for them. Daisianna asked about the woman who had been raped at Anse Rouge. Was she all right?

"I wonder," Charles said.

"Wonder what?"

"I wonder if she was raped."

"I didn't know there was any question," said Daisianna.

Charles laughed. "My only question is that she is one of the homeliest old ladies I've ever seen. Also she's an aggressive drunk. The day of your party she was trying to make one of the Dutch policemen, the big black one with the fancy mustache."

"Oh, Charles."

"She was. If she was raped, she should count it a conquest."

Daisianna wore her blond wig when they dined at the Casino that night, and afterward she played roulette, though gambling and gamblers bored Charles. Daisianna had cashed two checks for two hundred dollars each when Charles told her they had to leave. "It's my money," said Daisianna. The other people at the table pretended not to notice. "You're drunk," said Charles. Daisianna told him to go home if he wanted, that she was planning to stay. In an extravagantly elevated manner she asked the waiter to bring her another gin and tonic. Charles was sitting at the bar when she joined him an hour later. She made her way through the roulette and crap tables looking like a hostess at a royal tea. The brilliantly blond hair, which had once belonged to a Korean schoolgirl, shone in the fluorescent light. Daisianna seemed distant and calm, and she seemed to have forgotten the earlier disagreement. "How much did you lose?" said Charles. "I didn't keep track," said Daisianna. "If one has to keep track, one shouldn't gamble."

Said Charles: "What do you mean?" He laughed at her. "You hate to lose money. It makes you sick. You only gamble when you're drunk or high on something."

When they got home, Charles went into the bedroom with her and filled his pockets with her pill bottles, the Mithliums, the Seconals, the Tuinals, the Valiums. Daisianna took off her wig and placed it on its little stuffed, featureless head in the dressing room. She made no comment on what

Charles was doing. He kissed her on the forehead and went outside, up the terrace steps, through the drawing room to the library. Daisianna locked the shutters. She listened for Charles, heard nothing, and went to her make-up case on the bureau. In it she had duplicates of everything Charles had confiscated. She swallowed three Seconals without water and lay down on the bed. She turned off the lights. Deep, time-confused sleep was instantaneous. When she awoke she thought it was morning but the clock showed she had been asleep less than an hour. She thought of Monopoly, how she hadn't played Monopoly since she was a child. No, she had played it at Hickory Hollow. She got up from the bed and wobbled through the dressing room to the bathroom, where Charles had left the outside door open again. She slammed it shut against land crabs, mongooses, scorpions, bats, rats, mice, and lizards. She was at the center of a malignant landscape. Back in the bedroom she took another Seconal, which she chased with vodka from a small plastic bottle she had labeled rubbing alcohol. She turned off the lights again and lay down, but she was so excited it was physically impossible to stay prone. She got up once more and lit all the lamps. It had become clear to her that she was in the siege of strangers. It was also clear to her that if she did not protect herself, no one would. It was as simple as that. She looked at Mark H. Magnuson's elephant gun standing in the corner, Mark H. Magnuson's initials carved by some Italian craftsman on the highly polished wooden stock. Why an Italian craftsman for an elephant gun? She would ask Mary about it one day. She carried the gun to bed. She fetched a box of shells. Carl Crow Jolly and his BB gun. She loaded one barrel, then the other. She drew Mary Magnuson's chaise into position between the bed and the shuttered doors. She released the safety catches. She turned off the lights and waited. She was prepared to wait as long as it might take. She was not alone. The Little Lord Jesus was there.

68

The first morning of the inquest in Marigot, Hugh Kroeder, the big black Dutch policeman with the Zapata mustache, parked his car outside the Oranjestad police station. An old black farmer he knew by face only had been waiting for him in the shade of the building. The farmer told Hugh what he knew, never looking the policeman in the eyes, shrugging his shoulders frequently to emphasize his distance from the facts. That afternoon Hugh called Fonse Devanner, who, in turn, told Honoré Picard. Early that evening the three men, accompanied by Matthew Marcorelles, the gendarme who had found Charles the night he was killed, drove in a French jeep to Petite Case, a fishing village six miles from Marigot over the mountains by a once-paved road. The gendarme drove, with M. Picard sitting in front. Fonse Devanner and the Dutch policeman sat in back, hanging on to the roof struts to ease the bumps. It was a part of the island that Fonse Devanner had never seen. They passed the entrance to a dirt road. "I have been told," Hugh Kroeder said, "that there be a marble bridge up yonder. Pure white marble. I have been told also that it crosses neither river nor stream." Matthew Marcorelles said something in French and Honoré Picard turned around to speak to the policeman and Fonse. "He says there is a bridge up there, and it does not cross anything, not even a ditch. But it is not marble. It is fieldstone." There was no moon. The jeep's headlights flickered with each bump. The darkness was total. Once a long white dress froze by the side of the road as the jeep went past. The road at last dipped down toward the shore to Petite Case. The gendarme drove slowly along Petite Case's one street, which was a continuation of the road itself. One-room cabins on stilts faced the street like auto trailers. The appearance of the gendarmerie jeep interrupted the play of some children, who began to run after it. The gendarme stopped, asked directions of one little boy, who climbed on the running board to show the way. The nose of an old Packard limousine poked out of an alley. It was Billy White's taxi. The boy pointed to a house ahead on the left, away from the beach. The gendarme turned off the road into a small palm grove and parked. "That's it," said the boy. Like the others, it was a tiny rectangular shanty resting on spindly legs that raised it four feet from the sandy earth. Facing them was a large square window, and framed against the vermilion wall of the room was the silhouette of a nodding woman. The four men got out of the jeep and walked toward the house. As they drew closer, it seemed as if the silhouette were glowing with heavenly light. It was a halo. The woman was reading aloud from an unseen book. The gendarme knocked on the steps and climbed up, followed by Honoré Picard and Fonse Devanner. In a rocking chair by the window sat an old black lady dressed in a tattered Mother Hubbard and wearing a hood of lovely golden curls. The woman looked up slowly and squinted at them. She was wearing Daisianna's wig. Backward.

Lorette Fanchon's house was a treasure chest. In addition to sheets, pillowcases, and towels that she had picked up on her nighttime travels, they found six women's bathing suits that had disappeared from a clothesline at Oranje House several months before, including a gold lamé bikini that a secretary from New York had claimed cost her $225. They also found ashtrays, men's shirts, and several dozen pairs of men's undershorts, all neatly washed and ironed, with their flies sewn up. Lorette Fanchon, who was a Dutch citizen although she lived on the French side, denied nothing. She went further. She would admit everything that anyone might suggest to her. Yes, she said, she had been in the house the night of the shooting. She told the inquest that she had been doing God's business. She was His instrument. She had made her witness and she called on everyone present to follow His path. Daisianna listened to the testimony with immense sadness. She sobbed aloud and everyone understood her terrible loss. She held the hand of Dinny Murdock, who had flown over from Antigua the night before to be with her. She later asked Jimmy Barnes to speak to the police to see if she could possibly help Lorette Fanchon, who was to be sent back to the hospital in Curaçao from which she had been released a year earlier.

Daisianna did not return to New York immediately. Two days after the inquest, she moved from Mary Magnuson's town house, where she had been staying, to the Oranje House, in Oranjestad, where Dinny Murdock had a room. Père Gollanahan was not sorry to see her move. Daisianna frightened him. In Oranjestad, Dinny Murdock told her amusing stories. Dinny liked to go shopping. He liked the sun. When he had a lot of sun, he wanted to make love. One of the things that amused her about him was his guilelessness. He had failed at every job he'd ever attempted. He'd been in the merchant marine. He'd been an interior decorator. He'd worked in an uncle's brokerage house. He'd been a tennis pro. Several years earlier, his father, at wit's end, had sent him to a career consultant. They'd tested Dinny and found that he had an aptitude for absolutely nothing. At night he tossed and turned from one side of the bed to the other unless she cradled him in her arms. Then he fell immediately to sleep.

69

The letter was typed on the stationery of the DcDc Foundation of New York, but it had been mailed from San Miguel de Allende, Mexico. Daisianna had dictated the major part of it to someone who did not write English very well.

Dear Jimmy,

Of all people you should realize that I'm not made of money. The quarterly statements were wiating for me here and I was shocked at some of the expenditures. I cant believe that your last trip to Chicago should have cost $682.23. I do hope you save all your hotel receits etcetera for Mr. Loomis. Don't you ever stay in Lake Forest with Travis and his family? I dont mean to sound unapreciative but as you know better than I money is going out faster than it is coming in.

Charles's mother lives on and on. I don't mind that but I do think its a bit much when she asks me to finance Guy in some idiotic scheme to open another American drug store in Paris. After all, there are at least six all ready. She's close to 90 and should know better. By the way, do I own the appartment on the Avenue d'Iéna? Please check. I think we bought it for her the year Charles died. When she dies I'd rather there not be any litigation with Guy. I dont think she can leave it to him, but I'm not sure.

Isnt it to gastly what's been happening on St. Constance? Mary tells me her house in the country was completely gutted. Ive given up the idea of buying anything here. The prices are outrageous, the people except for Mary not very interesting and the Mexican government insists on a Mexican co-owner. Do you know an honest Mexican lawyer? Someone has told me that Costa Rica is the place to buy now. We may go there from here if it isnt the rainy season.

Heaven knows how to find out. Anyone who might know lies. Perhaps we'll just come back and hole up on the farm and eat sardines and raisins. I'd be willing but Dinny would miss the sun. He gets cranky when he's out of it for very long.

About the Sangamon County farm. Perhaps you should go there to find out what is going on. I couldnt understand a word of the letters you sent me. Does the University want to buy it from me or do they want me to present it to them? You were unclear. If I do give it to them, what would be the tax advantage? Loomis can probably figure this out. Would it be possible for me to give it to them now, for presentation after my death, while I retain the use of it in my lifetime? I realize that Ive never even seen it, but I dont want to rush into something I'll be sorry for later. Are they finding anything of value or just more beads and arrowheads? Ive always been fasinated by archeology but I confess that those reports and papers you sent me put me to sleep. Also I was surprised that if it is such an important find that its always refered to as the MacLeister Site and not the Barrett Site. After all, the land has been in the Barrett family for almost 150 years and MacLeister is only the name of the man who has been farming it. He rents it from me. I might be more interested in giving them the land if they called it the Barrett Site. Would they agree? See what they think. I'd hate to learn I had given away a potential Disneyland, if that is what it is. Go out there as soon as you can. Its probably easiest to fly to Springfield and rent a car there. Just dont go by limosine.

The postscript was in Daisianna's handwriting:

I was surprised by your note that you and Cleo have separated. I didn't think she'd ever let you go. What did you do to her? I still think she's a plush horse and always has been. I assume the boys are with her and not living in the Harvard Club with you (I hope it's neat). Dinny and I are —I think—as happy as can be expected. The demands are few. He's very good company, though some of the friends he picks up aren't, which may be why my letters sometimes sound more shrill than I intend. However, I have to make all the decisions. Yet it's an even sort of life for me. No more highs, but then no more lows. I'm still not sure what happened. It had to do with Mandelbaum and then Charles, but how I don't know. Perhaps it's best not to question it. Charles was the old life. I can't miss it, though I think of him all the time. It's sad because in those last months we weren't very good friends. One rather remarkable change: I'm suddenly possessed of a nearly faultless memory. It's as if I'd been given another eye and another ear. I feel haunted by truth. It doesn't necessarily make one more kind. That's a secret between us. Ever,

Daisianna.

70

Jimmy drove to the old Barrett farm on a hot still July afternoon after having checked into the Ann Rutledge Motor Inn near Springfield. The way was not difficult to find. White hand-painted arrows on pieces of weathered board pointed the route. The MacLeister Site had become a major tourist attraction for central and southern Illinois. Alongside dilapidated filling stations that might once have serviced the getaway car of Baby Face Nelson and the trucks of bootleggers, there were new souvenir stands, at one of which Jimmy bought two small grayish-blue spearheads embedded in cubes of Lucite, one for each boy. He picked up a mimeographed flyer that said in part: "In the MacLeister cornfield archaeologists have uncovered evidence of the fact that prehistoric man dwelled along the lower Illinois River Valley for more than 10,000 years, from about 9000 B.C. until A.D. 1200. In other words, men roamed the valleys of Illinois long before the pharaohs of ancient Egypt built their great pyramids at Giza and long before the construction of implacable Stonehenge in southwestern England."

The chief of the dig, a Professor Harovski—who said "Call me Bob"—guided Jimmy through the excavations, a series of square-cornered trenches that looked like giant-sized reproductions of the sort of constructions made by children with small shovels on the beach. The biggest trench was 80 feet wide, 200 feet long, and 5 to 30 feet deep. Others were 6 to 15 feet wide and 30 feet long. There were 120 people at work at the site, college students on summer vacations and amateur archaeologists. Like elves, they were burrowing, sorting, measuring, weighing, lifting, labeling, hauling, dumping. Ramps improvised of planks led into some of the deeper trenches. Said Jimmy: "It looks like strip mining." Said the professor: "It makes me think of the way the pyramids were built. Hundreds of people, each doing one small task. Too bad the Egyptians didn't have a computer to help them. I'll show you how that works later." On one side of the site, Farmer MacLeister was continuing to grow corn. The barns and other outbuildings had been turned into a communications and information center, offices, storerooms, and workrooms. "The old Barrett house stood over there," said the professor, "just beyond the barn. It burned down in the nineteen-twenties, which is when MacLeister began to farm the place. He's now eighty-four but you'd never know it. I think he must be the only E. V. Debs Socialist left in the state. There's a small graveyard on the other side of the site. Just two graves, and only one of them marked so that you can read it: 'Fanny,' dated either 1836 or 1838. A slave, I assume. The Barretts buried themselves elsewhere."

The professor paused in a trench where a young man was chipping while listening to very loud rock on a portable radio. The professor made a face. "My tastes run to the lightly classical," he said. "Now look up there, about nine feet from the top. You see that cut in the wall, shaped like the side of a big bowl? That's what we call a 'feature,' a nonportable artifact. That bowl was dug around 2500 B.C. to serve as a fire pit. The people who lived here used it for cooking."

At another part of the site: "So far we've found seventeen distinct horizons, which is what we call the strata that bear traces of human habitation. They show that man lived here on seventeen different occasions, including Paleo-Indian man, who lived in North America eight to ten thousand years before Christ."

Later, standing near a pretty young woman who was wearing blue jeans and a red bandanna as a minimum bra, the professor stopped again. In the side of the trench one could define the colors of earth that represented the different cultures. Some layers were no more than fourteen or fifteen inches thick. It was as if time, having finished with a people, had flattened them for the convenience of their successors. Each in turn was squashed by those who came later.

"We're all immigrants, aren't we?" said the professor, who looked as if he might be Slavic. "Even the Sangamon roundheads and the Mendinosian flexibles. Some immigrants were more successful than others. We're trying to discover causes for effects. Why some cultures endured for hundreds of years and others collapsed overnight. Was it plague? Some temporary shift in climate? Overpopulation? Genocide? An inability to adapt? Some process of organic rejection? Not knowing how to cope? Everything we've found indicates this valley has been a land of milk and honey throughout the millennia. There's always been plenty of water. The bluffs protect it from the severity of the winters elsewhere in the state. The people of Horizon Seventeen knew about corn but it wasn't until thousands of years later that anyone began to cultivate it. We've found the foundations of prehistoric houses at Horizon Six, going back to 2500 B.C., among the oldest ever found in North America, houses made of upright logs and insulated with clay. Yet we've discovered no dwellings at Horizon Five, which came afterward. What happened? Didn't they know? Is the collective subconscious such a fragile thing?"

The professor had arranged for Jimmy to dine that evening with five of his colleagues, one of whom, a member of the University's administration, had flown down from Chicago for the occasion. They sat at a large round table in a back room at Mrs. Parker's Home Cookery in Dempster, a small town five miles from the site. The professors treated Jimmy with the mixture of deference, hostility, and awe that bank examiners and some kinds of celebrities inspire when on official business. All the archaeologists ordered Mrs. Parker's home-fried catfish because one couldn't get them in Chicago, and they intimidated Jimmy into ordering them, too, though he classified home-fried catfish even lower than he did eel. These catfish were greasy and tough and the home-cooked vegetables were canned corn and canned string beans.

Harovski began the discussion: "Mr. Barnes has suggested that Mrs. du Chaudrun would consider presenting the site to the University if we renamed it the Barrett Site. Of course, it's not officially named anything now. We've called it the MacLeister Site simply because it's known as Mac-Leister's farm."

Said another professor: "It would break Tom MacLeister's heart if it were called anything else."

Another said: "Tom MacLeister likes to see his name on road signs."

Said Harovski: "It would be difficult to change the habits of the archaeological community. There have been dozens of papers written already, and dozens more are being written. It's one of the best-known sites in the United States, and probably one of the most important finds in North America in the last half-century."

Said the boy who that afternoon had been listening to rock and who turned out to be a full professor: "Why does she want to do this—Mrs. What's-her-name?"

Said Jimmy: "The property has been the Barrett farm for almost a hundred and fifty years. The Barretts were her mother's people. They pioneered the land."

"Not quite," said another professor. "The Barretts had a number of predecessors." Laughter. "I wonder why it makes any difference to her. It's not as if she's looking for tenure."

More laughter.

Said Jimmy: "I suppose she sees it as a kind of memorial."

"Why do you publish, Atwater?" someone asked over Jimmy's head. "You want to have your own little memorials, don't you?"

"It's not the same thing," said Atwater.

Said Harovski: "This place isn't a memorial to anyone."

The man representing the University's administration finally spoke. "What the hell," he said, "why not call it the Barrett Site? MacLeister won't know about it. These things take so long to effect he'll be gone by the time anyone seriously starts calling it the Barrett Site. If he isn't, he's so self-centered he'll think there's been a mistake. Mrs. du Chaudrun has been most generous. I find the argument ridiculous."

Said Professor Atwater: "And you have to get back to Chicago tonight."

"Yes."

Laughter.

Said Harovski to Jimmy: "Then it's agreed." He extended his hand to Jimmy and they shook on it.

Before Jimmy drove to Springfield, he returned with Harovski to the site where, in his office desk drawer, the professor found a small, badly tarnished silver spoon. "I picked this up two years ago when I was making some probes near the foundation of the farmhouse."

The spoon was engraved with a ram and initialed with a fancy Old English "J." "Mrs. du Chaudrun might like to have it," he said.

Said Jimmy: "Is it very old?"

"Depends on what you mean," Harovski said, laughing. "It's a baby spoon. The date, 1840, is on the back."

"Don't you want it?"

"It's not the sort of thing we're interested in."

At the Ann Rutledge Motor Inn Jimmy put the old spoon on his night table. He took a shower and turned up the air-conditioning so that he could sleep under blankets. In bed he reread the mimeographed flyer about the MacLeister Site. It concluded: "On a summer's evening in this placid, fertile corn country, one can sense the presence of lost peoples. Who were they? Where did they go? In the day, one can visit the site. Admission is free but contributions are accepted to help defray the costs of this unique archaeological endeavor." Before going to sleep, Jimmy Barnes masturbated. His life had come to this: it was the safest, most sensible way.

A Note on the Type

*This book was set in Caledonia, a Linotype
face designed by W. A. Dwiggins. It belongs to the family
of printing types called "modern face" by printers—
a term used to mark the change in style of type letters
that occurred about 1800. Caledonia borders on the general design of Scotch Modern, but is more freely drawn
than that letter.*

*Composed, printed and bound by
The Book Press, Brattleboro, Vermont.
Typography and binding design by*
VIRGINIA TAN